The

Counterfeiter

Dear Dr. Sherman —
Please accept this
modest thanks for
your expertise
and kindness
these past several
years.
With admiration
and affection
Ed Cone
11/27/20

The

Counterfeiter

ED CONE

New York 2020

Project Manager: Steven Hayes
Cover and interior design, cover art: Gilbert Fletcher
Editor: Barbara Hoffert
Copyeditor: Margo LaPierre

Library of Congress Cataloging-in-publication Data available upon request

ISBN 978-1-7332430-0-1
ebook ISBN 978-1-7332430-1-8

Epigraph and quote on page 118 from André Gide, *Les Faux-Monnayeurs* (Paris: Bibliothèque de la Pléiade, 1958). Translation on page 235 by Justin O'Brien, *The Counterfeiters* (New York: Vintage, 1955).

Manufactured in the United States of America

2 9 1 3 8 4 7 5 6

First Edition

This book is dedicated to my good friend and comrade,

My Wife

The
Counterfeiter

"La manière dont le monde des apparences s'impose à nous et dont nous tentons d'imposer au monde extérieur notre interprétation particulière, fait le drame de notre vie. La résistance des faits nous invite à transporter notre construction idéale dans le rêve, l'espérance, la vie future, en laquelle notre croyance s'alimente de tous nos déboires dans celle-ci."

—André Gide

Les Faux-Monnayeurs, p. 1096

PART I

Ocean House

CHAPTER
1

I T WAS A PROPITIOUS SETTING for their first meeting, an outside
room of a rambling home in the Hamptons, a house so big it
blocked your view of the ocean when you drove up the
driveway. A house you could mistake for an inn or hotel, if you
didn't know better. It was a clapboard dwelling that faced the sea;
the Atlantic was its view. The grand entrance, with its portico and
colonnade, looked out over the waves. Visitors in the middle of the
last century arrived in back through extensive gardens and a
spacious arbor, then entered through a central hall where the host
greeted his guests.

This outside room, so called because it was open on three
sides, was not a setting where the writer was accustomed to
receiving anyone but his sister. Like the sea, Fiona was there when
she was there; he'd no more have forbidden her entry than he'd have
asked the gulls to stop howling or the sea to roll back.

Edward's eyes were stuck to the sheet in his typewriter. He'd
been on that proverbial roll and ignored all distractions—scents,
sounds, and sea. The sea, of course, was a scent and a sound, but
their combination put it in a category of its own. The ever-present
sea was the chief constant in Edward's life, as vital as the blood in
his veins. He'd been immersed in his musings since sunup and heard
nothing, not a footstep, when someone entered the room. The

intruder had tiptoed into the writer's presence, taking care not to make a sound.

When he finally raised his eyes from the page, it was not Fiona he saw but a figure some four or five inches taller than his sister's five foot five and a good twenty years younger, around twenty years of age or so. At first he had no clue to the youth's identity, though his presence caused neither surprise nor disquiet. He pushed the typewriter aside and, after a few moments, realized he was staring intently, bad form to say the least. The youth hadn't flinched.

The single-syllable sound of the young man's voice broke the spell.

"Sir ...?"

The pleasing tenor helped Edward bridge the void between his writing and the world around him. Now he recognized the young man as the son of his groundskeeper. For a fleeting moment, he debated whether to be irked at the invasion and was surprised when he wasn't. It was a rare occasion when Edward Vann surprised himself.

"We'd agreed to meet this morning at ten, sir, ..." The young man, of fair skin and even features, stole a peek at his watch as if for verification.

"So we did, so we did indeed," returned the writer, in genial spirits now, yet as puzzled as ever that he'd agreed to meet with this homespun figure in jeans and shirt of a nondescript plaid, a pattern worn by farm boys and fishermen. Yet something told him he'd remember these moments.

"Won't you have a seat?" He pointed to a rattan chair across from his desk, its back to a splendid view of the ocean. "I'll ring for something to drink. Would you care for fresh lemonade ... and perhaps some muffins ...?"

Vann pushed a button at the side of his desk while the youth perched on the edge of the chair, as if he feared it wouldn't hold his weight. "As we were saying—?" He stopped abruptly, hoping for a reminder from his visitor.

"Yes, sir, my job ..."

"Yes, what about this job of yours ...?"

"My duties, sir, if you'd care to list them ..."

Vann pursed his lips and scratched the top of his head to provoke a smile from his listener. The gesture worked. His imitation of a puzzled chimp was said to be difficult to resist, perhaps because it was out of character with his somewhat saturnine disposition. It put them both at ease. He was still bargaining for time, trying to figure out what to do with this person who'd materialized in his private space. "What do you *think* they should be ...?"

It was coming back now. He'd offered the kid a job on the estate for the summer. He was home from college and needed to earn some money. That's how his dad, Silas Deane, had explained the situation two, three weeks ago. The subject might have never come to his attention if Fiona hadn't driven it into the conversation. She was going over the books and called Silas in for an accounting of certain expenses. "There's nothing untoward about them," she'd explained to Deane in the British accent she affected at her most officious. "Edward here didn't have a clue what they were for," she resumed, casting an unflattering light on him and drawing him in where he preferred not to go; the management of the estate had been her purview since the death of their father several years ago, though she didn't live on the premises. She made unannounced drop-ins, interrupting her brother's cherished solitude but relieving him from overseeing an extensive household.

After the groundskeeper gave his usual satisfactory account, she asked about his son, one of Fiona's strictly pro forma inquiries. "Oh, Neddy," he'd replied with an air of distraction, "if he can just stay in college and get that degree ...," the reluctant father paused. "Not much of a student, is he?" Fiona questioned, shining the worst possible light on the subject, provoking her brother to wince perceptibly as the proud father replied, "Oh, he's a fine student, my Ned. It's the cost that stands in his way. He's not at community college, you know. He goes off to Columbia University, in New York City."

Seeking to compensate for Fiona's gaucherie, Edward suggested, "Perhaps we might find work for him here ..."

The groundskeeper brightened, clasping the hands he'd been holding at his side. He reminded Edward of a man clutching his hat. Fiona's disapproving countenance—you couldn't call it a glare—only encouraged him. "Send him round to me. I'm sure we can find something to keep him occupied."

"I'll do just that, sir. He'll be home in little more than a week." The elated Silas Deane backed all the way to the door.

"Well," Ned resumed the discussion of his duties, "I've noticed you have someone to tend your lawn, trim the hedges, such as that. I don't know if I'm much good with dishes or polishing silver, but I have a bicycle, I can run errands. Inside the house, I can do the heavy stuff, and I'm also not bad with a paintbrush—"

The young man's self-assurance impressed Vann, and he tried to recall whether he was as composed at that age. This favorable impression prompted him to inquire,

"What are you studying in college, if I may ask?"

"English. I'm a literature major."

"English or American literature?"

"English and French. I'm doing a comparison of the characters in Balzac and Dickens."

"A kind of *Comédie Internationale* …?"

"Rather, a *Tragédie*."

Seized by an outlandish idea, Edward signaled the youth to scoot his chair closer, then pulled the sheet of paper from the Smith Corona. "What do you think of this …?"

Ned peered at the sheet, on which several paragraphs had been typed. Edward's eyes followed the youth's as they moved across and down, then returned to the top of the page.

"I like it, sir."

Edward felt himself go slack.

"There's a purple tinge to it …" Ned glanced up and resumed too quickly for the writer to respond, "but I imagine that's intended here."

He nodded. They'd exhausted the topic. At least, he now had one person's opinion, a stranger's at that, but somehow it mattered to him.

His visitor added, "I hope I may look forward to reading more ...?"

Again, the young man surprised him; he'd expected the deference of youth (*Gee, it's really swell*).

A flash of insight or inspiration—it struck so fast he hardly knew it hit—and Vann exclaimed, "When can you begin?"

"I've begun already, haven't I?"

Later that afternoon, as a breeze welled in off the sea, inviting the sheer curtains to dance in place around his study, he tried to resume the thread of his novel. But the sea, the sun, the sand were having their way with his imagination; his mind kept reverting to the young man, his new hired hand, his first employee. Until now, his sister had done the hiring and firing on the estate. Now he was responsible for one new worker, who had as yet only the most vaguely defined job description. He smiled inwardly at his new position: lord of the manor with vassal in tow. He'd avoided that role all his life, despite periodic lectures from his mother about a Vann's obligations to society. Mother expected things to be just so to avert chaos; she traced her lineage to the Stuart king who lost his head.

When young Deane had asked about his tasks, Edward had devised a rudimentary list. The image of a shed near the side gardens crystallized in his mind's eye. It could use a coat of paint and new windows. A package at the post office awaited picking up. Then, incredibly, there was his novel.

The two empty glasses on his desk reminded him of his visitor's presence earlier in the day. They'd consumed their lemonade with buttered muffins that Farleigh brought from the upstairs pantry. Their polite discussion soon meandered onto literary topics and grew heated, though it had nothing to do with the job. Or did it?

They were contrasting the odes of Keats with the sonnets of Shakespeare. "A comparison of the two," Ned asserted, "compels you to take a stand on the writer's point of view." The thread of their discussion matters little here, but Ned had finally asserted, "Our conception of beauty is too different for us to resolve this issue!"

Then it burst upon Vann, this flash of insight-light: "You shall review my novel periodically."

"*Me*—?"

"No, an alien from outer—!" He stopped himself, checking his sarcasm at the door. "Sorry, I don't mean to offend."

"No offense taken."

"Well," he declared, impressed with the youth's spunk, "You're a good man!"

Good man or not, he was entrusting his sacred text to a hobbledehoy. But why not? The young man offered an alternative vision that might check his excesses, exaggerations, illogicalities, repetitions, redundancies, anachronisms, and other literary pitfalls. No one need know, not his agent, not Olivia, certainly not Fiona, who'd bristle at the idea he was paying a yardboy to edit his work. All right, Deane was not an editor; he was only a sophomore at Columbia (with a sure understanding of literature). Yet now they were collaborating, and that was good enough for him.

"Collaborators, are you?" Alden Brooks was more amused than surprised when Vann reported his latest venture over drinks at The Gullet, the hideously named local watering hole. Brooks considered his client an original; leave it to Edward Vann to concoct an unconventional solution to a nonexistent problem.

"He's as good as any reader I could find around here," Vann replied a shade defensively.

"Will you mention him to your in-house editor?"

"In good time, if I deem it appropriate." Each took a sip of his martini, then Vann added, "They won't be working at cross-purposes, you know."

"What do I know?" came Alden's affable rejoinder. "My field is the law, not the alchemy of fiction. Your two books of essays got raves, and now you have this novel under contract. You have every reason for great expectations, no matter who edits you."

Edward lazed in bed for some time next morning before he recalled the deal he'd made with Silas Deane's son. He was overcome at first by fear that he'd done something foolish. But the sight and sound of the sea outside his bedroom windows tamed his roiling emotions and he sank back on the pillows, his immediate concern now whether to ring for breakfast or to dress and get it himself.

He hopped out of bed and threw on an old pair of linen trousers, a cotton shirt, and sandals. As he started downstairs, he couldn't suppress a grin, as if intrigued by something about to happen. His tight smiles usually stretched no more than into his cheeks; this one pushed beyond toward his ears. The receding line of light brown hair was holding but thinning. The salt-and-pepper mustache encroached on his upper lip, which was appreciably thinner than the lower. The mustache balanced them out. He drew the comb through his hair one more time, then descended to the kitchen.

"Mornin', Mr. Ed."

Farleigh looked up from the list he was composing of the next day's menu, his smile as invariable as the surf. This longtime family servant was the only acquaintance besides Alden Brooks allowed to abbreviate his name.

"Good morning, Mr. Granger, sir." Vann's mock formality brought a smile to his houseman's lips. "Could you pack me a lunch basket and a thermos of coffee, cream in the coffee, sugar on the side." Instructions Farleigh knew by heart.

Edward's eyes scanned the front page of the *Times* spread out on the counter.

ELIZABETH CROWNED QUEEN

"And, Farleigh, would you include two mugs ..."

With wicker basket, he stepped onto the front lawn to a blaze of light. The susurration of the sea urged him forward. Following the path that held close to the house, he walked eastward till he turned the corner to the side garden. He made his way through a bewildering variety of roses, then came to the shed that he'd asked Ned to repair. Shielding his eyes from the sun, he caught sight of the young man on a ladder, shaded by the overhang of the roof. He was wearing sneakers, faded jeans, and a sleeveless undershirt. When it appeared his worker hadn't noticed him, he called out, "Ready for a break—?"

There was no response, just the sound of the sea crashing onto the sand and filling the air, its impetuous waters clamoring to be heard.

"What's that you say?" Edward cried out.

"I didn't say a thing, sir."

"No wonder I couldn't hear you!" He smiled broadly and Ned returned his smile.

"Perhaps the ocean was talking. But come along and have a bite with me. I'm ravenous, and you must be, too—!"

As Ned climbed down the ladder, he admitted, "No coaxing necessary."

Edward led them beyond the shed to a flagstone patio. He placed the basket on a wrought-iron table and sank onto a lawn sofa. He expected his worker would take a chair across from him, but Ned joined him on the sofa.

The waxen scent of roses competed with the briny smell of the sea. Edward opened the basket and placed the provisions on the table. As he poured their coffee, Ned observed, "You've thought of everything, Mr. Vann ..."

"It's Farleigh who's thought of everything. And drop that Mr. Vann, would you—"

It was one of those perfect days, when the sun warmed but didn't burn and the wind refreshed without stinging. They ate in silence as the wind fluttered the napkins and blew their hair. At some point Edward declared, "We never decided what I'm to pay you, and when."

"Any amount, any time."

"Aren't you concerned I might take advantage of you?"

The painter looked about as if searching for words. The freckles dotting his bare shoulders mirrored the brown specks on his face. The summer sun had turned his pale complexion to a ruddy hue, and his thick brown hair looked in place even when tossed and tousled by the wind.

"You're fair and square, sir," he offered. "I think I should have nothing to fear from you."

"I admire your trust in me," replied his boss. "I shall attempt to be worthy of it."

Next morning the sea was flat and still, the wind having decamped toward the end of the island. It was going to be a hot day. When Ned reported for duty, the rim of his baseball cap shaded his eyes from a merciless sun. Again, he wore a white undershirt but had exchanged his jeans and sneakers for a pair of shorts and well-worn penny loafers. Edward had drawn up a list of things for him to do, but asked on impulse, "Would you care to take a look at these impoverished pages ...?" He wasn't sure why he'd introduced his novel at the start of the day; he'd planned to bring it up near the end.

Ned placed his hat on the floor and slid to the edge of the rattan chair when Edward pushed the typewriter toward him. His large brown eyes scanned the page, still in the machine, and he adjusted the carriage as he read, while Edward's fingers drummed the desktop. Soon the reader declared, "Are you ready ...?"

Edward nodded.

"Dramatic setting—a train station in Germany (standing for transition?) and Nazi guards stationed everywhere while security agents (possibly SS?) hustle unfortunates through the vast space (probably to concentration camps?) ... Mind a suggestion?"

"Why not?" he replied uncertainly.

"You give too much away with this beginning. We know the Nazis are thuggish brutes, and the scene reeks of evil, but, of course, that's what we'd expect."

He reached up and untwisted a strap of his undershirt as Edward's head bobbed imperceptibly. "What if you set the opening at a distance from the Reich, change the time frame to the start of hostilities, maybe earlier ...?"

The writer betrayed no reaction.

"I was thinking France—before the war, or just as it starts ... Refugees trapped at the border, ... while troops file past in the opposite direction ..."

➤❖➤

I used to think Fiona Vann was the most beautiful woman I ever saw. I'd watch her strolling on the beach in late afternoons of summer, the sun splaying the platinum strands of her hair. I'd fight the urge to dash after her, to sweep that hair from her face, then press my burning lips to hers and confess my love—to make sure she got the point. Several times I summoned the courage to follow her, at a respectable distance, *bien sûr*. I was afraid she'd catch on to me, but she never looked back, once she set out on her unvarying path.

One day she changed course, and I had to think fast to avoid detection.

Much to my disappointment, Fiona met up with a man—a romantic interest, I assumed—who would put an end to my dreams in all their folly, just as servicemen tear down the posters from their lockers of a movie star they idolize when the faithless girl ups and marries. But I soon saw I had nothing to fear—the man she met was her brother.

Edward Vann—tall, severe, aristocratic. Vann was a writer and said to be a recluse. After the death of his father some years ago, he inherited the family estate. His older brother and sister, Maximiliano and Fiona, had an interest in the house as well, but I didn't know the details. I only knew what Dad told me. For several years, Dad had managed the finances of a minor charity for the Vann family, and when Old Man Vann passed, his younger son became Dad's boss. If it weren't for that changing of the guard, I might never have been introduced to Edward Vann.

That seismic shift occurred when I was a sophomore at Columbia. I needed a summer job, and Dad said I should apply for work on the Vann estate; Dad knew they were forever hiring and firing over there. Why shouldn't I benefit from the château's largesse?

I said I didn't want to be pushy. I didn't even know the Vanns.

"Pushy-smushy," Dad retorted. "Don't you know you've gotta use your connections to get ahead in life, Ari?"

I wasn't sure I wanted to get ahead that way. Not that I'm not ambitious. What up-and-coming college boy on Long Island isn't? (Alas, my family pronounced it Lon' G'island.)

"If you don't get your ass over there pronto," Dad warned after his fourth Schlitz of the afternoon, "I'll go apply *for* you, Ari Edelman. Now, how d'you think *that'll* make you look, pal ...?"

Dad sniffed opportunity. He calculated that with my "connection," I could do better than at the local lumberyard or Dairy Queen, and maybe there'd be something down the road for him. I promised I'd hightail it to Ocean House next morning. Connection-smonnection.

"Wait here," said the man who answered the door, pissed and peremptory—because I'd come to the wrong entranceway? I couldn't tell front from back. You had a lawn worthy of Versailles as you approached Ocean House and the entire Atlantic on the other side.

So I waited in the grand foyer. And waited.

Until finally, who should waft down the stairs but Fiona herself. Her hair was piled on her regal head and she wore a plain black dress and high heels, plus a string of pearls. Pearls! When she got to the bottom of the stairs, she shot a glance at me and froze.

I threw myself at her feet and swore undying fealty.

Kidding!

I stood there before this Sultana Shiksa, clutching my hat in my hand, and I hadn't even worn one. My teeth clicked shut and trapped my tongue in my dry mouth. I was utterly without my most reliable weapon—words.

Fiona leaned forward as if trying to hear something I hadn't said. After dropping the hat I wasn't holding and almost stooping to pick it up, I summoned the courage to say, "I'd like to apply for work, if you please." I didn't tack on a "ma'am" because I didn't want her to think I thought she was much older than I was. I was afraid she'd never take me seriously—as a lover, I mean.

Just then, her brother entered from stage left. He seemed preoccupied, and if Fiona hadn't spoken up, I suspect he wouldn't have even noticed me.

"Edward, do you know of any jobs around here …?"

It was not an auspicious beginning. Fiona seemed about as interested in me as if I'd been the milkman or the gardener. I knew then and there I had no business in this fancy establishment; it was out of bounds to the likes of a poor Jewish boy from Nowhere, Lon G'island. That's what happens when you start messing with rich goyim.

But all was not lost. I thought the master of the house hadn't heard her, for he gave no sign that he had. He was dressed all in white and carried a stack of papers; you could have taken him for a priest or monk. Then he swept us in with his penetrating gaze, rather, swept *me* in. I can't remember when so much august attention had been focused on yours truly. Yet he didn't speak. That was when Fiona stepped in again.

"Edward, this young man wants a job. Can you find one for him? His dad does some accounting work for you."

"What can you do?" Edward Vann asked abruptly.

"Anything."

He exchanged glances with his sister. Was he suppressing a smile?

"… that is, anything you need doing," I emended.

Still facing his sister, he proclaimed, "At least you found someone qualified, Fiona." Then to me: "Come round tomorrow about ten o'clock. I'll speak to you then."

Vann's terse manner signified I was to exit pronto. But I wasn't quick enough to take my cue. I was still transfixed when his parting remark—he left the room the moment he said it—gave me my marching orders: "Good day."

CHAPTER 2

H
E REREAD HIS REWRITE, flipped back to the original, then scanned the rewrite once again. His fingers hovered over the keys preparing for more strikes, but instead he flipped the carriage to release the page. He was not possessive about his writing and took criticism well. So was it such a big deal that he'd accepted the suggestions of this new critic or adviser or whatever you want to call the young man he'd hired to run errands and clean-up paint-up fix-up?

He'd been at it all day, and the sun was painting its most brilliant colors across the horizon. A coating of gold underlay the rose and purple that it splashed up and down the Atlantic. Inspired by the profligate display, he went for a walk on the beach in his bare feet, relishing the feel of cool sand squishing through his toes. The salt tang filled him with well-being.

Just as he was wondering whether he'd meet up with anyone he knew, he noticed a figure approaching in the distance and wondered how long it would be before they came abreast. Soon enough he made out not one but two individuals coming toward him. He almost turned back—he preferred his walks in solitude—but he kept to his course.

A squall of gulls alighted from nowhere to broadcast their indecipherable tidings, and he reached up as if to brush them away. That involuntary gesture was caught by one of the pair up ahead, who surprised him by waving back. But it shouldn't have been such a surprise, for he soon found himself face-to-face with Ned Deane and a young woman in tow.

"This is my friend Sally," Ned explained. "Sally, Mr. Vann—he's a neighbor." It was neat captioning, entirely to the point. Is that how his new employee thought of him?

"I've heard amazing things about you, sir," Sally answered his unasked question as Edward extended his hand. She was a pretty thing—dark curls and heart-shaped face—polite and poised into the bargain. Somehow he found her irritating.

"We've been out to Montauk Point," Ned announced, as if he felt obliged to account for his actions off the job. He was wearing his baseball cap and a T-shirt over cutoffs. Sally wore sunglasses and flip-flops, plus a loose shift to cover her bathing suit.

"You've come all this distance on foot—?"

A boyish grin preceded the explanation. "Friends dropped us off so we could piddle on the way home."

"Ned said he was too tired to walk," declared Sally, "but I insisted, and I'm sure he's glad I did" (here a wink at her companion) "because he's done nothing but talk about you all afternoon."

"Not *all* afternoon," Ned objected. Perhaps he blushed at Sally's remark, but the brim of his hat shadowed his face.

"This bears out Oscar Wilde's famous dictum," returned an amused Vann. " 'The only thing worse than being talked about behind your back is *not* being talked about.' "

"Yes, sir," replied Sally. Her questioning tone made him wonder whether she'd grasped the humor. Ned's broad smile left no doubt.

"Well," said Vann, his gaze encompassing the two of them, "don't let me detain you. You must be eager to get back after such a busy day ..."

Before either could reply, a kamikaze gull nosedived Ned and knocked his hat to the ground, then a playful wind blew it along the water's edge. All three set off in pursuit, but Edward quickly outpaced his younger companions. Surprised by how easily he outdistanced them, he soon had the flyaway hat in hand.

"I can't run in these silly flip-flops," Sally offered her plausible excuse. But Ned had nothing to say for his performance. His sinewy legs looked as if they were made for racing. Yet he was gasping for breath.

Vann was about to hand over the hat but, submitting to impulse, placed it on the young man's head.

Ned reached up with both hands to adjust it. "Looks like I'm in your debt again, Mr. Vann."

"Edward, please."

"Edward—" Ned corrected.

"Don't worry, your credit's good."

Several messages awaited his return. Farleigh had left them in the center of his desk, anchored by a glass statuette of Aphrodite, a gift from his former wife, the sole remnant of that marriage. The first message was from Fiona. Recalling Farleigh's recent confession that she'd instructed him to put her messages always on top, he slipped it to the bottom of the pile and shuffled through the next three, until he came to one from Miss St.-John.

PLEASE RETURN CALL—NOTHING URGENT—OLIVIA

How like Olivia—the epitome of restraint and moderation. Were they too much alike? They'd been a number going on two years, but had no particular plans, when friends asked, as they invariably did, for tying the knot. The failure of his first marriage had left scars, and the convalescent lover wasn't ready to reenter the fray. Those who purported to know him opined that he was "testing the waters." His former wife had asked little but to be left alone. Caroline Sinclair came from the same kind of wealth as he did; she'd never had to fight for anything, except happiness, which had eluded her long before she was introduced to her future husband. Marriage, alas, proved not to be the magic bullet that would bring it to her—

or to him, though he'd never thought much about happiness till Caroline moved it to the top of the marriage agenda.

"I thought it would be you." The mellifluous voice assured him he'd dialed the correct number. Several times lately the wrong person had answered, he tried to explain when she asked why he hadn't returned her calls, to which she replied that he was a victim of Freudian slips, that he was actually avoiding her and, as a result, was dialing wrong numbers with "unconscious intent."

"Why would I be avoiding you?" he returned, wondering whether she knew a reason he might not be aware of.

"I'm not your analyst, just your girlfriend." One point for Olivia.

"Then may I see you tonight?"

"Only if you beg me."

He let himself in with the key she'd given him as a gift a year ago. "What's this …?" he'd asked.

"Our future," came the neutral reply.

He'd requested a copy because Olivia had locked herself out a couple of times and he suggested she give him a key for safekeeping. "If it's only for safekeeping, as you so poetically put it," she'd retorted, "why should I bother giving it to you?"

"Because I'll think you're locking us out on purpose."

He found her reclining on a sofa surrounded by countless cushions, their scarlets, heliotropes, and vermilions hinting at oriental decadence. Olivia was wearing black velvet slacks and a sequined vest. "You're a perfect Ingres, one I'd like to frame," he told her, his wishful thinking warming him with visions of naked female flesh that had been available for the taking in Parisian dens and brothels as the war in Europe was winding down. But that was then. Had Europe ruined him?

She played with the idea for a moment. "I'm probably not voluptuous enough for Monsieur Ingres." She tossed a copy of *The New Yorker* to the coffee table. "But tell me, Edward, what are you in the mood for …?"

"A night of searing love."

"That can be arranged."

For some time their lovemaking had been perfunctory. They'd fallen into a trap that seldom fails to put a damper on passion: routine. He'd start with one arm around her shoulder while holding her tight, so tight she felt imprisoned, as she later tried to explain. Then he'd bring her off with a deft touch here and there; it took only a few touches at the beginning, but they'd reached the stage where his touch had lost its touch. And by the time she was finished, he was drifting off. She'd told him recently, "When you make love it's as if you're in a dream." She was only partly right; he was asleep. Finally, she conjectured,

"I think someone's come between us."

"Who is this mythical beast?"

"Your writing.

His lips brushed the cheek of his sleeping lover, then he dressed and sped home before dawn, leaving his MG in the driveway for Farleigh to garage. While motoring through the morning mist, he wondered whether Olivia had only pretended to be asleep when he kissed her. They hadn't quarreled; there'd been no unpleasantness. But a "night of searing love" it was not. He felt guilty and put out at the same time: guilty for his underperformance, put out because she hadn't inspired him to greater heights, to any heights for that matter. He hadn't enjoyed what his army buddies called a "good lay" in months, and he had no clue whether their coupling satisfied Olivia. Like Caroline, she was quite adept at concealing her feelings and accomplished at faking it in bed. He'd overheard one of Caroline's phone calls in which his ex all but bragged about her ability to "pretend" between the sheets. Was history repeating itself?

When he entered his study, he recognized nothing at first and had to acclimate himself to the familiar, though he spent most of his waking hours there. Fiona called it his cocoon. "I keep fearing you'll turn into a butterfly," she'd chide, always urging him to get out and "see the world." He'd told her more than once, "There's world enough for me in here."

The sun was filtering through a cloud cover. It battered the surface of the sea to a dull silver of crinkled aluminum foil. The gulls were out in force but were more subdued than usual. He missed their raucous cries, often the only voices he heard till late in the day. The circled date on his desk calendar reminded him a caller was about to arrive. He phoned down to Farleigh and asked him to prepare breakfast for himself and Ned. His "editor" had a hearty appetite.

Within the hour he heard a light knock and Ned appeared in the doorway, baseball cap in hand. He held back before venturing in, even then his approach tentative. Was Ned intimidated by his editorial duties? It's not every day that a college boy is asked to review the manuscript of an experienced writer. Yet Ned seemed remarkably self-assured whenever they discussed his writing.

"I'm glad to see you." He rose to extend a cordial handshake.

Ned sank into the waiting chair and brushed his forehead with the back of his hand, as if the slightest effort tired him. He'd been perspiring though it was only morning, and the summer heat had not yet descended. He wore the same plaid shirt as at their first interview. It seemed less nondescript today. Edward recalled yesterday's encounter on the beach and superimposed a pink-and-purple sky behind his visitor now, as if he were viewing a portrait in a gallery, his hobbledehoy of a Hals transforming smartly into a Gainsborough.

"All set?"

"Ready as I'll ever be." Ned glanced around the room as if not sure where he was.

"Would you care for a bite to eat before we start?"

"No, Edward, I'm ready now."

This declared with little conviction, but it was the first time the young man had called him by his first name without prompting.

"I've redone the opener," Edward exclaimed with a show of pride. "I shifted the setting to France, as you suggested, right after the German invasion, and introduced the two romantic leads. ... Why are you smiling?"

"'Leads.' It sounds as if we're watching a movie."

Ned's eyes scanned the page, returned to the top, scanned again, a pattern he repeated page after page. The gulls had resumed their morning chatter and the boisterous waves slapped the sand with increasing impudence. These repeated sounds and the rising heat lulled Edward till his head began to droop.

He must have dozed off for several moments. When he came to, his new employee was staring at him unabashedly.

"Is something the matter, Ned …?"

His reader had stood and was backing away from the desk. "I think I'm not myself today …," he stammered. "Would you forgive me if I took a break …? I imagine I could probably come back later …"

"Yes, of course. May I see you out …?"

"I'll be okay," Ned replied then turned to go. Edward listened as his footsteps grew fainter. When they'd all but receded into silence, he heard a muffled sound as if a heavy object had dropped on thick carpet. He rushed from the room to the top of the stairway. In the chasm below, Ned sprawled against the floor. A distraught Farleigh hovered over him.

He took the stairs two at a time and at the bottom knelt by Ned's side. Ned's legs were drawn up and his arms splayed over the parquet. He thrust an arm under Ned's head and ordered, "Fetch some water." He pressed his head to the young man's chest as Farleigh scurried off to the kitchen. "His breathing sounds heavy," he uttered to no one in particular. One of the maids who'd been dusting in a nearby room joined them.

"Will he be all right sir?" Her face betrayed a mixture of concern and the curiosity of an onlooker at a car wreck.

"Yes, I'm sure." The reply sounded automatic, even to him.

"Your water, sir." Farleigh handed him the glass.

"Hold it to his lips while I raise his head," he directed. "Ned, can you hear me …?"

His eyes tight shut, Ned moved his lips for a sip, then barely murmured, "I'm so sick …"

"Farleigh, get Silas on the phone. Milly, fetch something to fan him with, please ..."

Farleigh returned to report that Mr. Deane was out for the day and was not expected home till much later.

"Take over here—will you?—while I call for an ambulance."

It wasn't the best of times, it wasn't the worst of times, but it was pretty close to the worst. I could hardly believe I was more intimidated on this, my second day at the job, than I was on the first. I had no idea what to expect that first day when I arrived at Ocean House. I assumed I'd have to carry a paintbrush, deliver packages, run errands, weed the garden, and other such menial tasks that might strike you as below the dignity of a Columbia Scholar. And that's exactly what transpired. But I mustn't leave out a life-changing event that also occurred that first day—and caused me such disquiet when I returned on the second.

I showed up shoes shined, hair brushed, tie on straight, hoping to make an indelibly brilliant impression. I was frankly fixating so much on how I was coming across that when Edward gestured for me to take a seat across the desk from him, I instead knocked a stack of papers onto the floor.

"My manuscript—!" he wailed, falling to his knees to collect the precious pages. Like a devout acolyte, I knelt beside him to display my zeal in the manuscript-restoration process. But in our fanaticism, grabbing pages right and left, we wound up with two separate manuscripts that had to be reintegrated.

"Please, sir, let me do the honors," I bleated, all but snatching the other half of the manuscript from his trembling hands.

He sat back and wiped his brow, as if he'd been at hard labor. "Very well," he replied, his reluctance insinuating that he didn't have the greatest expectations of my clerical skills. But as I sat at a side table with the jumbled manuscript before me, leafing the pages back in order, my sharp eye caught a word spelled three different ways on the same page–folderal, falderal, folderol.

"You might want to fix this, sir," I proclaimed, my voice blending subservience with authority.

Before he could respond, I added, "... and you've got double quotes here inside single quotes—it should be the other way around."

He was impressed—olé! And I could see that my work was cut out for me: the Illustrious EDWARD VANN was going to ask little ari edelman to edit his MAGNUM OPUS—!"

"You've given me an idea ...," he said under his breath. Then I knew it was coming: I was to be made editor in chief of his masterwork. Why not? Wasn't I that Scholar from Columbia?

"Would you please take these pages home and do a close proofreading? Whatever you do, don't change a thing, but keep a list of what you think might be improved. Get through as many pages as you can, and bring them in tomorrow"

I'd just been promoted to copy boy.

On Day II, I returned with a chunk of manuscript in hand and a list almost as long as the manuscript itself. (Vann was not a fluid writer.) Though my mandate was mainly to spell-correct and fact-check, someone was going to have to spin this pile of paper into gold. Put another way, I was starting to see myself as a Jewish Joe Gillis skittering wildly onto Sunset-Hampton Boulevard where Norma Vann Desmond's minimum opus awaited me.

At breakfast before I set out, Mama was going over a list of things she wanted me to accomplish on the job that day, none of them having a thing to do with my duties.

"I've never set foot over there," she repeated this well-known fact. She'd made the point so many times since learning that the master of Ocean House had hired me that this revelation had become a confession of her soul, masking a burgeoning pride that her little darling was on his way up in the world (with paintbrush and watering can in hand, oy).

While I was trying to focus on that first clutch of Edward Vann's novel of war and redemption (so he called it) that I'd brought home, Mama set a plate of blintzes and sour cream before me.

"You know what you can do for me, Ari …?" Her faraway look presaged a mishegas that would unfortunately involve yours truly. "I want you to find out if they use a kosher butcher over there." It struck me that in the two weeks since Edward Vann had hired me, Mama never once referred to his residence as Ocean House but always "over there." Perhaps she picked it up from Dad.

"Don't mean to tell you how to run your business," Dad often said the opposite of what he meant, "but I wouldn't let it go to your head that you're working this summer over there."

"Where would you like me to let it go?" I retorted.

"You know what I mean" came his laconic reply.

Mama took a seat at the table with us, no plate in front of her. (Family secret: she seldom ate a bite in the presence of the two men in our family, perhaps a hangover from our forbears' days in the shtetl; she took her meals alone only after we'd cleared out of the breakfast nook aka dining room, which we didn't have one of). "Our Ari, he's a smart boy—he knows his place."

Was that meant to be a compliment?

"Long as he doesn't wander out of it," advised Dad. "But don't let them put you down either, son. I've often told you that."

"Certainly not," agreed Mama. "What does our Ari have to be ashamed of already …?"

I was starting to get it. They were trying to build up my confidence before I set out for over there.

"Who said anything about *ashamed*?" said Dad.

My confidence was starting to perk up.

"Just remember," Dad rounded out his advice du jour: "You're not perfect." He added for good measure: "And no one expects you to be."

I hopped on my bike, a nervous wreck, and set out for over there, kosher smosher. At least I'd learned which were the front and back doors of Ocean House. I was not to use either. Servants and staff were expected to enter by a nebbishy side door.

"There you are," exclaimed Mr. Granger, butler-in-chief, when he saw me approach. I was about to be overwhelmed by what I took to be his hauteur, when I realized that Farleigh Granger had lived a life of servitude. He was only a stand-in for a real person (this realization came before the onset of my Marxist phase). I soon learned he was a decent fellow, totally devoted to his master, or should I say "lord"?

"Glad to see you," he declared, and I started to utter something sprightly, when I realized why he was "glad."

"Be a good lad and take this tray up to the study, would you. You'll save me a trip."

The tray was loaded with provisions for Edward's breakfast.

I tucked the manuscript under my arm and trod lightly from the kitchen down the hall to the great stairway, then mounted the stairs, my trepidation increasing by the step. What if my mind didn't work and I couldn't convince the Lord of the Manor to accept my suggestions? What if he hated them or, worse, they offended him? Whatifwhatifwhatif already …!

When he didn't look up, I cleared my throat, but it hardly mattered what I said, because my voice failed. I tried shuffling my feet but my feet didn't make a sound. I forgot that I was wearing my new loafers, which slid silently over the floor—a preppy yid. I tried clearing my throat again, but it sounded as if I was burping and, thank heaven, Edward didn't notice. I was about to leave the room and try a new entrance when I heard a loud sneeze and was so startled I didn't realize it was mine.

"God bless you," came Edward's primly Protestant reply.

I could use his blessing, thought I.

"Oh, that—" said Edward, noticing the tray I was carrying. Then his precise instruction: "Just put it anywhere."

As I lowered the tray onto a table near his desk, he declared, "You've had breakfast this morning …?"

Before I could reply, the phone rang. With utmost courtesy my new employer inquired, "Would you mind terribly if I took the call? It might be unimportant …"

His remark turned out to be my introduction to Edward's sense of humor. He was also trying to tell me, with utmost subtlety, that if the call were unimportant, it wouldn't last long.

"Oh, hi, Liv. … Yes, it's I … Yes, I'm here—otherwise I wouldn't have answered, would I? But that goes without saying, doesn't it …? … No, darling, you're not interrupting anything …" He looked up and winked at me, while I, his vassal, pretended I was not hanging on his every word.

"Yes, tonight is fine. … What …? Of course, I promise to be wild and passionate. … Of course, I can hardly wait. … "Wait—! I have to attend some board meeting (and I mean B-O-R-E-D, Liv). I'll be with Fiona and it could take all evening, so sorry, darling. … Thank you for understanding; we'll have a wild and passionate evening some other night … soon … I promise … you're a peach!"

He returned the phone to the receiver then declared, "How rude of me, assuming a growing boy like you would have no appetite even if you've already had your breakfast. Pull up that chair and break bread with me. We'll need fortification to get through my turgid mess of a manuscript."

"I couldn't agree more," I exclaimed, so eager to please that I spoke before I thought. Then trying to undo the damage of my verbal faux pas, "I meant, about the breakfast, uh, the growing boy part, … well, uh—"

With a wry smile and another wink, Edward proclaimed, "We understand each other."

Mishegas.

CHAPTER 3

W HEN HE HEARD THE WHINE of the ambulance, he tore himself from Ned's side and raced onto the porch. "In here, gentlemen—!" He signaled to the young stretcher bearer and his older companion, who was also the driver.

An eerie calm settled upon the foyer as the older attendant knelt beside the body athwart the parquet floor. "He just passed out?"

"He fell down the stairs." The scent of polish filled Edward's nostrils, and for a moment the walls seemed to be closing in.

Farleigh interjected, "He was almost at the bottom when he fell, sir, from what I observed."

The attendant put his ear to Ned's chest. "Feverish—and his pulse is fast. Let's get him to the hospital."

The attendants carried Ned's body to the ambulance with Edward close behind. When the doors clanged shut, Edward raced to the garage and revved the MG's motor, then tailed the ambulance along the road to town, its siren a dirge in the morning stillness. He parked in the shade of a welcoming elm before hastening to the hospital's entrance. At the information desk a clerk asked him to be seated while the patient was being admitted.

"Can I see him then—?"

"Are you family?"

"Neighbor."

"Then I'm afraid you won't be permitted to see the patient before visiting hours at the earliest, which are not until 5:00 p.m."

"But ... he has only me at the moment. We can't reach his dad." He added for good measure, "... there's nobody else."

"Regulations, sir." The clerk's tight bun and horn-rimmed spectacles enhanced her authority. But did he hear someone calling his name?

"Edward Vann, if I'm not mistaken ...?"

The familiar features of the gentleman standing before him brought a smile of recognition.

"This must be the first time I've seen you outside The Gullet, Ed." His lawyer, Alden Brooks, extended his hand, the straw offered to a drowning man.

"It's Silas Deane's son, Alden. He got sick at my place and I can't reach his dad. I'd like to stay with him but I'm not family ..."

Brooks approached the matron at the desk. After the briefest exchange he returned to his client. "You've got the green light. Proceed to his room."

"Thank you. And one more thing—if I'm not imposing ...?"

Brooks nodded evenly.

"Would you call Olivia St.-John and explain that I'll be tied up at the hospital ...?"

"Should I ask her to join you here ...?"

"Olivia will know what to do."

It was more than an hour before they finished examining Ned and brought him to his room. He appeared to be sleeping peacefully as Edward kept vigil beside him for the next two hours. When a nurse reported that the boy's father would arrive soon, Edward drove home to shower and shave then returned a short time later. Back at the hospital, he realized Brooks had reached Olivia because flowers filled Ned's room and all but concealed the lone figure by the bedside.

Silas Deane sat with head bowed, oblivious to the visitor who'd stepped into the room. He was holding a small envelope that he'd removed from one of the bouquets. A respectful pause then

Edward shuffled his feet. The groundskeeper handed the envelope to the new arrival without looking up from his son.

Edward opened the note.

WITH HIGHEST HOPES FOR YOUR SPEEDY RECOVERY — *Edward*

Olivia had struck just the right tone.

Ned stirred a couple of times and looked as if he might be trying to speak but remained impassive. A nurse came to check his pulse then took his temperature. She shook her head ever so slightly before she brushed out of the room.

Only when the doctor appeared in the doorway did Silas spring to life. He crowded next to him while Dr. Kirkpatrick examined his son, running a hand over his belly, checking his heartbeat, taking his pulse.

After finishing his examination the physician, a portly gentleman whose graying hair framed a kindly face, signaled his visitors to step into the hall. He put on a pair of black-framed glasses as if they came with his diagnosis and declaimed, "I'm sorry to tell you, Mr. Deane, very sorry indeed, but I fear we have a full-blown case of polio on our hands."

The father frowned but said nothing.

"The next seventy-two hours will be critical, I suspect. It could take that long for the crisis to pass."

Silas's hands were shaking. "But ... what is it that we must do in the meantime, doctor ...?"

"Pray," came the practiced reply.

"Pray—? What good will *that* do?"

Dr. Kirkpatrick stole a quick glance at his weary audience. "I'll keep a close watch on him, and God willing—" He broke off then added as he left the room, "Good evening to you, gentlemen."

Edward put a hand on his groundkeeper's shoulder. "He's going to pull through, Silas ..."

Deane reached up and scratched the back of his head. "I appreciate your optimism, Edward. How can you be sure ...?"

"He's young, he's healthy, he's the picture of life."

Deane betrayed no emotion, but he did glance up to convey his thanks.

"Why don't you go home and get some rest, Silas?" Edward urged. "I can wait with him."

"I won't leave my son."

The look on Deane's face told him it was futile to utter the usual nostrums. "I'll be back later, in case you wish to be relieved."

"Thanks for meeting me here."

To the plangent strains of "Lawdy Miss Clawdy," Edward slid into the booth across from Olivia. The crowd at The Gullet was unusually lively for a weeknight. Couples chattered at tables, singles were mooning at the bar, while a group of young men in tight white T-shirts and duck's ass haircuts whooped and hollered around a dicey pinball machine.

"I thought a drink might help you unwind," she offered, placing her small ivory hand over his as it rested on the checked tablecloth.

His hand slipped around hers and held it till the waiter took their order. A honky-tonk number played on the jukebox, about a woman wondering whether her man would show up. It sounded incongruous so soon after the sickroom. The wellbeing of Edward Deane had hardly mattered to him until recently. Now the young man occupied his thoughts to an extent that surprised him and made him wonder whether Silas Deane's devotion had seeped into him.

"Edward—?" Olivia regarded him quizzically. "The waiter is waiting to take our order ..."

"Sorry, dear—"

"You really *are* in another world this evening. Shall I order for us ...?"

They dined in near silence, two fish dinners with chips and pickles washed down by a Budweiser. When he paid the bill she asked, "Where to now, Edward ...?"

"Back to the hospital."

"You're a kind soul," she returned as they rose from the table.

"I promised his dad I'd be there."

He didn't mean to sound defensive but feared he might be disappointing her, if she'd planned to spend the evening with him. She wouldn't let on—Olivia never asked for anything. This refusal to put herself on the line exasperated him at times. He didn't realize that she was giving him just the rein he needed to negotiate their romance.

The night seemed especially black as he drove to the hospital past homes forlorn and forbidding. Few lights were on. Could everyone be asleep? The bright aura that was hovering about the hospital brought a welcome relief when he parked the MG. As he entered the building, he recalled the time his dad rushed him there as a kid when he fell off a seawall and cut his knee. The blood ran down his calf into his white socks, turning them a rusty pink. In the operating room a swarm of attendants hovered around the young intern sewing stitches into his knee. The fear of pain, the prick of the needle, the smell of alcohol almost made him pass out. Yet his overriding memory was of the warmth of his father's hand upon his shoulder. It was the only time that Dad ever touched him.

The door was partly ajar. A lone bulb at the head of his bed cast a gloomy shadow over Ned. Edward froze when he stepped into the room; the young man's face resembled a death mask. He sank onto the straight-backed chair by the bedside. Why were hospitals so uncomforting?

Eventually Ned's shoulders shifted slightly and furrows spread across his brow. Edward leaned over and said softly, "Hello, Ned ..." Ned's eyes flickered, then his lips moved. Edward thought he heard the word *water*. He filled a cup from the sink and lifted Ned's head off the pillow, bringing the rim of the cup to his lips. Ned barely wet them, then his head fell back. Edward gently disengaged and sank again onto the unconsoling chair.

He was about to doze off when a nurse entered the room. Her eyes swept over him and he thought he detected the trace of a smile, or at least a kindly expression, as she checked the patient's vital signs. When she turned to leave, Edward followed her into the hall.

"Might I inquire how our patient is doing?"

The comely nurse, who looked to be in her mid-thirties, asked, "Are you family?"

"I might as well be," he offered, standing his ground.

She hesitated. "His dad just left. I guess you're taking the night shift?" She glanced over her shoulder and resumed. "We're still waiting for him to turn the corner. This stage can last a few days. Other times, it's over before you know it."

"Over?" His alarm prompted her to take his hand.

"He's young, he's a fighter—I can tell you that much. You probably know it already." She glanced down the corridor. "The first thing to hope for is that he pulls through. The verdict will be in on that within, I'd say, twelve to twenty-four hours. The next thing to hope is that he'll be intact when he comes out on the other side."

"Intact—?"

Still holding his hand, she added, "The disease can be debilitating. Some patients make it through unscathed. Others bear the marks of their ordeal for some time afterward."

"But they eventually recover—?"

"Some do."

He released her hand and she turned to go, but he called after her, "You're a good woman—" She held his gaze for some time before resuming her rounds.

He returned to the room, leaned over Ned's bed, and wondered whether it made sense to pray. But no words came. Bending down until his lips nearly touched Ned's ear, he whispered, "Ned—it's me—Edward. ... I want you to get well. ... I'm counting on you. ... You hear me, Ned ...?"

He hovered over the patient, smoothing his covers, checking his breathing, fretting, hoping a miracle would come of his efforts. He'd never attended to someone else's needs so closely before. He made a fist and barely touched it to Ned's cheek before settling down for the night.

* * *

Dawn was ascending by the time he left Ned's bedside. When he stepped into the corridor, he encountered Silas Deane. The father grasped both his hands. "Thank you, Edward …"

"Our boy's on the winning team, Silas—that's for certain." He wondered where this burst of optimism originated. He'd still heard no definitive account of Ned's progress, though he'd finally cornered Dr. Kirkpatrick and badgered him into providing a brief update on Ned's condition. "At this point, we've brought his fever down and that's certainly something. It was up to 105 degrees." The doctor didn't look him in the eye. Edward struggled to suppress his frustration at the limitations of medical science by mid-twentieth century. "We're doing our very best to keep him comfortable, administering fluids, …" Sensing his listener's impatience, Dr. Kirkpatrick added, "This is my best medical opinion." He collapsed his arms over his chest and made to depart. He'd depleted his sympathy and compassion.

Best medical opinion, whatever that was worth. He was standing on the front porch of the hospital as the sun rose and the beachfront town resumed its daytime activities. Delivery trucks rumbled toward their destinations while sleek Oldsmobiles and Buicks sped off to the city. Once seated in the MG, he glanced back; the hospital with its unmatched wings looked strangely unfamiliar, though he'd driven past it countless times. Curious, he reflected, how an emotional experience can alter a familiar setting beyond recognition.

Let's be honest—Sadie and I stayed on the beach too long that day—sunburn was the problem, not infantile paralysis. We'd found a semi-secluded cove where I thought I had the best chance of getting into where every not entirely nice Jewish boy likes to get—the girl's pants. And I was almost there … when we ran into Edward. He was in his beachcomber mode. It was our first open-air encounter. Up till then, I'd been all reverence and humility before my idol. But something about the bright sun and salty sea air reduced us to our essentials that day, and I found myself surprisingly relaxed in his presence, though he almost caught us in flagrante. But I'm getting ahead of the story—my real story, that is.

I'd been pursuing Sadie Sonnenschein all summer. She wasn't exactly my type; my preferred type was Fiona Vann of the Hamptons, Long Island, New York. But when a piece of fruit exceeds your grasp, you reach for a lower branch, to be perfectly crass (if *crass* can ever be perfect). Sadie was a smart girl and she was a good-looker. She had the boobs and the butt to launch a guy into orbit, and with her fair skin and blond hair she could pass for a shiksa. She'd even lost the accent along the way, though to be around her folks was enough to transport you back to the bakeries and tanneries of Łódź and Białystok.

Her mama, Belle Sonnenschein, used to say about me, "He has a way with woids, that one." She always addressed me in the third person, and I never knew when, or whether, I was expected to respond. "What's he up to tonight?" she'd ask when I'd come to call for her daughter. At times like that, Sadie would put on her best WASP accent; I think she did it to spook her mom. "We shan't be late, *maman*," that French twist at the end the coup de grâce.

Sadie looked up to me because I had a scholarship from Columbia. The first thing her *maman* asked when Sadie broke the news was, "How much does it pay?" "It covers all his expenses," Sadie proudly proclaimed. When she divulged the amount, a low whistle issued from stage left. Papa Si (as in "sigh") peeked out from behind his copy of the *Wall Street Journal*. Simon Sonnenschein was responsible for turning sleeveless undershirts—his costume du jour, stretched over his sagging paunch—into objects of scorn and ridicule. Without tendering congratulations, he asked, "You ever think of putting that piece of change into something that'll pay big, then withdraw it down the road as you need it …?"

"No, sir. I don't have much of a head for business."

"Ari's interested in education, Papa, not stocks," Sadie informed him. There was something both hilarious and touching about the way she'd put the guy down. No matter how out of line he could be, it never seemed to embarrass her; it was as if she was correcting a child. Maybe she was.

The Sonnenscheins were the comic relief of our community. How could I forget the time when Edward came to their house (I never found out why) and Si met him at the door in his shirt-no-sleeves. I could almost feel Edward flinch from my perch on the stairs with Sadie. After the illustrious Mr. Vann had finished his business, he tossed a compliment to the missus by commenting on the jewelry—strictly costume—she was wearing. He proffered it in such a way that an astute listener (*moi*) would not necessarily take it as a compliment (as when a parent introduces you to a particularly homely child and, desperate to make nice, you respond, "He looks just like you"). "That's quite a collection of bracelets you're wearing, Mrs. S." Even I knew that the right thing to say when you get a compliment is "Thank you." Not the ineffable Belle S. She looked Edward straight in the eye and exclaimed, "Si says every time I go to the beauty parlor, I'm wearing a hundred dollars' worth of jewelry." I'd hoped that would end it all there, this flagrant inventory. But her husband was not to be outdone. "A hundred and fifty, Belle," he countered. At which she retorted, "I know what's on my body. A hundred bucks, Si—count it up yourself, ..." Holding her plump arm aloft and pointing to the first of a dozen bangles, then successively to the others, "You paid twenty-nine fifty for this one, thirty-two ninety-nine, for the next ...," as the ancient Romans used to say, "... et cetera." Later, I was reminded of Mrs. Sonnenschein in an anthropology course, where I read about those African tribes that wear their wealth wherever they go.

That day on the beach, my concupiscence brought the Lord's wrath upon me. Sadie and yours truly had finished our picnic lunch, and I'd been sweet-talking her for over an hour. Sadie had just won a scholarship from Barnard College, Columbia's neighbor, and I was promising to be her beau once we returned to the City. I guess it was my way of pledging my troth. Heedless of the sun's rays, I'd managed to caress the top of her bikini off her round, firm, fully packed breasts and to tease her pants down to her delta, when she caught sight of someone in the near distance. I was dying for a quickie, but we hadn't gone all the way (yet) and I knew time was running (out) because of that infernal vagabond coming toward us. With miles of sand between the Hamptons and Montauk, why did he have to encroach on *our* space?

Sadie squeezed back into her swimsuit and I made the necessary adjustments so my suit ceased to resemble a ship's prow. The sun shone directly in our eyes so I couldn't make out who was approaching, till he was almost upon us. When I recognized Edward Vann, I stood to attention and made ready to greet him.

"How nice to see that someone's taking advantage of this lovely strand." Edward leaned in and shook my hand. I'd been so hot for Sadie that I'd hardly noticed the setting. To me it was just two bands of blue and tan, sky and sand. (Later it struck me that Edward may have intended a double-entendre.)

"You're acquainted with Sadie Sonnenschein, Mr. Vann?" I asked to be polite. I still called him by his last name.

"Of course," he replied with impeccable aplomb. "Please don't get up," he insisted when he saw that Sadie was about to stand for the "introduction"; they'd surely met before.

I was quite taken by Edward au naturel, with his ruffled hair and glistening eyes, lit by a blaze of sun. They were the color of the sea, with an intense greenish cast. His gaze was fastened on us, and for a moment I felt the stab of jealousy. I wanted him to shower all his attention on *me*. We made small talk for several minutes, then he said he must get home. He shook both our hands this time. I thought he held mine longer than my companion's, and my eyes held his for the duration of the "shake." That night I had the worst case of sunburn of my life.

CHAPTER

4

H E SLEPT FITFULLY FOR A FEW HOURS and awakened before dawn. The enveloping silence felt like humidity on a hot summer day, when your skin warns you there's no escape from the weather closing in. Yet he was thankful for the break from worrying about Ned lying in that hospital bed; the oblivion of sleep was just what he needed. He'd not given much thought to parenthood, living much of his life isolated from society, despite his social position. But Ned's illness had opened a window on the travails of raising kids. This newfound sympathy reminded him of a late nineteenth-century painting. It depicted a doctor with limited resources hovering over a dying child. The mother lies prostrate while the father despairs by the bedside. He could see himself now inside that picture frame.

How had the young man come to matter so much to him in such a short time? They were even namesakes, though Ned didn't use "Edward." But what a thing to be thinking when Ned lay near death! A wave of irritation swept over him at the caprice of fate, which he was inclined to take personally. Why had it intervened just as this young man in his prime wandered into his solitary existence?

He slipped out of bed and rang Farleigh to prepare his breakfast, then took a shower. As the rough bar of soap grazed his skin, he imagined he was undergoing a medieval penance to restore the health of his friend. Yet rub as he might, the image of Ned's face—eyes shut, forehead bathed in sweat, lips drawn tight—hovered before his eyes. He threw on shirt, slacks, and sandals before hastening down to breakfast, then off to the hospital.

The sun shone benevolently, and a cool breeze was blowing off an indifferent sea as he turned onto the highway. A stream of commuters was flowing toward New York, gearing up for the drama that awaits the suburbanite in Gotham. He'd made that commute himself when he was an editor with his own imprint in Midtown Manhattan. His foot strained to press the accelerator. He couldn't remember the last time he'd felt the swift onrush of time.

At the exit he jammed the accelerator to the floor. The morning mist had evaporated, and when the hospital came into view, a halo of light illuminated it. He parked and raced to the front door, then took the stairs to Ned's room. The floor nurse on duty gave him a quick look but let him pass; his lawyer's open sesame must still be valid. He stole down the corridor till he came to Ned's door. Expecting to find him alone or with his dad, he was startled to see that the patient had a visitor.

"It was too early to ring you." Olivia had pulled her dark brown hair into a bun and covered it with a white kerchief. When she glanced up at him, her perfectly symmetrical face reminded him of Helen Hayes, perhaps as a nurse in some fantasia of war and redemption conjured by a Hemingway, or, in fact, by him when he remembered the novel he was writing.

"How did you get in to see him?" he wondered. "It's not regular visiting hours."

"Same as you," she replied. "Pull."

He took a seat beside her. "How's our patient?"

"You know as much as I do. He's been pretty inert since I arrived. Now and then his face contorts, if that's the right word ..."

"It was kind of you to come."

As he spoke Ned's eyelids flickered and he raised his head an inch off the pillow. Was he trying to speak? Edward moved closer to the bed. After an apparent struggle, Ned brought an arm out from under the covers and reached toward him. Edward clasped his hand, waiting for him to speak. But the effort seemed to have exhausted the patient. His eyes snapped shut like those of a doll when it lies back, and he said nothing. A nurse paused at the doorway, smiled, and passed on.

"Time for me to be on my way." Olivia rose and brushed Edward's cheek with her lips. "Let me know how he's doing. I'll be home most of the day."

Edward nodded, then watched her depart. Ned was still holding his hand.

My sunburn was so severe I didn't feel like going to work for the next two days. It was worse than a fever. Your fever gives off heat as you attempt to recover; my sunburn radiated into me, the heat seeking out my core to lodge there and torment me for my transgressions of the flesh. It was fate's or the deity's punishment for my concupiscence on the beach with Sadie. Everything hurt but my hard-ons. I tried to suffer in silence. I failed.

"If you feel *that* bad," advised Mama, "someone better call that Mr. Vann of yours and tell him you can't work today."

"Ohh," I groaned, "oh, *ooh*–!"

"All right, already—!" Mama declared. "I'll make the call."

She dutifully reported my "perilous condition" to my employer. I didn't have to tell her to play it for all it was worth. "We're hoping he'll come out of it ... No, he's much too sore to move him to the hospital ... He just lies there ... No, he's not talking ... hardly a word ... I'll be glad to give you an update when I can leave his side ..."

Mama's Academy Award–winning performance did the trick. In the afternoon of my second day off work—I was feeling much better by then, thanks to liberal applications of Heinz vinegar—who should come calling on me but Olivia St.-John.

"I told Edward I'd be in your neck of the woods, and he asked me to stop by and see how you're feeling."

"Won't you stay for tea?" asked my startled mama. (Was she stalling for time? We never drank tea at our house.)

"I thought maybe Ari might enjoy some fresh air ..."

"Oh, I don't know whether he's up to it—"

"I'd love to," I broke in, catching sight on our driveway of her Impala convertible with the lid down.

Olivia had removed the velvet ribbon she usually tied in her hair. Her tresses blew in the breeze as if their sole aim was to taunt me. It was the first time I realized that Edward's paramour was beautiful. Up till now, I'd had eyes only for Fiona Vann—plus, of course, Sadie's body.

"Is there some place you'd especially like to go—my treat?" she asked after we'd driven along the shore for several minutes. "How about a Dairy Queen?"

I took a breath. "May I make a daring suggestion—?"

"I could be up for a dare."

Her reply was encouraging—judicious with a streak of go-for-it.

"How about The Gullet? I'm kinda thirsty."

"From that sunburn, of course," she replied, her trademark tact putting me at ease.

We parked at the curb and I hopped out to open her door.

She looked pleased. "I must tell Edward you're a gentleman as well as a scholar."

"Thanks. Did Edward send you to report on me ...?"

Bad me! It was a ruse: I used my pretended (at this point) infirmity to probe for info I'd otherwise not be free to gather. I was dying to find out more about our Edward—specifically, what he thought of *me*.

Like, when they seated us at The Gullet and we ordered martinis (Dairy Queens be damned!), I asked, "Does Edward often use you as ambassador ...?"

"Why do you ask?"

"Well, it was kind of him to check on how I'm feeling—by sending the most attractive emissary." I hoped she'd reply that Edward thought of me day and night, that he was worried sick about my terminal tumor—I mean, my oversize ego … I mean, my sunburn … !

"Edward is given to great causes," she replied, her neutrality worthy of Solomon.

I couldn't recall that she'd ever criticized our writer friend those few times we'd met, though she'd never praised him either. This caused me to question the nature of their commitment. How much did Olivia know of Edward's former wife, "the woman who wasn't there," Edward had let slip during one of our editing sessions. Local gossip had it that the bloodless marriage left Edward distrustful of the institution itself. Others said that Olivia was a carbon copy of his first wife. They both came from a moneyed background, though Caroline from bigger bucks. Olivia sprang from less exalted but more reliable stock—doctors, professors, a lawyer or two. It wasn't my business to crack the safe of her mind, though after several sips of my martini, I began to jimmy the lock.

"I suppose you're one of Edward's causes …?"

Her eyes shot to mine as if I'd said "Let's have sex under this table!" Her lips quivered, and I thought she was about to make a confession. Without a word, she directed her attention to the stage at the back of the room, where local talent appeared when it moved the management to showcase it. A young man in jeans and T-shirt was holding the mike, announcing the first "act" of the evening. He muttered and mumbled like the local yokel he was, but the place became silent the moment the first performer appeared onstage.

A woman of light dark skin with a full figure swathed in a silvery sheath took the mike from the MC. She looked out of place in our dump, more like a performer at a Manhattan dive. I'd say she must have been in her forties and betrayed not a trace of self-consciousness. She probably had little desire to please her audience. In truth, some of the gents had arrived straight from their farm swaddled in flannel shirts and overalls.

But then the singer's voice came within hearing, introducing her first song. There was something ingratiating about her accent, which I couldn't quite place; she didn't come from around here. She was quite a showman. "Have you ever regretted something you did for love?" she asked, warming us up. I thought of my hand in Sadie's pants and the sunburn from it. She next inquired, "Would you forgo a single pleasure you've tasted in love's name?" (This was getting good!) She then led into her first song, "I'd Rather Be Burned As A Witch."

I ordered another round for us over Olivia's mild objection. She was scrutinizing the woman on stage and paid no attention to anything else. Our second round arrived and I was glad for the fortification, because the singer had wound up her song and was heading in our direction. She made her way past admiring onlookers without seeming to notice a soul, then stopped at our table. Her proud demeanor centered upon a sculpted nose that was small from north to south but projected prominently over full lips. But the eyes were her most arresting feature, black as jet with a fixity of gaze that could stop a man in his tracks.

She said not a word but exchanged glances with Olivia, and I thought she smiled before leaving us.

"You've heard her sing before?" I asked when the performer was safely out of earshot.

All Olivia replied was "What was that …?"

Edward wandered onto the beach, and his feet sought the shifting strip where the waves wet the sand, the "line" crossed by sea creatures when they first ventured onto land to become at some point beings like, frankly speaking, us. He followed that ever-shifting line eastward toward Montauk Point, walking with no purpose but to get away. Though Ned's condition had stabilized, he was no better than when they first rushed him to the hospital. The hours of bedside worry were taking their toll and he needed release. On impulse, he started to call Olivia; an evening in the sack might do the trick. But the call of the sea lured him from the house to the beach.

A stranger encountering the wanderer would have observed a fortyish man who could pass for younger, his shoulders slightly bent, you might think prematurely. His light brown hair still had volume enough for the wind to tousle, coarseness enough to fall in place when the wind tired of its sport. His eyes would have met a passer-by's without looking away, but he would not be the first to show a sign of recognition. The growth of beard was all but habitual, as was the mustache. Olivia said it gave him character. When he'd asked her whether she thought his character was weak, she'd replied, "You have character enough, but it adds to your heft."

He returned to Ocean House at peace with himself for the first time since polio struck Ned. He'd ask Farleigh to mix him a gin and tonic. It was too late to write; his creative juices seemed to start up only at sunrise or before. But just before he turned to go in, Farleigh approached him from the house and handed him a nondescript envelope. It was smaller than letter-size and looked as if it might have been stuck in a woman's purse for some time, a faint crease running across one corner and a smudge on the backside— lipstick or blood, it was hard to tell. It was addressed to no one and contained a single sheet of paper creased down the middle. When unfolded, it read simply

IN TOWN

He stuffed the envelope in his pocket. A spike of alarm that his houseman might know about the letter's origin prompted the nonchalant observation, "I think it's going to rain, Farleigh." He was dying to ask who delivered the missive, but instead turned his eyes to the sea. "I won't be having supper here tonight."

He returned to the house and restrained himself from taking the stairs two at a time. Once inside his bedroom he hastened to the shower. As he stood under its soothing waters, a tumescence arose in his groin. It had been a while since that happened of its own. He watched his member rise, aiming toward the right. Dimitris, his older brother's best friend, had once told him that his penis had special talent; most of them pointed to the left. He recalled the occasion, they were adolescents, when Maxi's friend came to know this about him. Dimitris often wandered through the house when he tired of Maxi's company, but Edward never expected he'd follow him into the bathroom. He was taking a shower when Dimitris stepped into the room and pulled the shower curtain aside. "Caught you!" the rascal exclaimed, wild with delight at his prank. Edward clasped his privates with both hands and expected Dimitris to run out of the room. But the interloper took a seat on the bench beneath the window and watched him finish bathing. The bather was just young enough that he didn't know whether to be indignant or aroused at the unseemly attention. Then Maxi appeared in the doorway. He shut out the next thought.

He followed the road from Ocean House to the highway, then turned onto a back street after a few miles. Dusk was falling and lights were flickering inside the houses he passed; they became smaller, less well tended, and farther apart as the MG penetrated the warren of narrow, unpaved roads. Then it came in view, a dwelling whose size was difficult to determine amid the conspiring trees. He left the car at the side of the road and proceeded up the dirt driveway.

While he was deciding whether to ring the bell or just walk in, the front door opened, as if of its own, and a figure in shadow faced him. The man wore only a T-shirt that didn't reach to his waist and tight-fitting trousers that exposed his ankles. He wore nothing on his feet.

Edward entered the living room and the phantom melded away, leaving him alone. He stood by a window that looked onto obscurity and waited. Until a voice asked,

"Do I thank you for coming ...?"

She had stepped just inside the room, as if she were unsure whether to remain.

"I'll do the thanking," he replied, then left the window and sank to his knees before her.

He heard a car passing in the distance and a sound he didn't recognize from a nearby room. The woman, who was about his age, stood motionless before him. He encircled her with his arms. Soon he was running eager hands up and down her legs, seeking the inside of her thighs as he pushed aside her silvery gown. He nuzzled her triangle, inhaling the scent of brine and ash that never failed to remind him of the sea.

"Liane!" he gasped, running lips and tongue up and down, across and over her exposure. His heavy breathing drowned out all other sounds as he roamed across her body.

She continued to hold him fast as his hands wrestled with his trouser buttons. He managed to unfasten them, then yanked them to his knees along with his undershorts. He leaned in to her once more and tried to pull her to the floor, but she shoved her knee to his chin and knocked him over. She stepped on his chest, increasing the pressure as she brought more of her weight to bear on him.

"Do you have it?" Her voice was devoid of tone.

He tried to speak but his throat contracted. Only later did he remember catching sight of the phantom's feet in a nearby doorway as he squirmed under her weight. He tried to nod, to signal an affirmative response, if only to lighten the pressure.

"Cat got your tongue, baby ...?" She was peering down at him, a smile curving her lips. It was not reflected in her jet-black eyes.

She removed her foot and he raised his head off the floor. "I'll get it for you."

"Five figures ...?"

"We'll have to see about that," he returned, sensing that she'd begun to relent. She gave a nod to the man who'd let him in. He approached silently and knelt beside their prey, then reached for Edward's member. He stroked it till it rose to full measure. This took only seconds.

I'm abandoning our writer to this femme brutale and her sidekick. He needs a vigorous shaking up after wallowing in his whitebread existence.

Why would a respectable guy like Edward Vann get mixed up with such a character? Who can say whether the intemperate pursuit of pleasure isn't the best way to slake desire? Aren't such "odd" couplings the stuff of sexual history? Think of the French bourgeois of the nineteenth century with his many whores. Edward's not a thrill seeker in the conventional sense. My take is that he's trapped between his life in society and a wide-ranging libido he keeps under wraps most of the time, but when it bursts forth there's no stopping it.

Though he's highly refined—he was made for society—he usually prefers to fly solo. Perhaps that's why he became a writer. He started off in nonfiction, scribbling about beach life in the Hamptons—pleasures of the idle rich. His books found their niche among them and among Upper West Side literary types. And now he has this novel under contract, and needs more help than he realized. That might have been the end of our story, a recluse immured in his seaside mansion, writing day and night with time off for his lady friend, Olivia, a respectable kind of woman for a man of Edward's status, despite his sorties to the likes of Liane Devereux.

Yet what more is there to say about a hermit scribbler whose attention I've tried to reel in all summer? Enter Edward "Ned" Deane, offspring of the Vann's long-serving groundskeeper, Silas. Of course, it stretches credulity that a college youth would be asked to critique the work of a seasoned author, a man old enough to be his father. But this is Vann's first attempt at fiction, creating "something out of nothing," as he told his lawyer, Alden Brooks, a whole new playing field …

… And here's where I came in. When I reported for work on Day III, things were looking up for me. I'd arrived armed with my list of "suggestions." Among the countless misspellings and verbal infelicities in Edward's manuscript nestled numerous anachronistic nuggets, for example, truces declared before battles began, a soldier the same age as his parents, and a dog at least fifty years old. Bringing these anachronisms to my exalted Edward's attention was my bucket of cold water in his face. He sat for some time pondering my editorial markings, marginal notations, deletions, underlinings, and the like, his lower lip shifting from side to side. Was he going to have a fit? Fire me on the spot? Call the police …?

"I see here …," he temporized, "that I should be putting your editorial skills to greater use."

Thus began our collaboration as writer and editor.

CHAPTER 5

NEXT MORNING HE DROVE to the hospital as the sun was rising. Recalling the events of the evening before, he wondered what his young friend would think of him now. He had reason to believe Ned held him in high regard. But if Ned knew how he'd passed the previous night, would he still want to work for him?

As things stood, Ned Deane was in no condition to worry about his employer's nocturnal forays. Ned remained semiconscious while Dr. Kirkpatrick and the nurses watched over him, and family and friends prayed for his recovery. He'd awake for only moments at a time; twice he asked where he was. After the disease had begun to subside, he confessed that his main recollection was of two faces hovering at his bedside.

That very morning, the two heads appeared again. His dad was gazing down at him. But it wasn't Dad, it was another man—Edward, sitting where Dad had formerly been. But perhaps that was yesterday …? Then he dimly recalled it *was* Edward because Dad's hair is gray and Edward's has only streaks of it. And it was not the first time, he'd noticed Edward there before, because his shirts changed. One was a cream color. The other looked like orange rust. A little wild for Edward, who didn't seem to wear many colors.

So Edward had been at his side, perhaps all along? He struggled to sit up, partly for appearances' sake, partly to show his gratitude to this kind, extraordinary man. He gripped the bedrail, and his back rose a couple of inches off the mattress. He could hear his labored breathing; the effort had exhausted him, but he was finally sitting upright for the first time since he was admitted to the hospital.

Straining to raise himself farther, he promptly fell back. But the effort exhilarated him, reminding him of the long shots he'd taken on the court—and made a basket. Seizing the rail again, he heaved himself into a sitting position and this time managed to stay upright. Sweat dripped down his brow and his vision blurred. Then Edward appeared in the doorway. He'd never seen him look so happy before.

"Going somewhere?" came his visitor's excited greeting.

"Soon, not immediately."

Edward put his hand over the patient's, which held fast to the bedrail. "This is quite a sight—a cause for celebration—!"

"Break out the champagne—"

"We *will* be breaking out that champagne, my friend—and before you know it!" He sank onto a chair by the bedside.

"I'm waiting," came the good-natured retort. "Seems I've gotten to be quite good at waiting lately."

"Don't be hard on yourself. You've been working more than any of us these past few days."

Ned reflected. "What's come over me, anyway ...?"

Vann's voice dropped to just above a whisper. "The doctor says a nasty case of polio."

"*Polio*—?"

Edward barely nodded, not sure he should have been the bearer of such news.

"Shit."

"Couldn't have put it better myself."

He left the hospital under a burning sun. The seats of the MG were almost too hot to touch, but what did it matter in the grander scheme of things? His prayers had been answered—Ned was going to recover! Not that he actually prayed; he'd given up praying soon after he was absorbed into the Episcopal faith. He'd attended confirmation classes and knew what he needed to know to pass muster with the presiding bishop. He'd even begun to embrace the faith. But then his mother died, and he left the church. From that day to this, he didn't know whether her death was from illness or by her own hand. Dad refused to say and no one else seemed to know. In fairness, he'd hardly inquired; it wasn't something a young man seeks out with much enthusiasm, especially when that death was tainted by scandal.

She'd been unstable, Cecelia Vann. He'd caught on from an early age, veiled allusions uttered by distant and not-so-distant relatives—even their housekeeper. He made his own teen-boy inquiries, but the most he'd gleaned was, "She had her moods." But everyone had moods. And there was the falling out with Fiona over her daughter's loss of a valuable heirloom tiara. Their mother never forgave her for that. Several times over the years he'd caught Fiona sobbing, not about the tiara but about the loss of her mother's love. So what had befallen his mother? The question still hung over him.

He was approaching the home stretch now, and his eyes were veering toward the blue-green sea that had just surged into view. They settled next on the steeple of the Episcopal church that had been his family's refuge from worldly affairs. This landmark was so familiar that he seldom noticed it while driving past, but today it caught his attention. Its spire reminded him that Ned, too, had lost his mom at an early age. A scene from the funeral at that church crossed his mind—a boy and a somewhat older girl running about the churchyard after the service as if they hadn't a care, as if nothing had changed in their young lives. That was the first time he'd laid eyes on Ned Deane. Dad had asked him to represent the family at the funeral; it was "inconvenient" for anyone else. Fiona was mired in the finishing touches of her (second attempted) wedding, which failed to fall through in time for her to be the family's ambassador, and Maximiliano didn't represent well, Dad had confided without elaboration. Dad's rare show of confidence took the sting out of his new assignment. Dad's excuse for missing the event was, of course, always the same: Business. He suspected Dad didn't want to be reminded in public of his own wife's demise.

As he headed for his automobile after the service, he came face to face with young Deane. Ned was the typical rapscallion—shoes untied, hair mussed, shirt splotched with dirt. He had little idea what to say to the scamp, who couldn't have been more than ten or eleven to his thirty-two years. But he wasn't the first to speak; the youngster preempted him.

"You must be Mr. Vann."

"Yes," he replied, kneeling down to be on eye-level with the reluctant mourner. He wanted to say something comforting but had no practice in showing his feelings in that age of polio, world communism, and atom bombs. He managed to come up with "But you may call me Edward."

The boy replied without any hesitation, "All right, Edward Vann."

They'd not said another word to each other from that time till the recent morning when he took on the "rapscallion" as his helper.

He parked the MG and entered Ocean House to be accosted by a too familiar voice.

"And where do you think you've been?" Fiona was in high dudgeon. He'd forgotten their date to "go over the books," as she dubbed their trying, all-too-frequent ritual.

"Sorry, Sis—I was at the hospital."

"Nothing serious, I trust …?"

"Young Edward Deane—he has polio."

"At such an inconvenient time," she reflected.

"What time *would* be convenient for polio …?"

"You know what I mean, Edward."

He knew all too well. His sister was a creature of habit who looked unfavorably on interruptions of her routine. Yet she had her better side, and her best. Had he stressed that Ned needed round-the-clock vigils at the hospital, Fiona would have willingly stood in for him. And sent a check.

"A good morning to you, Edward." A second voice echoed his sister's.

Melville Mellon-Glade stood on the stairs one step from the bottom, as if he couldn't decide whether to join them or return upstairs to the suite of rooms reserved for Fiona when she visited. He was clad in jodhpurs and linen shirt, with a pair of riding boots on his size-twelve feet. Tall and spare, with fading brown hair parted down the middle and a mustache of matching hue, he might have stepped off a page from Fitzgerald. He'd made his money in the wine import trade, which is to say he'd inherited a substantial share of the family business. This allowed him to devote much of his energies to tennis and polo. And now, to Fiona.

Edward started to shake hands with his sister's fiancé but couldn't bring himself to formally acknowledge someone caught between upstairs and down. He gave a nod instead. He was anxious to put in a call to Dr. Kirkpatrick, then get back to his writing, which he hadn't touched since Ned took ill. Like the sea, writing was his life's blood. If he neglected it, he'd soon be overcome by restlessness and entangled in the loose ends of his existence. His sister's visit was one of those loose ends.

Treating his apparent preoccupation as but a minor inconvenience, Fiona relented. "We can meet later in the day or even tomorrow," she offered. "Besides," she added with a trace of coyness, "I have news to announce: you'll be interested to know we've set a date for the wedding."

"*A* date or *the* date…?" quipped the writer. Before she could reply he added, "That *is* news." He'd caught himself before calling it "good" for fear of patronizing her, though it was certainly *good* for him—he'd long ago decided that holy matrimony might get her off his back.

When he returned to the hospital that afternoon, the sound of laughter was rippling from Ned's room. At least someone seemed happy. He'd reached Dr. Kirkpatrick and teased a wary, sketchy prognosis out of him. His young friend was definitely out of the "danger zone," as the physician put it, but the "end" wasn't yet in sight. When he pressed Kirkpatrick for details, the doctor explained that recovery was likely to occur in stages. One of those involved mobility. Ned had not been able to move his left leg since he'd recovered consciousness and his fever abated.

He stood in the doorway waiting to be noticed. Ned soon flashed him a broad grin. Before he could return it, he recognized Ned's visitor, the young woman he'd met on the beach with Ned, right before polio struck. She was sitting next to Silas Deane.

"You remember my friend …," Ned prompted her.

"Of course I do—Mr. Vann!"

Sally Sunshine's cheery expression made him wince. Was there anything to smile about at the moment?

"Edward, please," he insisted with exaggerated politeness. He recalled the irritation she'd provoked when they met on the beach. It was rearing its head again, and the poor girl had hardly done a thing to arouse it.

He took a seat beside her. "How is our patient faring …?"

"Couldn't be better," came the self-assured reply. Ned was sitting up and the color was returning to his cheeks; rather, the redness of fever had abated and his complexion, if not rosy, was no longer pale. Perhaps the lurid green hospital gown made him look worse than he felt.

"I'm sure he'll be back on the court before we know it," chimed Sally. "Won't you, Ned …?"

Edward wondered whether she'd heard the latest prognosis and was trying to keep Ned's spirits up. She probably had little to go on but hopeless optimism. But perhaps optimism wasn't a bad thing at this turn.

Despite Ned's brave front for visitors, he soon drifted off to sleep. When he seemed at rest, Sally whispered it was time to leave. She approached the bed and bent over as if to kiss the now drowsing patient, but Silas stopped her. "He may still be contagious you know."

"I'm not worried," said Sally, but she didn't try to brush past the father's protective arm. "I'll see you soon, Edward." Vann stood and nodded as the devoted girlfriend left the room.

When they were alone together, Silas informed him that he'd just received a substantial check after lunch, delivered in person, by Fiona. "She said it was to ... what was her word? ... to *alleviate* my expenses. Had to use a dictionary to figure that one out," the groundskeeper added with a wink, perhaps to brush back a tear.

"I can't vouch for my sister's lingo," mused Edward, "but I can definitely vouch for her credit."

"Whatever the word she used," returned Deane, "it was mighty kind of her, and I'd be dishonest to pretend I don't need it, losing time up here at the hospital—not that I wouldn't want to be by Neddy's side as much as possible ..." The groundskeeper's eyes were indeed welling now.

"You don't have to justify your situation to me, Silas."

Deane coughed self-consciously. "Listen to me, goin' on about money when my son's health is on the line and who knows how he'll come out of this ordeal ..."

"Have you spoken with Dr. Kirkpatrick?"

"This morning. He ran into me while he was making his rounds before I got to the room."

Vann nodded encouragingly.

"Said my boy had come along good as could be expected. Said he'd passed the crisis." Deane lowered his voice before resuming. "I had a question or two for him, Dr. Kirkpatrick—I asked him what he thought the final outcome would be. He started scratchin' his head, you know, the way folks do when they're afraid to tell you somethin' you should know but they don't want to be the one to tell you."

"I understand," said Edward.

"It was about the boy's ability to walk afterward."

"Walk ...?"

"Well, sir, I knew the doc didn't want to go any further than that, but I figured it's my son, and I need to know ..."

"What did he tell you?"

Silas took a deep breath. "He wasn't sure the boy would walk normal again."

CHAPTER

6

A GENTLE BREEZE RIPPLED THE SHEER CURTAINS of Edward's bedroom and they were dancing in place when he awoke. A loose shutter on one of the windows also competed for his attention as it clacked against the wall at irregular intervals. It was a large room; the family once allocated it to guests because of its spacious bathroom and nearby pantry. It was certainly too big for one man, according to Fiona. That's why he chose it when he moved back "home" from the city, where he still kept a pied-à-terre.

The smell of the sea was a soporific for his early-morning musings. But without warning he was wrenched from his reverie by a voice expostulating "God damn—!"

A heavy mass had dropped on top of him, and the voice was his own.

"Maxi! What the hell are you doing here—?"

"You and I need to have a talk, Eddie." His brother skewered him with his gaze. The sound of his nickname careened him back to their childhood, when his older brother used to lord it over him. In those days Fiona acted as intercessor in lieu of their mother. Was his mother ever there, or was she but a supernumerary walking through his life?

He couldn't imagine what Maxi wanted, but it had to be something out of the ordinary. Maxi retreated to the foot of the bed and propped a pillow behind his back. He resembled a ruffian who'd been caught breaking into the house. His thick hair stained gray was seldom combed, as if he'd just risen from bed. His skin verged on sallow, while his craggy features could have been those of a hardened convict. Edward pictured him as a kind of malevolent Jean Valjean. Yet Maximiliano Vann was considered by many to be strikingly handsome. His absurdly long first name was one of those compromises that married couples make to compensate for a perceived slight; it was entirely Cecelia's idea. Cyrus had called it "affected and effeminate." But Cecelia insisted that the name was a way for her husband to compensate for his absurdly "truncated" surname.

"I'll come straight to the point," said Maxi, brushing a shock of hair from his forehead. The room shrank as Edward eyed his brother. "I trust this will cost you very little." Maxi put his hand on Edward's knee. "You think I'm going to ask for something outrageous—? Not at all, Eddie, just the local address of Liane Devereux."

He wasn't ready to confront Maxi head-on. At best he could keep him at bay. Maxi was adept at playing the bon vivant; he could also strike like a viper. To hold him off till he could decide on his next move, he declared, "I'll need a little time."

He had to get away. He didn't know how long his brother planned to squat at the house, and he didn't want to ask. Despite its vast size, Ocean House seemed to be teeming with denizens since Fiona's encampment and Maxi's invasion. To escape from his brother, he'd call Vincenzo and make a date for dinner in the city. Vincenzo, an architect, had just returned from a trip abroad; he was unlikely to have plans for the evening.

"My trip? It was a total success," explained Vincenzo Molinas over drinks at a glass-front restaurant in a subdued corner of Greenwich Village. His black eyes sparkled under thick eyebrows and brought his placid countenance alive. Edward thought it was the most handsome face he'd ever seen. His best friend, whose jet-black hair, trim mustache, and fair skin reminded him of a Spanish grandee, a foil to the ascetic Yankee that Edward saw himself to be.

"In a nutshell," Vincenzo resumed, "I fell head over heels in love while there, was seduced—and abandoned—all within a few days."

"Nice work." Edward smiled. "You never do anything by halves, Vin—that's what I love about you."

Vincenzo raised his wine glass and the light pierced it, spilling its deep claret hue across the tablecloth.

"Ah, my level-headed buddy." Vin's sharp eye caught the glow of well-being on Edward's face that might have been poured from a bottle of wine. It had engulfed them both. "I can't image you ever disgracing yourself in such a fashion."

Edward shuddered. "You can't conceive of me lying on the floor at the feet of a dominatrix while her sidekick jerks me off ...?"

A taut smile broke across Vincenzo's face. "Your propriety is exceeded only by your imagination, my friend. Shall we dine?"

No sooner had the waiter taken their order than Vincenzo asked, "Why do you go to her?"

"Then you *did* believe me—!"

"I read your mind." A pause: "But why are you smiling like that ...?"

The strain of a familiar aria from *Don Giovanni* was playing in the background. It reminded Vann of his friend because an orchestra had played the same melody at his wedding, where Vin was his best man. Best man? It was Vincenzo who'd introduced him to Caroline Sinclair while they were still roommates at Yale. "After trying her out yourself?" he'd quipped while Vin sang her praises. "She's not *that* kind of girl—!" his friend had replied. In retrospect, he wished he'd known somewhat more about the "kind of girl" Caroline was before he'd taken the plunge.

"I'm smiling *like that* because ..." He interrupted himself, not quite certain how to proceed. Would Vin find him mawkish if he'd mention the coincidence of the Mozart aria at this time? "... because you know me so well."

Vincenzo Molinas knew him better than anyone else did. He'd withheld virtually nothing from Vin. For all his friend's mocking wit and caustic sense of humor, he'd always felt safe to confide in him, and Vin had never let him down.

"Why *did* you go to her?"

"Because I couldn't help myself." Edward's eyes swept the small dining room as if to be sure no one was overhearing them.

Vincenzo looked away long enough to give him time to collect his thoughts.

"She had something I needed—badly."

"What was it …?"

"I don't know."

He slept over at Vincenzo's, then took the jitney back to the Island early next morning. He was in a state of arousal the entire trip. Being with Vin did that to him. He'd even aired the subject with his friend one evening, after several drinks too many. Vincenzo wrote it off to the excitement of a close friendship. "We open endless possibilities to each other," Vin had remarked. He'd removed his contacts and was wearing a pair of heavy black spectacles. They made him look avuncular.

"*What* possibilities?"

"It seems to me," Vin elaborated, "we hold back little or nothing from each other. We take risks. Then when the gamble turns out to have been worth the risk, something liberating happens. And when we feel liberated, our imaginations are free to go wherever they want."

"So you think my imagination wants me to go after you?"

"Have another drink," Vin had countered. "Your *imagination* can go wherever it wishes."

The steady vibration of the jitney nearly lulled him to sleep, till he spotted Farleigh hailing him from curbside.

"Good morning, Mr. Ed." His houseman's unfailingly cheerful greeting sucked him back to reality.

"Can you drop me off at the hospital, Farleigh?"

It was the day Ned was due to be released. He'd offered to drive him home, but Silas wanted to be with his son when he was discharged.

He was now accepted as a regular by the nursing staff. As he approached the room of his rapscallion-editor, laughter and raised voices issued from inside. He stepped in to find himself face to face with the patient and his dad, plus Sally, Olivia, and a woman he'd not seen before—a physical therapist.

Despite the chorus of friendly greetings, he felt remiss for not arriving sooner. Would Ned think he was uncaring, just a "social butterfly," as Fiona sometimes called him, a do-gooder who had nothing better to do but do good …?

Then he saw the awful object. How was Ned supposed to walk with that hideous brace clamped to his leg? His eyes began to brim. Why was everyone smiling?

"Thanks for showing up, Edward. I knew you'd be here!"

Ned's valiant smile threatened to break the dam welling in his eyes. He turned away and forced a cough. "Would you listen to me—!" he exclaimed, patting his chest while faking another cough.

"Maybe we should get *you* a room in the hospital, Mr. Vann." Sally's good humor dispelled the tension. Even Olivia got in her two cents. "When was your last checkup, Edward?"

He took her hand while Sally joined Silas at the bedside and helped Ned to rise. Grasping his crutches and struggling to gain his balance, Ned took a tentative step, then another. Wavering for a moment or two, he righted himself and turned toward the door, his left leg trailing behind him. The exertion was apparent; his face had flushed scarlet.

On the way home from the hospital, Olivia suggested lunch at a drive-in. After they finished their burgers and fries, she took him for a Dairy Queen. While licking their cones she remarked, "How thoughtful that you offered to look in on the boy later today. I'm sure his dad appreciates your concern."

"He's a good kid," he replied, embarrassed because he'd shown Olivia so little attention lately. His life was spools of thread unwinding at every turn. Wasn't it time to show her how much he cared for *her*? He'd have to think of a way, when time permitted.

"Will you save me an evening this coming weekend?"

"Take your pick, any night," she obliged.

"I'll let you know" was all he said before disappearing into the house.

He took a quick shower then dressed in Bermudas, polo shirt, and docksiders. The MG awaited him when he left Ocean House for the drive to the Deane residence.

A grove of birch trees sheltered that house, a modest brown-shingled affair that had weathered many seasons. It was the kind of house that would welcome wayfarers, where anyone of goodwill would find acceptance. Cyrus Vann helped Deane make the down payment on it, shortly before Ned's birth.

He approached the front door of the bungalow in trepidation, wondering once more why polio had chosen Ned and not him as its victim. He'd had his chance at life—a successful publishing career, a contract for his first novel, a crack at marriage. The question was, would Ned be able to continue his studies in the fall? Would he lose his scholarship? Would he walk again unaided? And of more immediate concern, would he be able to take up his duties on the Vann estate—and his manuscript, what about *it* …?

"I'll tell the boy you're here." Silas ushered him through a sparely furnished parlor and led him down the hall to his son's room. There he called out, "Neddy—you have a visitor …"

The door to Ned's room was closed. Before turning the knob, Silas gave Edward a knowing look, knocked (no reply), then opened it.

The blinds were pulled though it was still daytime. When his eyes fell on Ned, Edward forced a smile. The convalescent lay on his back, while a plastic "bubble" covered his chest. "To help him breathe," explained his father.

He approached the bed as Silas receded behind him. Ned's eyes were closed, and his visitor wasn't sure whether he was awake. Then the eyes blinked once, twice. He wished to utter words of encouragement and promises of help, but all he said was, "Good to see you, old man."

Ned trained his soft brown eyes on him and blinked again. He saw himself as a burden now, fearing that Edward was paying his respects from a sense of duty and might even resent him for falling down on the job. He said nothing.

Backing out of the room, Silas whispered, "I'll leave you two alone ..."

Edward waited for Ned to speak. In the protracted silence they caught each other's eye. Each started to say something, without uttering a word. Edward's gaze came to rest on the breathing apparatus over Ned's chest. He'd heard frightful accounts of the iron lung, which imprisoned polio victims for life. Thank heaven Ned wasn't trapped in one of those!

Ned took his silence for boredom at having to make a courtesy call. When he perceived that Edward seemed fixated on the breathing machine, he declared, "Oh, *that*—it's to help me through the next few days, so I don't get pneumonia. I won't have to use it forever."

Edward drew up a stool and took a seat at the bedside.

"I'm breathing just fine, really," Ned encouraged, as if Edward were the patient in need of consolation.

"That's good," said Edward, resenting the inadequacy of words at such a time. "I mean, it's good that you're breathing ..."

"I know what you mean." Ned stared hard at him. "Thank you."

"You're welcome. I mean—" His eyes wandered aimlessly about the room. "Ned, I wanted to tell you—"

Ned's unwavering gaze broke his train of thought. At length Edward asked, his voice wavering,

"What can I do to help you?"

"You've already done it."

Have you ever heard such a sob story? Really, Edward, you were on

the verge of tears! Shouldn't you, the consummate WASP, have more self-control? It defies credulity that a buttoned-down gent like you would lose it at a sick man's bedside, of all places. Think of how you must have made poor Ned feel. He was probably more worried about you than you were about him!

Not that it's a bad thing to show some sympathy now and then, for someone who really needs—and deserves—it. Moi—for instance, who'd been slaving over your manuscript. And I had a splitting hangover from several too many at The Gullet last night. Then you appear on my doorstep unannounced in the glaring morning light with no greeting other than, "Could you help me with something?"

Why don't WASPs use the telephone before they pay a call? It took all the noblesse oblige I could marshal to let this seigneur enter my humble abode. And it was only because my folks weren't home that I invited my distinguished caller inside. My parents would have no idea how to behave around the scion of Ocean House. Imagine a circus with my dad as ringmaster and my mama riding bareback. You get the idea.

Edward brightened as soon as I said "Come in." (I think my words were Won't you please enter? I sprinkled in the interrogative for the occasion.) I agreed to review a new chapter he'd added to his tome (without first consulting me!). But I froze in horror when we crossed the threshold to my roomette. I was so used to its décor that I failed to anticipate the impression it would make on Edward Vann: three days' worth of underpants strewn about the floor, plus shirts and slacks lounging on the uneasy chair and the bed, not to mention the beer bottle, half-filled coffee cup, and girlie magazines that completed the tableau mort.

The writer plopped down on my bed as if unaware of the clutter around him, while I said a quick prayer to the god of unbelievers to guide me through the ordeal.

Edward could hardly conceal his excitement (usually a bad sign when it came to his writing). "I've also added a new section on D-day."

"You can't do that," I exclaimed in shock and awe.

"Why ever not ...?"

"It's an anachronism—Day-d was launched in 1944. You're still in 1942—!"

"This is art—"

"No," I stood my ground, sidling next to him, determined to prevail, "It's license ..."

"I love you, Ari."

"Why, pray ...?"

"You say the most outrageous things ..." He added after a moment, "... without batting an eyelid!"

I blinked several times to usher us back to reality.

That made him crumple. "All that work for nothing."

"Nonsense," I encouraged. "Hang onto it, we'll use it later."

He broke into a smile. "You have a solution for everything."

"And you, my friend, have a problem for everything. That's why we're the perfect team." Was I laying it on too thick?

My visitor seemed to be considering my last salvo. Then rising and clutching his manuscript, he said, "I must be going." Had he finally noticed all the mess around us? "But, tell me, Ari, what can I do for you ...?"

"Just keep writing," I encouraged him. I was now his muse, *n'est-ce pas*?

CHAPTER
7

DRIVING OVER TO THE DEANE COTTAGE NEXT MORNING, he reflected that Ned was no longer his summer employee—they were on a new footing. Did Ned realize, he wondered as he approached the front door.

Silas stood stolid in the doorway, as if caught in a picture frame. "We're having a bit of a time, the boy and I …"

He marveled at the father's restraint. He knew Deane was purposely vague, to cushion him from bad news. He followed his groundskeeper through the homey bungalow to Ned's room. Ned's leg brace lay on the floor beside his bed, his crutches stiff as sentinels against the headboard. Silas withdrew as soon as he'd ushered their visitor into the darkened room.

Edward took a seat at the foot of the bed. The breathing machine no longer covered Ned's chest. With a hand to his heart, the visitor asked, "Your breather—?"

"Got rid of it." Ned's voice had an edge he'd not heard before.

"And you're breathing just fine …?"

"Come listen if you wish." Ned raised himself. "I'm not spending my life in a breathing bubble—!"

"Good for you!" A crisis had passed: Ned would recover substantially.

"And you know what else—?"

Edward's expression mingled hope, mirth, admiration.

"I'm going to be up, I'll be walking soon."

"And shooting hoops …?"

"Hole in one!"

"You're talking golf, man—!" Ned slapped him on the rump, the whop guys give each other in the thrill of victory. His bold gesture astonished him—whopping a man twice his age—but it was a time of triumph! He'd coaxed the capricious ball into the basket with Edward's adroit support. They'd removed his leg brace for their "game," and Edward kept close by to help him balance. It was awkward at first. He'd struggled to show he was quite capable of staying on his feet, despite those first steps and the near tumble when his friend let go of him.

"Son of a bitch—!"

Edward grabbed him by the shoulders to prevent a fall.

"Excuse me, Edward—I don't normally talk that way."

"These aren't normal times." Edward squelched a smile. "Back to our game—!"

He released his companion, but his hands hovered inches from his sides. Ned struggled toward the basket, dribbling, sweating, the ball rebounding with force, nearly escaping, but he retrieved it, lurched toward the basket—Edward right behind—and tossed it in.

"Whoopee!" Edward's cry startled the nearby gulls, whose flapping wings appeared to be cheering for Ned. "You see what you did, man—?"

That war whoop—it was the first time Edward had let go around him. The master of Ocean House—stiff and unyielding—had come alive. They were equals now, and something loosened in his chest.

"I don't know about you, but I'm absolutely beat," Edward fibbed, fearing Ned was pushing so hard just to impress him. "Should we take a break …?"

Slinging a casual arm around Ned's waist, he helped him to a bench at the edge of the court. It was a breezy morning, yet both were perspiring profusely. As they hobbled off the court together, he caught a whiff of Ned's sweat. Later that day as he was about to shower, the scent came back to him, and he paused for a moment before stepping under the showerhead.

He'd left a cooler of soda and sandwiches on the bench when they arrived at the court. He opened a bottle of soda for each of them, then drink in hand, raised his in a toast. "To our friendship."

"I *hope* you consider me a friend, Edward." Ned's face tinged toward rose. "I haven't been much of an employee ..."

"Don't be absurd. How could you work when you were sick?"

"Dad says you brought a check to the house every week."

"Workers compensation."

"It embarrasses me."

"Get over it."

Ned's eyebrows raised a soundless protest. He placed his hand on Edward's arm. Edward clamped his hand over Ned's and they sat in silence while the assembly of gulls rehearsed their squalls for the afternoon.

After biting his lip several times, Edward asked, "Would you like to move in for a while?"

"Live at your place?"

"I spoke with your dad about it—I hope you don't object? You'd be more comfortable, I think. What I mean is, we have the facilities, and there's hired help when needed ..."

Ned's face was blank but his eyes searched the distance as if seeking something.

"There's an elevator, you know—"

"No, I didn't know." The defensive reply intimated, *How in the hell would I know ...?*

"Well, you know now. And Farleigh can put a ramp at the front door. He's good at that sort of thing. You wouldn't have to worry about the stairs."

Ned withdrew his hand before he spoke. "Edward, you've done far too much for me already. I can't accept such a proposal."

"You can't?" said Edward. "Fine—I'll send for your things this afternoon."

≥❋≤

Have I ever told you about Super-Guy, my black Columbia that Dad won at a county fair? He was the alter ego between my legs. Dad was going to donate this fair prize to our temple's spring raffle, but I persuaded him to keep the noble steed for me (for a price: two weeks' allowance). My dad sought profit everywhere and turned one whenever he could.

After blowing another week's allowance on bells & whistles, I rode that bike all over the Island. My friend Barney—his dad was a fisherman, as you might guess from the name—Barney said I got my jollies with Super-Guy. It was a bizarre thing to say. What did anyone named "Barney" know about sex? But he wasn't far off the mark or, maybe I should say, the crotch. Often after I'd taken The Guy out for a spin then raced him home, this titillating tingle would start up my groin. It happened once when I ran into Sadie on Main Street, and she signaled me to pull over to the curb.

"What've you been up to, pray?" That "pray" business was another of her verbal tics that might have maddened me to extinction if it weren't so comical.

It was all I could do to keep from squeezing my balls to stop the sensations brought on courtesy of Super-Guy (and Sadie wasn't helping). I had to suppress the hard-on before it got out of hand (actually, *into* hand); otherwise, Sadie would think *she*'d brought it up.

"Oh, me?" I said, looking around for whatever she might choose to imagine. "Having sex with my bicycle." An extravagant confession is never believed.

She hardly blinked, to her credit. So I added, going on offense, "Well, fancy meeting you here."

"Fancy, indeed," she temporized and all but curtsied. (Did she think we were on a sound stage?)

I refused to play gallant, despite Mama's many lessons on how to ask a young lady for a date (e.g., "I'd be pleased if you were free to …"). I blurted out, "You doing anything tonight?"

Of course she was busy; that's why she'd pulled me over. "Wouldn't you like to know?"

"It's why I asked. Well, see you around." I got back in the Super Saddle.

"Wait—!"

I could hear it coming. "I expect to be home part of the day tomorrow."

"What part?" I was already peddling away from the curb.

"The part when you come by."

That Sadie was a pistol. She had a way of ensnaring me when she caught me off guard. It didn't hurt that I was horny after all the jiggling from The Guy. Barney told me I should exchange my bike's bony seat for the padded variety. "Nah," said manly me, "I can take it." Frankly, I liked the seat-job.

One day a couple of weeks after Edward hired me to work at Ocean House, Super-Guy and I were returning from town when a breeze off the sea urged me to circle past the estate. As I turned into the lane to Edward's property, I got cold feet—what if I ran into my employer and he thought I'd taken to spying on him? I almost turned back, but that seductive breeze kept egging me on, and I soon found myself entering the pristine preserve where the Vann mansion sprawls.

As soon as that Moby-Dick of a house came in view, I heard excited voices. I didn't think folks in this part of the Island got worked up over anything but stock prices. But as I drew closer, there they stood, some dozen slender males six feet tall with wavy blond hair—multiple copies of Van Johnson—arrayed on the mansion's basketball court.

Kidding, of course, but that's how a stand of lank, rich Gentiles look to a stocky Jewish boy who careens unwittingly into their midst. Several turned to gape as I drew near—I was too surprised to wheel and go back the way I came. I coasted closer toward my destiny—eternal shame and damnation—till a familiar voice cried out, "Hey, Ari—!"

Edward broke from the ranks and walked toward me in Tsar Nicholas II mode (there *was* a resemblance to that hapless autocrat). My heart sank as I heard him spew the ukase: *Be gone from this court, wandering Jew, and never return!*

That's what I *thought* I'd hear. What he actually *said* was, "You play ball—?"

"Sure," I said, figuring that verbal economy was the best riposte.

"Want to play—?"

"Yep," I nodded as twenty-four pair of cerulean eyes settled on my sweaty Sephardic curls.

"Back to the game—!" Edward ordered as we turned on the testosterone and resumed the play.

I'm no pro on the court—what do you expect from a guy who's hardly more than five six? But I'm lithe and quick and make smart moves. And I made a startling discovery as we caromed from one end of that court to the other: WASPs sweat! Soon they were sweating with the best of me.

When the game came to an end, I elected to make a quick exit so Edward wouldn't think hoi polloi was trying to foist himself on the crème de la crème. "Good game," I called out to the assembled players, who'd assumed almost human proportions with their mussed locks and fair, hairless skin gleaming with salt-free sweat. I hopped on Super-Guy ready to roll, but Edward came running after me.

"How fortunate you dropped by," he began in his stately cadence. "Is there anything you can't do, Ari ...?" He brushed a hand through my hair. "Come early tomorrow, will you? I've hit a damn snag with our book."

Our book. Was ever a possessive pronoun more entrancing?

"I've been trying to reach you all day." Olivia's voice came cool and steady through the receiver. Why was she never angry? He'd been remiss and was the first to admit it. But she leveled no accusation. He started to explain that he'd spent the day helping Ned settle into his new digs. But Olivia knew this and approved of his offer. And speaking of offers, she'd asked, "Why didn't you accept mine to help with the move?" The question gave him pause, and he tacked to another subject.

"Want to join us for dinner tonight, Liv?" Olivia could help Ned feel at home in the sprawling mansion. "It's a gorgeous night, dear. We'll have the sea for music and the stars for lighting. Doesn't that sound romantic …?"

"A romantic threesome—why not?"

A breeze had picked up as the sun was tumbling into the sea, dispersing the humidity that had hung about for the day. The small patio where they dined was exposed to the elements. Edward had recommended it over the much larger, protected terrace next to the house. "More intimate, don't you think …?" he'd encouraged.

Olivia caught the sparkle in his eyes. Was it the air of early evening bringing out this change in her lover? She'd never seen Edward so animated, so happy, and, it would seem, so at peace.

"I'm all for intimacy," she returned, gazing out to sea, her eyes steadily fixed on the horizon as if watching for a ship to come in.

Ned had said very little but seemed to be having a good time. The only thing to disturb his composure was the sound of his leg brace clanking to the ground. He'd worn it to the table but Edward removed it before they sat down; he'd propped it against the rock wall at the side of the patio.

"What was that?" exclaimed Olivia, her gaze swiveling back from the sea.

"My infernal brace."

She reached for Ned's hand as Edward sprang up to set the device against the wall again. "I want you to know how proud we are of you." She continued to hold Ned's hand.

"I don't want anyone to be proud of me," Ned rejoined with perhaps more feeling than intended. "I'm just doing what I have to do to get back to normal."

"Olivia means that she hopes—"

"I *know* what she means, Edward."

"Of course he does," she soothed. "Perhaps Edward can tell us what time we can start counting the stars tonight ...?"

Edward searched the heavens as if the answer were to be sought on high. "I predict we can begin the census as soon as someone gives me a kiss."

Only then did Olivia release Ned's hand. "Are you ready to start counting ...?"

She rose from her chair and brushed his cheeks with her lips, while Ned's enigmatic smile revealed nothing of what he thought of their little act. Edward was pleased he'd persuaded him to stay at Ocean House. Heaven knew it was empty enough.

Earlier that day, after he'd given Ned the "grand tour" and settled him in his room, he dropped by to make sure his guest had all he needed. Ned was seated in a chair by the window, the brace on his leg, a book in hand.

"What are you reading?" asked Edward, recalling that he'd left Ned to browse in the extensive library of Ocean House.

"This—" said Ned, holding up the leather-bound volume. "A copy of *The Counterfeiters*, by André Gide. Have you read it?"

"Yes, I have."

"Did you appreciate it?"

Ned's choice of verb piqued his curiosity. "If you mean, did I enjoy it, I did."

"Why?"

"The novel within a novel, that was a clever idea."

"Who was your favorite character?"

Edward perched on the window-seat across from his new lodger. Shafts of late-day sun streaked Ned's face, deconstructing it as his features lost their relation to one another in the play of light. "I guess I'd have to say Edward, strange as it may seem."

"Why strange?"

"Because that's *my* name."

"I don't think it's strange. It's a good choice." After a pause, "It's my name, too, as a matter of fact."

He was debating whether to ask Ned who his favorite character was when the young man said, "There's one more thing I'd like to know …"

Edward strained to recall his impressions of the novel that he'd read an age ago. He didn't want Ned to show him up. "What is it …?"

"Where's the bathroom around here?"

"Behind that door."

Ned glanced across the room to the wall with the windows.

"I thought it was another closet."

Edward opened the door, revealing a spacious bathroom in tiles depicting buoys and anchors. A round window carried out the nautical motif. It afforded a view of the Atlantic.

"Do you actually have a bathroom for every bedroom in this place …?"

"You might say we have a bedroom for every bath."

The stars did come out to be counted by the time Farleigh served dessert, a rum-soaked sponge cake accompanied by cordials.

Enjoying a second helping and his second cordial, Ned asked dreamily, "What is this delicious concoction, anyway?"

"Tiramisu," said his host.

"It means 'pick me up,' " explained Olivia.

"It's to help you get back on your feet." Edward did his imitation chimp routine so Ned wouldn't think he was patronizing him.

But Ned's spirits showed no sign of slacking when he replied, "I'll remember that."

It would have been the perfect way to end the evening before they went their separate ways. But fate's timing was off by a minute or two. As they were rising from the table, Farleigh's cautious approach diverted Edward from his company.

"Phone call for you, Mr. Ed." He lowered his voice. "She says it's urgent …"

* * *

The MG hugged the roadway as Edward kept his foot on the gas. He'd delayed his departure just long enough for Olivia to make a graceful exit. But now that they were both on the road, he had to hold back from floor-boarding, otherwise he'd overtake her Impala. No telling what she thought of his abrupt departure. And Ned, what would his houseguest think of his sudden disappearance, fobbed off with a mumbled excuse about "business to attend to"? Could his charge manage by himself with the heavy leg brace? He pulled over to the side of the road and switched off his lights so Olivia could make headway without detecting him.

The blackness of a Suffolk night engulfed him. He waited for a song on the radio to end, then switched on the headlights and followed the twisting road till he came to his destination. He could feel his heart thumping as he parked the MG and removed the key from the ignition. The key uttered a warning *carrrefulll* as he withdrew it.

He knocked a couple of times, but no one answered. He let himself in. A dim light suffused the front room. His eyes were slow to adjust, and for a moment he wondered whether he was alone. Then she appeared in the doorway, leaning against the frame. That was when he noticed the man behind her in the hallway. His slight frame, coffee skin, and rumpled hair suggested more a kitchen helper than a bodyguard.

"Good evening, Liane." It was an inauspicious beginning, ridiculously formal, even for Edward Vann. And he was staring as she advanced on him, clad in a yellow sarong that showed off her figure. Her feet were bare.

"Did you bring it?"

He removed the checkbook from his trouser pocket and laid it on the coffee table.

She was standing only a foot from him now. He envisioned her body pressing into his. He cherished these moments, when imagination surges ahead of time and place.

She grasped his hand and led him to the sofa, where she sat on the edge and pulled him toward her. He nuzzled against her as her arms enfolded his hips, undulating, pressing him into her breasts.

She unzipped him, pulled his trousers down with his undershorts. His dick popped out and throbbed before her as she commenced a humming sound while she swallowed, her voice-vibrations a current streaking through his member to his bowels.

Though she'd undressed him before their sofa-sex, she'd not removed her sarong. Now in the aftermath, she pulled it together when he heard footsteps from the hallway. Her man should be appearing now, an abject doorway-filler. But another figure in bathrobe and slippers occupied his place. "Nice work," declared Maxi, glancing down at them.

CHAPTER
8

THE DENSE NIGHT AIR closed in around him, while the moon's anemic rays barely lit the road. The only sound but for his MG was the humming of the sea. He drove more by instinct than vision. It was dead of night, and all were abed but drunks and blackmailers. When he arrived home, the staff had retired, and nothing was stirring at the property but the waves.

He was about to mount the stairs, but the long hallway beckoned to the wing where he'd offered Ned a room. Regret over his unceremonious departure that evening fashioned a clinging cloak he couldn't remove: he'd abandoned Ned and Olivia with barely a word of explanation. How *does* one excuse oneself to guests when off to an assignation? And weren't Olivia and Ned more than guests—?

The door to Ned's room was ajar, and he stepped inside. With his leg brace prone on the floor beside him, Ned looked like a soldier asleep with his rifle in the battle for France, his chiseled profile suggesting the nobles sculpted on sarcophagi of feudal Europe. God, Edward thought, his imagination was having its way.

A chill had seeped into the room and he was tempted to pull the covers up to Ned's shoulders, but he was afraid of waking him. In that tender, worried hesitation he caught himself wondering again what Ned would think of him if he knew where he'd spent the evening.

He was feeling sleepy, lulled by the sea's sighs and whispers. Yet as he rose to leave, he thought the sea called out to him.

"Edward …?"

Ned shifted and propped on his elbows.

"Did I wake you—?" He knelt by the youth's side.

"No, I don't think so. Perhaps it was the sea—calling to us." (Was Ned grinning?)

"At this hour? I'll have to speak to the sea about that."

"If anyone could stop the sea from making a racket, I'm sure it's you, Edward."

"My powers may be great, my boy, but you overrate them."

Could Ned see he was blushing? He gave Ned's shoulder a pat, then returned to his room. He fell into bed hoping that sleep would quell the jumble of his mind. As he sank into oblivion, he was thinking that all his life he'd lived only for himself, seeking out floozies and whores for pleasure. But thanks to some inexplicable grace, he was at last watching over someone else.

"Edward, did anyone ever tell you, you look distinguished and dapper in a tux …?"

Ned stole a glance at his friend in the mirror opposite, then his eyes fell to the magazine he was perusing. Edward indeed looked strikingly handsome in his tuxedo, hair slicked back and chin aloft as he prepared to greet his company.

Before he could reply Ned resumed, "I know, real men aren't supposed to say such things to each other."

"There's lots of things 'real men' aren't supposed to do," interposed Olivia, who was sitting on the settee next to Ned, "… but do you think the best of them refrain because of it?"

The three had gathered in the vestibule off the small parlor, awaiting the arrival of friends for a drop-by before Edward and Olivia would leave for the dance at Hardscrabble Country Club. The cozy corner, as regular visitors to Ocean House called it, was one of the few rooms in the mansion you might consider intimate. The settee lounged beneath a picture window, and a gilded mirror all but covered one wall. The mirror was installed under protest by Cyrus

Vann at his wife's behest. "It's just a convenient way station when our female guests need to check their hair, their face, or their hemline—" Her husband had retorted, "There's room here for an X-ray machine as well, pet, if you think they might need a closer look." Cecelia sniffed, "It's not as if you didn't have your billiard room, your smoking room, your poker room. Anyway—" she settled the matter briskly (the servants might be listening), "the women you invite to the house are perfect Medusas, with little concern for their appearance. I don't want them cluttering my living room and frightening the children."

Ned took another sip of Harvey's Bristol Cream and held it on his tongue. "You don't know Harvey's?" Edward had asked when he'd offered Ned the drink. Was Edward putting him down? "How would I know about your Harley's, or whatever you call it?" said Ned pugnaciously. Edward then realized his mistake, his presumption that his young friend noticed immediately. That's when he invited him to the dance at the club, but Ned demurred.

"I'm serious," he'd said. "I have a tux you could fit into."

"Nah, I'd be out of place."

"You'd be the best man there!"

"That's your belief, my friend."

"I'd rather spend an evening with you than with all the men at that club put together."

"Then you must join another club," Ned parried. Edward seized him in a bear hug and raised him off the floor.

The doorbell rang and Edward let Ned slip through his arms to answer it. Ned took advantage of his absence to ask Olivia, "Are you madly in love with Edward?"

Perhaps the amusement tinged with concern that crossed her face prompted Ned to add, "It's this delectable sherry speaking, Liv—I'm just a bystander to my own remarks." A bystander, in fact, who'd never before called her by the nickname Edward favored.

A black silk sheath clung to Olivia's body without looking tight. She'd clipped on a pair of diamond earrings, and the hint of Shalimar that hung about her fired Ned's imagination, abetted by the Harvey's. He'd grown unduly fond of Olivia—she was a frequent visitor at his hospital bedside. But he'd not yet had a meaningful conversation with her, not about herself. The sherry put an end to that.

"Do you mean," she began, "do I love, or am I in love with, the gentleman in question …what was his name again …?"

Taken in by the twist at the end, he declared with comical overemphasis, "Edwa-a-a-rd."

"At your service—" echoed their host, who had reappeared before them.

Ned colored at Edward's sudden return, but Olivia saved the situation.

"Ned was wanting to know whether you prefer the sonnets of Shakespeare or Keats …"

"That's an odd question. He already knows what I think about those sonnets."

"Of course he does," rejoined Olivia. Edward had told her about his interview with Ned before he offered him the job. "I meant to say, the poetry of Wordsworth or Shelley—a slip of the tongue."

Edward's opinion on that topic might be of considerable interest, but more guests were arriving and he excused himself to greet them.

When he was out of hearing range, Olivia took Ned's hand. "Careful what you ask me next time."

"You mustn't put limits on me, Olivia," he pressed her hand, "… or I'll fall in love with you—honestly!"

You couldn't hear Olivia's response because of the conversation mingled with snorts and gasps of laughter from nearby guests. Ned wasn't looking forward to this raft of strangers—Edward insisted he be present, he didn't say why. But he was glad he didn't have to account for his tongue to Olivia. The wayward remark had slipped out on its own. Why *had* he made such a declaration?

Couples were advancing on them now. Olivia stepped into her role as hostess, nodding to some, introducing Ned to others as if he were her date. He thought he recognized one of the callers, an imposing gentleman with wavy black hair and mustache who'd stopped by the house a couple of times to consult with Edward, likely his attorney. The first time, he and Edward were in the study when Farleigh ushered the man in. Edward hadn't bothered to introduce him, and this led him to wonder whether Edward was ashamed of him. Yet when he and Edward shopped at the market a few days later—their first such outing, to buy groceries on Farleigh's day off—Edward introduced him with fanfare to a couple of acquaintances on the sidewalk in front of the market. It would have been easy enough to avoid the women, but Edward had called out, "Adele, Sophia—come meet an illustrious friend of mine ..."

The room was filling and he was wondering whether it was time to exit, when someone called out, "I say, haven't I seen you somewhere before ...?"

A small man with impish features—large ears, turned-up nose, curling lips, the kind of guy women call joli-laid—was staring hard at him.

The sherry prompted his forthright response, "If you have, you'll have to remind me."

When the man continued to stare past him as if he were not present, Ned tacked on, "I'm sure it'll come back to me."

The man's insolent eyes scanned him up and down, but he still held his tongue.

"All right, then," Ned challenged, "so are you a friend of Edward's?"

"A *friend* ...? Good heavens *no*—Edward *detests* me!"

A smirk came over his lips but flitted off when Ned offered politely, "I'm sure you must be mistaken about that."

"I'm a friend of his brother."

"Maximiliano?"

"You're quite the astute one."

"I see you finally made it, old boy," Edward joined them. The impudent one refused the hand that Edward didn't offer and withdrew a step before declaring,

"As I was saying to this clever young fellow here, you hate me, Edward—don't dare deny it—I detest insincerity." Then turning to Ned, "It's quite apparent, as you can see for yourself."

"Why does he hate you?" Ned's tone mixed doubt with whimsy.

"Because I used to watch him beat off in the shower."

"You watched me one time, Dimitris." Edward kept his sangfroid.

"I watched him only once," Dimitris retorted, "because he began to charge admission."

Edward took Dimitris by the arm to lead him away. Over his shoulder he called to Ned, "If you haven't been formally introduced to Mr. Onassis here, I urge you to keep it that way."

It was as good a time as any to leave. More couples were spilling into the house and Edward wouldn't notice his departure. To avoid all these guests, he hastened onto the terrace and followed the moon toward his quarters. The sound of merrymaking mingled with the droning of the waves, and he suddenly felt quite weary; he'd not been on his feet this long since his illness struck. Collapsing onto a chaise longue inexplicably awaiting him on the lawn beyond the terrace, he breathed in the black velvet air.

Yet troubling thoughts beset him when he'd expected to relax. Why had he engaged in amorous wordplay with Olivia, and listened in while a family friend (what else to call him?) cast Edward in a lewd light? He could have turned his back or walked away, to show his disapproval.

Besides these concerns, he'd started to worry about Dad. Dad's frequent visits to the hospital had kept him from his work, though Dad went to extravagant lengths to conceal this from him. Edward's hospitality was a godsend, but now that he was able to resume his activities, wasn't his place with his father? They had only summers to be together. Otherwise he was in the city and couldn't afford the time or money for frequent visits home. His sister was tied down with her own family since she'd married and moved to the Westchester suburbs. Dad was alone now. Wasn't it time to leave Ocean House and return to him?

Eventually he felt himself going slack beneath the blue-black firmament pierced by the pinpoints of a gazillion stars. He tried making words of the heavenly alphabet soup, deciphering a **D** here, a **WA** there, maybe another **D**, yes, definitely two **D**'s, and hoping to find a message sent by fate or God, he wasn't sure which he believed in, when he felt a hand on his shoulder, intrusive but somehow reassuring.

"Found you—at last!"

The man stood before him, at first indistinct in the night. Yet didn't he recognize him, not from personal acquaintance, but just where had he seen that face—in photographs … a grouping of family photos on a piano in the music room …?

"Maximiliano …?"

"At your service."

Edward's brother wore a black shirt, black trousers, and black sneakers, the attire rendering him all but invisible against the backdrop of night. Maxi was clearly not dressed for the confab in the parlor. Why had Edward excluded him? And why was he staring at him now, his head tilted to the side?

"How did you know I'd be sitting here—?"

"May I help myself to a seat?"

Before he could reply, Maxi sank down on the chaise beside him. "I had no idea you'd be here, my friend—I'm no sorcerer. But I knew you were camping out at the house. I was making my way to your suite when I had the good fortune to stumble onto you." A smile of satisfaction lit his face. "I suppose Edward sent you out to count the stars—?"

"Actually, I was—"

"Does it matter? I've *found* you—we've found each *other*, if you will."

Maxi lit up a Lucky, its scarlet tip dotting the dark. He offered the pack to Ned, who declined.

"As you were saying," Maxi resumed, "Edward sent you out to count stars—that's *so* like Edward—but I was hoping I could entice you with a more practical and, shall we say, lucrative proposition."

Ned made no attempt to mask his skepticism. "State your proposition."

"You're interested—good!" Maxi leaned closer, as if wary of being overheard on the deserted beach. "You recently met my friend Dimitris …?"

"Mr. Onassis?"

"Sharp memory. Your attentiveness will stand you in good stead."

"Glad to hear it—"

"—once you've got the job."

Ned's puzzled expression seemed to amuse him. "Just what was I saying …? He wants to offer you a position as personal secretary. Big office in the city—you can work as much as your schedule allows, once school is in session." After a second: "Your reply—?"

"I'll have to think about it."

"You haven't thought about it already? My word, you're not as quick a study as Edward led me to believe. That's Edward for you."

"But, you see—"

"Don't make excuses for him. I know my brother better than you do—at least for now. Of course, you're in charge here, but I shouldn't flaunt it if I were you. Edward is horrified by overt displays of anything."

Ned's head was starting to spin from the mix of sherry and Maxi's patter. But before he could reply, Maxi resumed, "I've kept you far too long. May I help you back to your room? I know about your brush with that nasty virus—dreadful business. You can go it alone? Very well—you're the best judge of that; I won't detain you further. But don't forget to let me have your response to my proposition—I'll be waiting for it."

Maxi started to leave but Ned raised a hand.

"You don't even know me …"

"I have no need to *know* you, though I'm sure you're a most charming fellow."

"How am I to get back to you?"

"You'll find a way, of course."

⇒✲⇐

Sometimes I wondered why Edward invited me now and then to rub shoulders with the elect. I was quite flattered, of course, but I was also puzzled why he didn't include me more often. Were those just random invitations, which he thought about no more than you'd think about opening a refrigerator or crossing the street? Or was Edward intent on keeping me at arm's length, except when he needed me? That makes poor Edward seem crass and calculating, which I don't think he was. And he never showed a trace of that bugaboo anti-Semitism in those days of racism, homophobia, and anti-communist hysteria in America the Beautiful.

Olivia was the bridge that enabled me to cross over at times into Edward's exalted realm. Her social status lay somewhere in that gulf between Edward's and mine. He must have noticed how well I got on with his lady fair, who, I believe, was quite taken with me (why not?). I'm reminded of the time I complimented him on his Halloween costume. It felt as if my patron and I had changed roles and I was the one granting approval.

He'd invited a crowd of friends to a costume party he threw at Ocean House on Halloween and, to my great surprise, included yours truly.

Edward, a costume party?

A master stroke. It allowed the Lord of the Manner to mix genteel rabble with the gratin, because everyone was required to cover the face with a mask or other device. When Edward appeared before Olivia and me in the small parlor as we were awaiting the arrival of the guests, I couldn't keep from rattling off, "Well, if it isn't Asclepius incarnate."

He was costumed as a physician, in long white smock, stethoscope around his neck, and doctor's mirror covering his forehead.

"Not half bad, don't you agree, Liv?" I couldn't resist calling her "Liv" as often as possible, to signal Edward that his paramour and I were becoming bosom buddies, ahem.

Edward broke into a grin. "Thanks for the compliment, Little Lord Fauntleroy." He surveyed my getup with approving eyes. I was dressed as Gainsborough's Blue Boy (Jewboy?), and I must say I looked the part. All I lacked was a gilt frame.

"What do you think, Liv?" He asked her.

"A pretty piece of perfection, if you want my opinion." Her nonchalant tone masked the fact that she herself had dolled me up. My fittings for that costume had been quite an adventure. Liv had to make several alterations, and I found myself slipping in and out of my clothes to the point where I stood before her one afternoon in nothing but my tighty whities. Bosom buddies indeed!

At that moment a large brown bear lumbered into our midst. Had it not been for the sneakers on his feet, he might have been the real thing. Besides the sneakers, the voice gave him away. He spoke in a commanding baritone that somehow lacked authority.

"Oh, here you are Edward," Maxi began. "Can I have a word with you—?"

"Yes."

The bear sidled next to the doctor and took him by the sleeve.

"I said you could have a *word*," Edward hissed, "but I haven't said when. Now, run along and be a good bear or I'll send a hunter after you."

"But this is a matter of urgency—it can't wait!" whined the bear, who'd lost any menace he had and now seemed quite comical.

Several guests had arrived and were heading toward us from the grand foyer. With a sigh of desperation, Edward turned to me. "Take him outside or somewhere, would you, please, Ari?"

His pleading expression signified that I was the man of the hour—BlueJewBoy to the rescue!

"Excuse me, Mr. Bear," I temporized, having no idea what was about to come out of my mouth, "speaking of *urgency*, there's something I've been meaning to ask you, and I crave an expert opinion." When the bear offered no resistance, I gestured for him to follow me. At that moment someone handed me a lasso and I slipped it over the bear's head (he was on all fours now). Then I led him through the grand foyer to the double doors giving onto the terrace behind the house.

The crisp evening air enveloped us as *Blue Boy with Bear in Tow* stepped through the picture frame, I mean, the double doorway and into the night. There my charge slipped off the lasso, slumped onto a chair, and pulled a pack of cigarettes from a concealed pocket of his bearsuit (hirsute?). While he fumbled with a book of matches, Mr. Helpful took them and lit his cig, then I slipped into a chair across from him.

Sucking in a couple of drags, the bear inquired, "Now, this urgent issue you brought me out here for …?"

It was imperative to be quick—and bold.

"No issue at all. It was just a ruse to get you outside here."

He blew out a couple of smoke rings, giving me a moment to think.

"We've never had a tête-à-tête—"

"What's that—?"

"I guess you could say it's kind of like a tête-à-bête—"

"You're losing me—"

"A heart-to-heart."

There was no wind, so the smoke rings the bear continued to emit hovered between us like ellipses between thoughts.

"You're a curious sort of fellow, a kind of amalgam …"

"You're losing me."

"I have the sense—through limited observation, mind you—that you're good at several things …"

Moi?

"… the curious part is that you don't want this to be known—necessarily."

"Necessarily," I repeated.

"But, say—" he lurched forward, his paws clutching the table as if he meant to wrest it away, "I know Eddie makes use of you in several ways …"

My head bobbed obligingly.

"At your service," I replied, perhaps too rashly. I was still buying time.

"I think I've found a way to put to advantage" (dramatic pause) "… your diplomatic skills."

Diplomatic?

"I see you as a wily ambassador, good at negotiating through a maze of, shall we call them, delicate situations."

Where was this heading? "I see," said the blind man.

"I'd be counting on your eyes, your ears …"

Was I to surrender my body?

"… and most of all, your incomparable discretion."

Flattery is a powerful aphrodisiac.

"There's been some concern among certain members of the family—I'm speaking of Fiona here, and of myself, of course …"

"Concern …?"

He flipped his cigarette onto the terrace and tried to retrieve another from the pack. I took the pack from his "claws" and lit another for him.

"You see, you're becoming useful already," he quipped, removing his head-hood. His human form was more intimidating than the bear outfit—the wild eyes and rumpled hair. "What I'm getting at is that you'd be tracking Edward's movements and, of course, reporting them."

"To—?"

"Me—"

It was time for Blue Boy to speak truth to flattery. "I think I'm not qualified for this job—"

"Nonsense."

"I may be a wily diplomat—*your* words, Mr. Bear—but what you need is a gumshoe."

I rose to return to Ocean House. From that moment forward, my relations with Maximiliano Vann were decidedly cool.

CHAPTER

9

I T WAS AN OVERCAST DAY of low-drifting clouds and brisk winds laden with intimations that things couldn't continue as they were. Fiona was on the warpath. The last two times she'd checked the accounts, she found the bills lying fallow on Edward's desk, as if they were meant for ornamentation only. The accounts were in hardly better shape than the bills he'd filed away in the "already paid" container: they were in chronological order and the amounts owed clearly indicated by a red circle. But nothing had been paid! The avenging goddess was in no mood to knock on doors or wait to be announced, not Fiona Vann, soon to be Mellon-Glade if her third engagement was to proceed without mishap to holy-smokes matrimony.

"What is the meaning of this—?"

She'd burst into his study and accosted him with a sheaf of bills that she held aloft as a child exhibits a prize she'd won to her parents.

The Vann siblings had been raised not to quarrel in public, but the lesson took feebly with Fiona. Ignoring Ned's presence—he was seated on the leather sofa across the room—she thrust the unpaid bills under Edward's nose.

With a quick glance at Ned, the miscreant readied his reply. It didn't help that he had a hangover. He'd ignored his better judgment at the Hardscrabble dance the night before and downed several scotches in succession. Although a canny judge of character and capable of reading the heart of another, he was not so shrewd when the heart was his own. Not even this morning, when he had time to reflect before Ned arrived, had he understood his malaise of the evening before, that he'd misinterpreted Ned's disappearance. Ned was much on his mind then as he greeted his guests, because he was looking forward to showing him off. His adoption of the young man of modest origins would reveal to his fancy friends that he, Edward Vann, was no snob but had the common touch. It's not clear why he felt the need to do this.

While awaiting his guests' arrival with Ned and Olivia in the vestibule, he was quietly pleased to be the object of their affection as he adjusted tie and cummerbund—Olivia making big eyes, Ned calling him "dapper," of all things. But on reflection, had he misconstrued their attention? Maybe they were only humoring him. Maybe they were poking fun at him preening before the mirror. And why did Ned leave early without a good-bye to anyone but Olivia?

And now Fiona was haranguing him in front of Ned.

"If you have an excuse for yourself," (the bills still reeking beneath his nose) "I'll deign to hear it."

"First of all, dear—do have a seat—" He gestured to the rattan chair at the side of his desk, but she continued to glower.

"In the first place, you were always better at arithmetic and numbers than I was …"

"This has nothing to do with arithmetic and numbers," she retorted, "which, by the way, are one and the same."

"They are …?" replied the writer, conscious of Ned's eyes on him. "Perhaps that explains the mystery of these unpaid bills."

"You are derelict," fumed Fiona. "Mystery solved!"

"If I'm indeed derelict," he was standing now, "then I insist you take a seat so I can explain everything."

But how could he tell her he'd been preoccupied with Ned, not the bills? Ned—a young man of undistinguished background, his groundskeeper's son at that, to the exclusion of everything else—except Maxi? How to explain that he'd been hiding the extortionate outlays to their brother by letting the bills slide, a "reassignment" of funds?

Fiona sat reluctantly in the offered chair. Though the room was drafty, the silk scarf around her neck refused to flutter, even as her feathers began to settle. She waited for the explanation but not before directing a penetrating gaze at Ned. Under her breath, though audibly, she inquired, "What is *he* doing here?"

Ned left the room after exchanging glances with Edward, then wandered outside to the beach. There he found the chaise that had witnessed his stargazing before Maxi's rude interruption. How innocuous it looked in the light of day. Maxi would want him to keep mum about their exchange, but wasn't his silence a betrayal? How could he have secrets from Edward? Why hadn't he gone to Edward straightaway and related the bizarre encounter of the previous evening? Would Edward think he'd led Maxi on, or would he at least wonder why he hadn't cut him off? Maybe Edward hardly thought about him. How else to explain his sudden disappearance last night, losing himself among his guests and leaving him to shift for himself? Was Edward ashamed of him, appearances to the contrary? (He hadn't forgotten how Edward had grabbed him and raised him off the floor.) Maybe Edward just got cold feet when the upper crust arrived at Ocean House?

He wandered down to the sea and removed his shoes so the waves could lap at his feet. The clouds had done a fine job of keeping the sun off the beach, despite the pushing and shoving of the wind. He wanted to walk along the water's edge but didn't wish to carry his shoes. He could leave them in the sand till he returned. And if they got washed away or stolen—Edward had loaned them to him; they wore the same size—Edward would replace them.

Yet he kept the shoes firmly in hand as he headed down the beach, wondering how he'd come to depend so much on Edward. Edward was even furnishing his clothing, and he felt free to discard it on a whim? "You don't want to be a moocher," Dad taught him from an early age. Was he turning into a parasite? What else did you call someone who took much but gave back little? As his feet sank into the sand, he noticed that he barely cast a shadow.

They were chance remarks, casual asides. Yet they triggered a chain reaction that brought them both to the brink of despair.

It happened later that day, just as dusk was descending, when they came upon each other in the grand foyer. Edward had left his study and Ned was returning from a nap. When Edward's blank expression fell upon him, the young man jumped to the conclusion that his friend-host-employer was perturbed about something he'd done; perhaps he'd overstayed his welcome in the study this morning and thus was unintentionally privy to the dressing down that Fiona gave her brother. Or worse, had Maximiliano divulged his nighttime "proposition" to Edward?

"You okay?"

The remark, well intended and intentionally unspecific, was the kind of verbal filler at which Edward excelled. It left his listener free to respond however he wished.

But Ned decided to say nothing. He'd wait to hear what Edward might have on his mind.

For his part, Edward took Ned's diffidence as a brushoff. Hadn't Ned ignored him the evening before while making up to Olivia? Was his modest young friend a go-getter after all? He asked abruptly, "I'm going for a walk—want to come along ...?"

"Why not?" Ned's tone suggested *I've nothing better to do.*

The stars had forced their way through the fading cloud cover and the moon had appeared at the eastern reaches of the beach. They exchanged hardly a word as they moved beyond the perimeter of the property, till Edward said, "The sea seems calmer tonight than I'd expected."

Ned took the remark as merely a prelude and waited for his taciturn companion to say more. But when the silence became uncomfortable, he blurted out, "Yes, it is."

Could Ned be out of sorts with him, Edward wondered, for dragging him along? Had Ned joined him just to oblige? He'd have to cut the walk short. He'd hoped to speak with Ned about his novel, particularly a key passage involving Berlin's Anhalter Bahnhof, the enormous train station all but destroyed during the war. The phrase "Anhalter Bahnhof" had been boring through his mind ever since his last discussion with Ned about the book, his own personal "metempsychosis." But, clearly, this was not the time to go into it.

"Should we head back ...?" he asked.

"Ready when you are."

Perhaps Edward had nothing to say to him after all. On the return trip Ned tried to kindle a conversation, but nothing caught. He trudged through the sand holding back so Edward could maintain a slight lead.

The house was looming up ahead. In a last-ditch attempt to reach out, Edward asked, "Did you have a nice time last night?"

He merely nodded at what he took to be a polite question. Edward wasn't sure he'd even heard him.

At the house, he started to hold the screen door for Ned but, to avoid the appearance of condescension, he let it go. Too late—it swished back and struck Ned's arm. It took Ned by surprise; the "blow" felt intentional.

Once inside Edward declared, "I'll be seeing you." Then he turned to go.

"Ciao," said Ned, watching him disappear up the stairway.

Ned returned to his room. It felt empty, if empty has a feel. His stomach was rumbling and he realized he'd eaten nothing since noon. Farleigh would be off duty now, but he could rustle up something to eat. He stole down the hallway from the guest wing toward the kitchen and made himself a sandwich. On the way back to his room, his eye lit upon a flight of stairs inside a cubbyhole off the hallway. He'd not noticed it before; it was most likely used by the maids. Grasping the unvarnished wooden handrail and wondering why the rich always cut back on amenities for their servants, he soon found himself on the second floor in the pantry, down the hall from Edward's bedroom.

A soft light was escaping from there. On impulse he stepped inside, wondering whether Edward would hear his footsteps, just as he'd wondered on that day when he first reported for work at Ocean

House. Edward lay in bed surrounded by a stack of books and magazines. The writer looked up as soon as he entered.

Neither spoke, each waiting for the other to take the initiative. But Edward was in his pajamas, and Ned didn't have the heart to breach the Maginot Line of all that reading material. Yet Edward seemed to nod encouragement.

He crept a bit closer. "I have something to say." He had absolutely no idea what was about to come out of his mouth. Edward maintained a steady gaze.

"I think it's time for me to move out now." His own words astonished him.

"You know what's best. I'll have your things packed up and sent to your house as soon as you wish."

"Thank you." He turned to go. "I appreciate it."

Edward nodded.

At the door Ned turned back. "I actually meant to say, thank you for *everything*."

"You're welcome," said Edward, trying to force a smile.

The sensation of suffocating made Ned cough.

"Is something the matter, Ned?"

"No, Edward. … Everything's the matter."

This time Edward's smile came more easily. "What is it?"

"It wouldn't do any good to say—I've ruined everything."

"Sit down." Edward brushed aside a pile of magazines. "*What* have you ruined …?"

Ned slid onto the edge of the bed. But when he tried to speak, tears came.

"What could you possibly have ruined—?"

"I haven't been much of a friend." Ned's voice caught in his throat. "I've sponged off you all summer—I've had nothing to give in return …"

Edward raised himself off the pillows. "Ned, I've been marooned in a desert for ever so long, and you've come to drown me with your goodwill and friendship. You've brought me alive after years in the wilderness. How could I not care for you enormously, Ned ...?"

He couldn't match Edward's eloquence, but his heart was overflowing. His hand grasped at the bed covers, as if he needed something to hold on to. Barely audibly, he whispered, "I'm drowning, too."

Reaching out, Edward's hand grazed Ned's shoulder, gently stroked it, and came to rest there. Their eyes met, and Ned leaned back, feeling the benevolent pressure of Edward's hand that, nonetheless, surprised and confused him. He kept still, as if frozen. Edward was watching him so intently that he shrank away. Perhaps his withdrawal prompted the older man to wrap both arms around him.

Edward—!" He lurched back and Edward's arms slipped off his body. Edward raised his hand as if to make a decla-ration, but Ned exclaimed, "Don't!"

Their eyes met again in a prolonged confrontation that al-lowed of no spoken word.

Then he began to sob, his convulsive shoulders rocking the bed. "I don't ... don't know what's going on with us, Edward ..."

"Ned—I'm sorry I upset you. Don't leave while you're distraught—"

"*Please*, Edward, let me be—"

When Edward shrank away, Ned spoke haltingly, as if inventing the words as he said them. "You're the most wonderful man I've ever known.... I worship you, Edward—you must know that by now.... But I'm scared, scared to death—"

"I understand."

But *what* did he understand? Ned would soon leave him, his protégé, sidekick, collaborator, the hobbledehoy who had crept into his study and invaded his impregnable heart, the kid in the nondescript plaid shirt who'd rewritten his fictional fantasies about the stink and din of battle and whorehouses on the Western Front. Ned was about to leave him, he who had everything and needed nothing in that cocoon of his, with its seven windows and their view of infinity … And it might have ended there, Ned slinking off to some indeterminate future when they'd make polite conversation on the off chance they'd ever meet again.

And that was to be it? Dismissing every inhibition ground in by family, friends, and society, he urged with unsurpassable fervor, "Come to me, Neddy."

➤❈➤

So it's cool to be gay in this day and age? I get it, but back to our protagonists. One is scared to death by his own admission, the other flummoxed. Being gay didn't feel very cool in those days. Back then, you could expect the sheriff's knock on the door or a police officer to haul you off for engaging in lewd, immoral, or indecent behavior, no matter who was consenting in the privacy of wherever.

But the point is, Edward and Ned are as hetero as a quiche lorraine, if not the apple pie that mother used to buy. So what's going on here? There seems to be a labeling issue. Does one night of lovemaking—scratch that—lewd, immoral, and indecent behavior change one's sexuality ipso facto from hetero to homo? Well, you might say, not if the people in question go right back to screwing members of the opposite sex the next day. Okay, granted, but what if they repeat the lewd, etc. behavior two nights in a row? three nights? four …? How many nights (or afternoons, or mornings) does it take to transmute your sexuality from straight to gay? What's the alchemy here …? Hmm—

Put another way, to continue the labeling issue, what if you applied the label "gay" (or "homo" or "fag" or "queer," your choice) *not* to the participants but to the act itself (we shall leave undefined what such "acts" shall consist of). Thus, you might say that Edward and Ned engaged in homosexual activity one night. Of course, we don't know what they actually did. Maybe they just lay next to each other. (Does that make it homosexual?) Or cuddled a bit. Or cuddled a lot. Or fucked their heads off, who knows? Do you know what goes on behind your neighbor's door? In fact, is it any business of yours, no matter what your own particular creed and inclinations might be?

But you might reply, *If we're going to label someone, we must know what they're doing.*

Why, and why?

So back to our perverts, or miscreants, or however the psychology profession's *Diagnostic and Statistical Manual* has labeled them: that tome is about as forthcoming as a closeted congressman in a gay bar. So, what are we to decide here?

It's been observed that when confined to prison, straight men often have sexual relations with other men; psychologists consider such relations "normal." Soldiers of the Red Army have written that relationships forged in the heat of such battles as Stalingrad and Kursk were the most meaningful of their lives. Okay, but Ned and Edward haven't been in jail or war together. Does that disqualify them from having same-sex relations without changing their sexuality? They don't get a pass for being merely intimate of mind (the turgid mess of a manuscript) and body (the basketball court)? The struggle of one for his life in that hospital bed and the struggle of the other to pull him through (the hospital bed again)—isn't that a battle worthy of Kursk?

Your call.

PART II

Reconciliation

CHAPTER

10

E DWARD WAS NOT ONE TO AWAKE in a new world each morning—the lot of dreamers and the adventurous. But as the sun flooded the room and the clacking of a loose shutter roused him from sleep, he wondered at the unfamiliar surroundings. Was he in someone else's house? Then it came to him; he was staring into Ned's eyes—they were awaking together in his own bedroom, and the events of the night before came rushing back.

It wasn't because they'd had too much to drink—they'd drunk nothing the evening before. They were in their right minds, their right bodies—weren't they? Lying beside him, Ned yawned and stretched.

"Happy to be here?" Edward asked.

"Here …?"

"No, on Jupiter."

Ned elbowed him gently, his leg against Edward's, then asked, "What are you thinking …"

"I was thinking that, well, what might once have seemed inconceivable now seems inevitable … though I'm supposed to be a battle-hardened army captain."

Ned raised himself on his elbows, the same pose in which Edward often caught him while he was recovering from polio. A rough stubble covered his cheeks. If Ned was no stylocrat, his appearance was what the discriminating call presentable. Ned's "new look" took him by surprise, and he almost stroked his young friend's face, but stayed his hand. Yet his palm "felt" the friction of that would-be touch to Ned's cheek.

"Where are we …?" Ned asked after several moments.

"I'm still trying to figure that out," he replied to the pinging of the drawstrings of the blinds against the window frames, a metronome clicking in counter rhythm to the murmuring of the sea.

Ned glanced around to get his bearings. He recalled his first tentative steps when he came to work at Ocean House. He'd hardly noticed his surroundings then; he was concentrating on making a favorable impression on his new employer. By now, the luxurious setting of Ocean House had become familiar—he'd spent countless hours here—but lying in bed with that employer? And why was Edward staring at him like that? Eventually he said, "I've never done anything like this."

"Like what—?"

"Like, you know, wake up in bed with another man." His eyes swept the room again. "Have you?"

"Many times."

"Edward—!" The metronome ticked more insistently as the wind teased the waves ashore.

"And with dozens of guys. Why do you stare at me, Ned—does that surprise you?"

Ned's eyes widened, and he pulled the covers to his chin.

"In the army, you goose! We bedded down in twos, threes, sometimes fours—wherever we found an empty bed."

"You caught me by surprise there," Ned began, but before he could say more an insistent knock at the door cued him to retreat beneath the covers. The counterpane enveloped him as Maximiliano strode into the room.

"Thought I'd find you lying about here, Eddie." Maxi propped his foot on the edge of the bed. "Are you aware I've been knocking?"

"I'm aware you haven't shaved, combed your hair, or changed your shirt in God knows how long."

"The budding novelist—and what an eye for detail," Maxi sneered.

The warmth of Ned's body against him and the fear of imminent discovery provoked a maddening erection. "What do you want?"

"It's a money matter—"

"I'm hardly surprised—"

"Ten grand."

"Tomorrow morning." He cut off the fulsome thanks that might have followed. "Would you leave now—I have business in town."

"I wouldn't think of staying a moment longer," Maxi drawled. He turned to go but hesitated. "You haven't put on weight, Eddie …?"

Edward bolted up and pulled the covers with him, forming a deceitful tent over his body and Ned, the bed not creaking but silently complicit. "It's the same hundred and sixty pounds of a year ago, and the year before that."

He exhaled audibly as Maxi withdrew but then wrenched the covers tighter as someone else appeared in the doorway.

"Miss Fiona phoned to say that she'd be arriving later this afternoon," Farleigh announced. "Said she wishes to discuss some matter with you, Mr. Ed."

He clutched the covers as if he feared Farleigh meant to wrench them away.

"Said she'd tried to ring you, but you didn't answer, sir."

"Good, very good, Farleigh," he returned, appalled by all this commotion in his private domain. "Don't bother with breakfast. We'll … *I'll* grab something later."

"Very good, Mr. Ed …" Farleigh stood his ground.

"Yes—?"

"And young Deane?"

"What about him—?"

"He must've got up and out before I opened the kitchen."

"Most likely went to see his dad, Farleigh. Thank you."

Farleigh's footsteps diminuendoed into the distance as Ned emerged from beneath the counterpane, the sheet partly covering his head.

"You can come out now." Edward suppressed a grin. Ned reminded him of a novice beneath her wimple.

His companion dressed quickly while Edward stationed himself at his desk. When Ned was about to leave Edward reminded, "Our theater date is coming up in two days."

"Did you think I'd forget?"

Ned's words echoed away, and Edward wondered whether he'd give a sign that anything had changed between them. He began to dig through a desk drawer in search of nothing while waiting out the eternity of Ned's footfall. When Ned made for the door, he rose to follow. Ned patted his arm and slipped into the hall.

Edward returned to his desk and stared out the window, his eyes following a flurry of gulls fleeing landward then veering wildly toward the high-hanging heavens.

Ned did not appear again till suppertime. Though the weather was temperate and the beach beckoned, Edward opted not to go for his daily stroll, to avoid running into him. His young friend's words had stuck in his mind: "I've never done this before." Was Ned feeling guilty? Was he attempting to absolve himself of responsibility for the incident, or whatever you want to call it? Was he, Edward, feeling guilty …?

That evening they were to meet in the small dining room off the kitchen. A bouquet of crimson-purple anemones graced the table.

"Gift from Miss St.-John," Farleigh explained. "Said to tell you she'd be at the house tomorrow at nine, to drive you to the train station."

How like Olivia to offer a gift, then disappear before he could thank her. What would she think if she knew how he'd passed the night? Were those blood-filled anemones a rebuke?

"Good evening, Edward."

He tensed at Ned's formality. Did Farleigh sense it?

"Glad to see you. Have a busy day?"

He waited for Ned's reply as they sat down to a meal of steamed mussels with pasta served by the houseman, who returned with a lime-and-carrot Jell-O mold and a basket of hot rolls. The overpowering silence braked attempts at conversation. Till Ned came out with, "I'm off to my dad's. Haven't seen him in a while. I've been a bad son."

"Don't beat yourself up." He searched Ned's face for any clues to his mood. "It's been hard for you to get around."

"That's no excuse."

They ate in silence but for the irksome banalities each felt obliged to utter, till Ned announced,

"I won't be back tonight."

"You're staying out—?"

"… at my dad's."

Ned held his eye for the first time since they came to the table.

"Good plan."

Ned barely nodded.

"I mean, that you want to visit your dad. He must miss you."

Ned nodded again, more gravely.

After another pause Edward thought to say, "Give your dad my regards." He added after considered hesitation, "I'll miss you."

Ned was almost out the door when he turned and all but whispered, "Miss you, too."

The cool, sunny morning promised a perfect day for their theater outing. Olivia had insisted on driving them to the station. She was tactful enough not to question why they were taking the train to the city, instead of the customary chauffeur + limo. If she'd inquired, he'd have explained that he suspected Ned would be more at ease without the trappings of the high life.

But where *was* Ned? Had he returned from home? Would Ned stand him up? Olivia had already parked her Impala when he came out to find her waiting on the driveway. She wore a hat with a floppy brim that hid her face from the brilliant sun.

His lips brushed her cheek, then he stumbled, righting himself while Olivia took his arm.

"Sorry, Liv—guess I'm not myself today ..."

"You're always yourself, Edward. It's your most endearing trait."

He smiled wanly. (Where was Ned?)

"Is your young man ready to leave?"

"Oh, Ned ...?" he questioned, as if she might have meant someone else. "He's around somewhere ..."

It was literally true, if unforthcoming. *Your young man*, her accusatory term?

"Everyone's been talking about how kind you've been to look after him. It's a great relief to his dad, I'm sure."

Everyone's been talking? "It's nothing to even think about." (Please.) (Where was Ned?)

They were standing in the shade now. He pushed her hat back to expose her face. She wore no makeup, but her creamy skin allowed her to dispense with cosmetics.

"You *are* a pretty creature ..." he hesitated.

"... when you take the time to look—?"

"Am I such an inconstant lover?" He glanced toward the house again in hopes of spotting Ned.

"You're only inconstant, dear." Before he could rebut her, she exclaimed, "Here comes our conquering hero ..."

A black Ford he didn't recognize was approaching. Sally Sunshine waved to them through the open window.

Ned hobbled out and joined them on the driveway, giving Olivia a kiss but avoiding Edward's eye. "Sally says she can drive us to the station," he announced to no one in particular.

"Olivia's here to drive us," said Edward, irritation prickling up the back of his neck. Did Ned think he'd neglect to arrange transportation for their trip?

"The station's not out of my way," Olivia offered.

"It's on my way as well," countered Sally.

After an awkward moment, Ned exclaimed, "Then I'll ride with Olivia." He winked at his newly appointed chauffeur, then opened the Impala's door for her. "You go with Sally," he directed Edward, not addressing him by name.

Olivia led the way to the station. There was no traffic, the road was easy. Sally rested her arm on the window frame as the wind rushing into the Ford caressed her curls. Though he'd not heard of the young woman till Ned introduced them that day on the beach, a lifetime ago, it had come to his attention that her dad worked at the local lumberyard and her mom was a beautician. Sally herself volunteered at the community library. He'd also learned she'd won a full scholarship to Barnard College. Barnard was right across the street from Columbia.

Tangled in his thoughts, Edward came close to forgetting he was riding beside her, till she said,

"Ned seems to be thriving since you took him in."

Took him in? The Ford hit a bump, and as he slid back on the seat he realized he didn't know whether Ned was her steady or only a sometimes date. The knowledge that he didn't know made him uneasy. Was *he* jealous?

"I've enjoyed watching him recover," said Edward. "You were very kind to spend so much time with him when he was incarcerated."

"Ned's a sweetheart. He expects so little. I suppose it comes from losing his mom at a young age. He's protecting himself from the disappointments that life doles out—usually without warning."

"Have you suffered such disappointments?"

"Maybe." She swerved to avoid a large hole in the roadway. "And now you're taking him to New York for a show. Aren't *you* the nice one!"

"I hope he enjoys it."

"He will. Ned has an inquiring mind, as you surely know by now …"

Her remark, self-assured and unassailable, put him even more on guard. They circled a roundabout then veered onto a back road to the station.

When Sally pulled up to the curb, Olivia had already parked a space ahead of them. "I hope you have a great trip, Edward. Would you like me to pick you up on your return?"

"That's very kind, Sally, but no need. Thanks for the lift."

"And thanks again for taking such good care of Ned. He's talked about nothing but this trip for the past week."

The train was approaching. Each woman kissed her man good-bye, then stepped back so as not to block other passengers waiting to board.

On the platform Ned stood several paces away from him. He kept his eye peeled to the distance as the train chugged to a stop. Over the hiss and steam Edward asked,

"Anything the matter?"

"Since you asked ... yes, there is."

"Want to talk about it?"

"It won't do any good."

"Try me."

They were about to mount the stepstool at the entrance to their car when Ned ventured, "I think I'm falling in love with you."

CHAPTER

11

I N THE CROWDED CAR a pair of seats awaited them as if reserved by fate. As soon as they settled in, Ned removed a book from his backpack, then started to jot the margins. Edward leaned in to see what he was writing but couldn't lean far enough for a view. It crossed his mind that Ned might just be scribbling.

They rode in silence as the commuter train seemed to go slower and slower. He hoped to start a conversation, but Ned had transferred his attention from the book to the moving picture of the window. As the train sped toward the city while seeming to move away from it, he considered giving Ned a sign that they were on track together. But then he wondered why he hadn't matched Ned's declaration on the station platform with a quid pro quo. Was he trapped within what Olivia called the "membrane" of his self?

The train was drawing closer to the city—Islip–Bay Shore–Babylon—for once the Long Island Rail Road was keeping to schedule. As the train plunged under the East River in its approach to Penn Station, a flash of light came to him in the darkness of the tunnel. He'd not address the issue head on but simply act as if nothing had changed between them.

He was lost as soon as they disembarked within the Greek Revival temple of Penn Station. He'd not taken the train since his teens.

Redcaps and passengers wove past them in every direction, while loudspeakers droned Last Call for ..., Arriving Late on Track ...

"This way," ordered Ned, who was used to taking the train from the Island to Columbia. "I know a quick way out of this maze." He dove into the milling crowd, glancing over his shoulder now and then to be sure he hadn't lost his companion. Soon they emerged into the cacophony of midday traffic on Seventh Avenue. The blare of horns blended with sirens and the screech of tires on pavement. The city was out to make as much noise as it could.

When Edward came abreast, he asked him, "How's your appetite—?"

"Raging."

"Ever been to a Horn & Hardart?"

"I'm game," Ned replied. He didn't have the heart to admit he ate at the popular chain whenever he was downtown with his Columbia buddies.

They found their eatery nearby, and Edward exchanged a couple of bills for a handful of nickels, half of which he gave to Ned. "The thing to do is look through those little glass doors along the wall," he directed, "to find your soup, sandwich, pies and cakes behind them—whatever you're in the mood for—they have just about everything here."

"I put a nickel in this slot ...?"

"... the glass door opens and—presto! You're a quick study, my friend!"

"Who would have thought ...?" Ned humored his kind, generous friend who anticipated his every need. He was still wondering why he unburdened himself on the train platform, and why Edward had said nothing in return.

They feasted on vegetable soup and ham sandwiches, with apple pie and ice cream cups for dessert. "It's like Grand Central Station here," Edward commented, both impressed and bewildered by the sea of humanity surging through the premises—secretaries buying lunch for the boss, office workers gossiping in twos and threes, construction workers in soiled undershirts grabbing a bite, all to the *click-clicking* of little glass doors opening and closing around them.

"Have you ever been to Grand Central Station?" asked Ned, a wooden spoon of ice cream held aloft while he awaited a reply.

"Once," returned Edward, "on a guided tour."

The lights went down, the curtain rose, and the actors took their places for the final act. Edward stole several peeks at Ned but, each time, the latter's eyes were fixed on the stage. As the play was nearing its end—the fatal shot was about to be fired by the enraged husband—he brushed Ned's arm with the tips of his fingers. Ned recoiled—a reflex? Later, Ned's arm brushed against his and neither moved away.

"Did the play make you sad?" Edward asked as they left the theater.

"It was a sad play, Edward ... but I can't be sad when we're together."

Outside, cigarette lighters clinked open as patrons lit up and spilled off the sidewalk into the street, clogged with five o'clock traffic. Checker and Yellow cabs flashed heartless off-duty signs, while those still empty honked and lurched in hopes of snaring fares. A chilling wind blew off the Hudson, yet amid the cold and din, Edward could hardly remember when he'd been so keyed up and happy.

On inspiration, he exclaimed, "Would you care to stay in town for dinner, maybe spend the night ...?"

"Can you make a hotel reservation at this hour ...?"

He'd resolved not to mention his apartment on the East Side, for fear Ned would think it was a setup. He had another idea. He'd call a friend. But he was out of change.

"Could you spare a nickel?" he asked.

Ned fished out several coins from his pocket. "Honored to be your banker for a *change*, sir, no pun intended."

They proceeded to the corner and turned onto the avenue, where a glass-paneled phone booth awaited them.

Ned watched his friend insert the coin, dial a number, then cup his free hand to his ear to shut out the roar of traffic up Eighth Avenue. Gotham loomed around him as dusk fell and the lights of nearby office towers flickered or dimmed. Though he'd come to know the city as a student at Columbia, he felt lost now amid the canyons of Midtown Manhattan. He was weary from the excitement of the day, his first big outing since he'd left the hospital.

But Edward had now left the phone booth and was walking toward him sporting a broad grin that clipped years off his age. "It's all arranged," he confided, taking Ned's arm and leading him to the curb, where he hailed a cab.

A boxy Checker with its pair of pull-down seats swerved to curbside. Inside the cab, Ned asked, "Where are we off to—?"

"Wouldn't you rather be surprised?"

"Sure."

But then Edward had second thoughts. "It's not fair of me to impose on your good nature. I could have nefarious plans in mind."

"Just don't forget to include me."

"You're a rascal!"

"For going along with you—?"

"Technically speaking, you're going along with the cabbie."

"Touché," Ned returned. "But you're an accessory."

"Is that all I am? I'll have to be more ambitious the next time around."

"And just when do you think that'll be … the next time … around …?"

"You know something?" Edward became very intent. "I'm having such a fantastic time—I wish we could sit here in this cab forever!"

"No imposition, no imposition at *all*—who cares about last-minute *intrusions*, to use your word? We were planning a dull evening at home. You couldn't have called at a better time …"

Vincenzo Molinas was awaiting them in the restaurant that he'd designated, and the first thing he did when Edward and Ned approached was introduce them to the gorgeous blonde at his side. "Miss Alexandra Cabot."

Edward fixed his eye on her, then declared, "I can't buy the 'dull evening' part of our phone chat, Vin, not with the lady in question."

The implied compliment broke the ice and all four joined in hesitant, then rolling laughter as they took their seats.

"Now you must let me introduce this remarkable young man to my left," Vann's face was flush with excitement. "Edward Deane, my neighbor on Long Island—I've recently hired him as my literary executor."

"Such talent in one so young," quipped Vin, who seemed to be enjoying himself immensely.

"Well, actually—" Ned broke in, "I do odd jobs around the house. My dad works for Edward."

"That's got to be the most modest biography I've ever heard," proclaimed Alexandra, "especially from a literary executor. Do you write?"

"Me? I'm a student at Columbia."

"Then you *will* write—?"

"Who knows the future?"

"*I* do," exclaimed Vin, "and we're ordering a round of drinks before we sink into sobriety and anyone but me says another word. *Garçon*—!" he signaled the waiter.

Alex gently elbowed his side. "Your French is impeccable, mon ami."

"Merci—next time I'll try two words."

That night the cozy Village bistro was amurmur with lively conversation at the dozen tables. The scotch, gin, bourbon, and vodka arrived soon enough, but not before the conversation had morphed into a verbal free-for-all. Although the glass-fronted corner restaurant was a virtual fishbowl, its diners seemed unmindful of the stares from passersby.

At the second round of drinks, Ned asked, "What do you do for a living, Miss Cabot, if I might inquire ...?" The awkwardly polite question and formal honorific brought a smile to her face. She was deciding she'd like the young man wholeheartedly.

"I'm a designer," she replied, "primarily for books, and some magazine work."

"Then you're an artist," Ned affirmed. "Pleased to know you." She could not tell from his broad smile whether Ned was teasing, flirting, or just being irresistible.

"Not to dash your high opinion, but I'm a designer."

"She's a designing woman," added Vincenzo. He wrapped his arm around her shoulders and pulled her in as she made a face that signified *Would you listen to this guy—!*

As they were finishing their meal Vin asked, "Are you going back to the Hamptons, Edward, or staying in town tonight?"

Edward cleared his throat, a tic since childhood when put on the spot. "That hasn't been decided," he replied. He hoped he didn't look as sheepish as he felt. When he'd invited Vin to meet them for dinner, he considered asking whether they could crash at Vin's place. But he hadn't broached the subject because he wasn't sure how the evening would play out. He wondered what Vin would think of his squiring a young man around town. But Vin was clearly enamored of his "designing woman"; he wasn't paying a lot of attention to anyone else. Yet he did offer, "There's plenty of room at my pad."

"I've got to be going," said Alexandra. "Big day tomorrow."

"Too bad." Ned's gaze lingered on the older woman.

"We'll meet again, I'm sure. Vincenzo will see to it—won't you, Vince?"

She was so self-assured that Edward was certain she meant what she said. He felt a twinge that she already had a nickname for Vincenzo. It sounded odd when she called him "Vince"; his best friend had always been "Vin" to him. They made a striking couple. The statuesque blond with her deep-blue eyes and fair skin was a fitting counterpart to her companion, whose dashing Latin features partly overwrote the fine porcelain of his aristocratic English mother.

Alex stood to go and the three men along with her. She shook hands with Edward and Ned, then brushed Vin's cheek with a kiss. "Call me, okay?"

"Take the guest bedroom, Edward; your executor can sleep on the couch in the living room," their host directed. The three of them were having a nightcap in Vin's Village apartment. The perfect bachelor roost, on the top floor of one of the newer apartments near Hudson Street, afforded views over Greenwich Village. The lights of downtown Manhattan were ablaze now, imparting a festive backdrop for all manner of human folly.

"You have an incredibly beautiful apartment, Vincenzo." Ned's admiring eyes swept over the modernist décor of the deep umber walls, one of them covered in black-and-white prints, another with sepia photographs.

"Thank you, Mr. Executor. I'm glad you can share it with me ."

The cocktails and wine had relaxed Ned, and he ventured, "I liked Alexandra. I liked her a lot."

"She liked you too, Ned. You made a sterling showing."

"You make Ned sound like a racehorse," injected Edward.

Vin added, "I just hope she likes *me*. I'll call her soon and find out."

"Was this your first date—?" Ned pressed.

"Yes, it was."

"But you've known her a while …?"

"Yes, I have—a couple of hours. That's a while, isn't it, in this day and age?"

Ned's mouth gaped as Vin added, "I met her this afternoon, at an exhibition of rare prints at the Morgan Library."

"You two seem like you've always been together."

"I hope we soon will have been."

Vincenzo poured another round of Madeira, then announced he was retiring for the night. "Come with me, Ned, I'll get your bedding for the sofa."

Edward followed their host to the linen closet. "What are you doing here?" asked Vin. "Don't you think the kid is able to carry his own stuff …?"

"I'll be sleeping on the couch tonight," said Edward. "Ned will sleep in the bedroom."

"The sofa's fine with me, Edward."

"You'll sleep better in a regular bed." Then in an aside to Vin, "Ned's been sick. He's well on the road to recovery but he still needs his beauty rest."

"Beauty rest …?"

"What Edward is trying to tell you is that I had polio this summer."

"Oh, my god!" Vin was clearly moved.

"He's going to be fine," affirmed Edward.

"No doubt about that," Ned agreed. "I have the best nurse in the world."

Each made his way to bed, and Edward was soon dreaming of a silvery sheath that fluttered around him, while Fiona was breathing down his neck, and Maxi was pinioning him to a thin mattress as Liane's pimp stroked him to climax. Or almost, for he was waking and, for a moment, thought he was at the house where he had his assignations.

As it dawned on him that he'd been immersed in a dream, it also dawned that he was not alone. Through the dimness, he made out a head at his eye level. Someone was seated on the floor next to the sofa.

"What are you doing up?" he exclaimed, to which Ned replied tentatively, as if reciting something he'd only recently memorized,

"Près de toi, je suis trop heureux pour dormir."[1]

---

[1] "When I'm near you, I'm too happy to sleep." Olivier to Édouard, *Les Faux-Monnayeurs*, p. 1190. Translation by the author.

≳❋≲

Imagine my surprise when I reported for desk duty at Ocean House one morning and my eminent employer announced, out of the blue, that we were jaunting to New York for the day.

"But—"

I was wearing a pair of cut-off jeans, a white T-shirt, the kind usually worn as an undershirt, and a pair of ratty tennis shoes. I'd eschewed my usual sartorial splendor because this was the day when I was assigned to heavy-duty stuff around the grounds of Ocean House—Farleigh's idea. "But my manuscript—?" Edward had protested to his martinet-in-chief the day before. "It'll have to wait, sir," came the reply, with supreme equanimity, as my hapless gaze strayed around the room. The tyranny of Butlers! When Farleigh left, Edward told me to drop by his study next morning anyway— we could have a "quickie." Despite what you might be thinking, he meant one more pass at his precious prose. But now this trip to New York—?

"I'm not dressed for the occasion," I vociferated, brimming with indignation.

"Who said anything about an *occasion*—?" quipped Edward, serenely oblivious to my discomfiture.

"I could run home and change—"

"Nonsense, there's not a moment to lose." (Why all the urgency?) "Besides, you look fine as you are."

"Edward, have you consulted an ophthalmologist lately …?"

The reply of my overweening patron: "I've never been able to pronounce that word."

Occasion osmaishun.

When I tell you Edward took me for a ride that day, I kid you not. He drove the MG like a fugitive determined to put as much distance as possible between his past life and the next, if I may state it apocalyptically (again, Edward's inflated prose creeps into my writing). Even his speech became slurred and slangy as we barreled down the back roads of Long Island. "Cat got your tongue, baby?" (He was puzzled by my very uncustomary silence. It was all I could do to draw breath.)

Becoming faintly nauseated from the twists and turns of the MG, which was like an unamusing ride at an amusement park, I suggested meekly, "Would we get there faster on the Long Island Expressway? It's a straight run ..."

"Nah."

In fact, we made it to the city in what must have been record time, hardly slowing our breakneck pace till we got to the Queensboro Bridge into Manhattan.

I love that grand entrance into Gotham from Lon' G-island. Here we emerge from the flatness, in every sense of the word, of the Island to the grandeur of the City, as residents of the Outer Boroughs call Manhattan, as if they weren't part of New York. The dinosaur-skeleton of a bridge lifts you above Queens and the Quotidian, till you feel you're soaring as high as the fabled towers of Midtown (Edward's disastrous influence on my prose persists).

Our stalwart MG shot down the avenue with little regard for other vehicles, a ferocious minnow among drifting sharks in New York City traffic. And before I knew it, we'd arrived at the heart of the city, landing in one of the seedier stretches of Times Square, near the Port Authority bus station.

Two types of individuals populate this stretch of avenue: the denizens who hang out here—hookers, pimps, rent boys, adult book store patrons—and the transients, scurrying through the zone as fast as they can to the bus station, subway, or theater.

There's something desolate about this stretch of Forty-Second Street. It resembles a Texas border town. I half-expect to cross paths with a tumbleweed every time I misadventure here. Many of the buildings that line this unsavory expanse are only one or two stories, as makeshift as the merchandise they purvey.

"I'll be back in a jiffy or two—" My lordly chauffeur took off and melted into the melee of the city, leaving yours truly to face the flotsam and jetsam. He'd deposited me near a row of adult bookstores and headshops that have been swept into the dustbin of history, courtesy Disney and Co., which has carried out its own appalling malling (mauling?) of the urban landscape. I'd ventured down here a few times with buddies from Columbia for a raunchy night out, but never alone. As a disingenuous breeze off the Hudson wafted around me, I imagined it was addressing me personally, uttering sounds that sounded like *m-u-c-h*. The wind repeated its mantra—*much much much*—then added something like *pow* or *wow*.

As I attempted to decipher this whispered missive, a blaze of colors assaulted my blinking eyes.

"How much—?" asked the man in the garish Hawaiian shirt.

"How much what—?"

I presumed I was dealing with an immigrant (i.e., a non–New Yorker) negotiating his way through the vagaries of the city.

"How much?" he repeated.

As I continued to stare at him, he regaled me with a menu of linguistic fare consisting of such expressions as "Cuánto cuesta?" "Combien?" "Wieviel, bitte schön?"

I figured out that he was a tourist asking for directions, till he put a hand on my chest and drawled under his breath, "How much you fixin' to charge me, son?"

So it was *I* he was after …?

"You've got me wrong, pal—"

"Who you think you tryin' to kid, kid—?" inquired his Southern accent. "It's plain as that schnoz on your pretty face whatchus out here for. You cain't make no monkey outta me—!"

"I don't mean to make anything out of you, sir," I returned (certainly not a silk purse), coloring scarlet from toes to fingertips (wasn't everyone watching?). "I'm just minding my own business." (Edward, where are you—?!)

"In that outfit …?" He eyed me up and down. "You must take me for a moron—!"

"I'm not taking you for anything, sir—" (But come to think of it …)

"Now, don't you be a smartass, son," he persevered. "My money's as good as the next guy's. Name a price, or we kin settle up afterwa'd. I'm presuming you've got a room in the v'cinity …?"

It was time to think fast. "We can go wherever you like after I make a quick stop at the Department of Health."

"*Health*—?!"

"I just have to get my shots."

"*Shots*—!?" It was as if I'd said the magic word on the *Groucho Marx Show*. No little bird fluttered down to hand me fifty bucks, but at least I was rid of my—do I dare say it?—admirer.

It was almost an hour before Edward returned to pick up his glorified streetwalker. During that time, I fended off three more would-be clients, two prostitutes who offered to eat me for lunch, and a pimp who assured me I could make more money freelancing for him than as a student at Columbia University, formerly Kings College, founded 1791.

"You okay …?" inquired a familiar voice, sounding as if he'd stumbled onto me by accident.

"Who, me—?"

"Good! Hop in—I know a diner you might like. You must be famished …"

My Knight in Shining MG parked his vehicle in a lot nearby, then we perambulated to a glorified greasy spoon whose glaring neon sign proclaimed Betty's Burgers. He requested a table for three, and before long a gentleman (I supposed) joined us. He wore a tweed suit that neither covered his wrists nor concealed the tacky white socks jammed inside a pair of well-worn wingtips. Yet he looked no more forlorn than the other diners. Edward presented yours truly as "my brilliant editor." In undershirt and cutoffs, Mr. Lawson took scant notice of me, but he engaged Edward in a murmuring conversation of which I hardly caught a word. Both seemed unaware of my presence, so I tried to look deep in thought whenever the waitress came near. At length, she stopped and asked,

"What'll it be, hon?" The time-honored refrain of a waitress yearning for the end of her shift.

"Hamburger steak, medium rare," I chirped.

She frowned. "We only make 'em one way here."

"How is that …?"

"Cooked."

As was my goose, I was about to learn. No sooner had we finished our repast than Edward, with a look at Lord Lawson, announced, "I must spend the evening in the city, Ari. If you can make it on your own down to Penn Station, I'll phone Farleigh to wait for your train."

I managed not to blink when he handed me a crisp twenty.

CHAPTER 12

I T WAS ONE OF THOSE HOT, CLAMMY DAYS, the day after their excursion to the city, a day that sticks to you like wallpaper. Even the beach offered scant relief from the heat and humidity. The wind was on furlough, leaving beachcombers and everyone else on the Island in the lurch. The day was meant for the very young and, as always, lovers who can't get enough of each other.

Edward was having a hard time. He'd looked forward to his afternoon walk with Ned. They had reached the midpoint in their review of his novel and agreed it was time for a break—no more sessions for a couple of days! He'd imagined this walk against a horizon of rose and gold. But their trek along the shore, far from lifting his spirits, had sunk them, and he didn't know why. As they trudged over the sand, he withdrew into himself, unmindful of the effect on his companion.

Ned, too, seemed adrift, as if he were detached from his surroundings. The perfunctory *yes* or *no* he returned to Edward's occasional observations only increased the distance between them. Until he paused as they were approaching the house, shaded his eyes from the glare off the clouds, and exclaimed, "You see that chair up there—?"

"The chaise longue …?"

"Something special happened there the night of your party. I hadn't mentioned it because it just came to me."

"You skipped out early, as I recall."

"You noticed …?"

"I was worried."

"Why—?"

"I wanted to be sure you were at ease and having a good time. But tell me what happened?"

"I was resting in that chaise, as you call it, watching the night sky, when I made out a string of letters formed by the stars."

"Like alphabet soup?"

"More of a jumble."

"A jumbalaya, then …?"

"Please be serious."

Edward cuffed him on the back of the neck. "I'm always serious. Proceed."

"I tried to make something of the letters, but I couldn't figure them out—until just now."

"What were the letters?"

"There was an *A*, a *W*, a couple of *D*'s …"

"Let's see whether I can solve this big mystery …" Edward pursed his lips and squnched his forehead. "*WAD*, of course, with a superfluous *D*."

"Guess again."

"I'm guessed out."

"It spelled your name."

"WADD with two *D*'s … isn't that's odd? Why didn't I recognize it immediately?"

"Come on—I had to supply the missing letters."

"How do you know your stars weren't spelling 'waddle'?"

"Because that's not how stars work."

They resumed their walk, Ned still wondering whether Edward was taking him seriously.

The sultry air thick and inescapable importuned Edward like a tiresome lover. He fell back till Ned moved ahead of him, marching with steady gait over the sand. Ned seemed unaware they were no longer in stride. Edward's eyes hovered over Ned's legs, partly covered by a pair of worn Bermuda shorts. He recalled that day on the basketball court, when Ned took his first halting steps back to life. It was just a short time ago that Ned was wearing that awful brace. Now his sinewy legs were regaining muscle tone. They'd come a long way together, he and this wayfarer who'd shown up on his doorstep hoping for a job. Now he seemed more like a son, the patient he'd helped recover from polio. He observed Ned's movements with the satisfaction of a Pygmalion.

After several paces Ned wheeled around.

"By the way, are you ever truly serious?"

"I'm a serious writer, you ought to know that. You tease me enough about cloistering myself in a cocoon. You're as bad as Fiona."

"I mean, serious about, well, us …?"

"What about us?"

Edward faced him off as if expecting a contretemps.

"You know," Ned began, hoping his friend would rescue him with a declaration or clarification of some kind. He deserved as much, didn't he, after revealing the incident with the heavenly alphabet soup, or jumble, or whatever the heavens were trying to communicate, not to mention his declaration on the train platform? "… I'm still waiting."

Still, Edward remained silent, till Ned asked point-blank, "Do you love me, Edward?"

His companion's face brightened in the onset of evening. He drew Ned to his chest and murmured, "Here's one for you, my little friend: Is water blue?" Ned's arms encircled his waist. "Of course, I love you, you goose. How could I have spent weeks at your side sharing the intimacy of my creation—my writing—and at your hospital bed, hoping and praying for your recovery—if I didn't love you?"

"That's good to hear," Ned whispered.

When they returned to Ocean House, Edward exclaimed, "Would you look at me—I'm a sweaty mess!"

Ned brushed the perspiration from his forehead. "Me too."

"Care to shower …?"

"Why not?"

They took the stairs two at a time, racing to an undefined finish line. He held back so Ned could keep his lead. He'd not felt this young or foolish in years, maybe ever.

They stripped off their clothes and Edward led the way to the shower. He turned on the water, yanked a towel from the rack, and swatted Ned on the behind.

Ned wheeled around then grabbed the towel from his friend. "Fucking bastard—!" He looped the towel around Edward's waist and dragged him to the shower floor, where he tumbled down beside him.

Steam rose from the cool tiles as the water struck. The vapors filled the space, reminding Edward of Wotan's descent into Nibelheim, from *Das Rheingold*, without, in the present case, all the gnomes scurrying about, *Gott sei Dank*. The enticing jet of water prickled their skin and "combed" their hair flat to their foreheads, prompting Edward to observe,

"You look different with bangs."

"You look different with a hard-on."

Edward glanced down at his swollen member, then his gaze fell back on Ned as his young friend reached over and grasped his erection.

As if making an excuse for himself, or for his member, Edward declared, "He's a wild creature—I have absolutely no control over him."

"Do you want to have control …?"

"I never thought I had a choice, about controlling him."

"*Him*—?"

"Don't you call yours 'him'?"

"I don't call him anything…"

"You don't …?"

"He does the calling …"

"Touché."

"We're already touchéing."

Edward took Ned's hand and pulled him up from the floor as Ned released his cock. He grabbed a bar of soap and started lathering Ned's face, soaping around the eyes as his fingers spread the suds across his cheeks, forehead, neck and ears, transforming Ned into a clown fit for the circus.

The clown stood steady as the bar of soap slithered over shoulders, chest, belly. Edward dropped to his knees and clasped Ned's warm, slippery flesh to his chest. His hands ran up and down Ned's haunches, pressing and kneading as if reshaping him to a new form. A vision of Liane appearing nude before him raced through his mind and he took Ned in to the back of his throat.

Afterward, as they sprawled beneath the water jet baptizing their bodies, Edward declared, "When we were in the city, I told you that I could ride beside you forever in that cab. Well, you know something? This is even better..."

My Edward was a stickler for things in their place, and not just physical items you could stash in chests and cubbyholes, but all the gestures and code words that bind WASPs together in that great collusion known to Us Outsiders as High Society. My idol and I interacted closely, some might call it intimately. Yet we hadn't yet blended into each other's world, not entirely.

I never expected to become one of THEM, of course. I had neither the clothes nor the prose for that transmigration to WASPdom. Ari Edelman living the High Life in the Hamptons? I was no Charles Swann, *croyez-moi*. But when Edward and yours truly collaborated on his writing, I can tell you that we became soulmates—*shudder*—the most clichéd term in modern English. But what else am I to call us? There on the level playing field of literature, my soul merged with Edward's and we shared every major human experience.

I even scrubbed his shower down one afternoon. Why me, O Lord? Because I couldn't break away from him. I was a satellite held in orbit around Sun King Edward Vann. I'd do anything to be near my star. I was but a lowly asteroid, a tailless comet who couldn't break free of his gravitational pull. Let Edward have the limelight; I was more than happy to bask—even languish—in his shadow (a first for me).

For all the hero worship, I was not above teasing my lord and master. On an afternoon after we'd sweated and sworn over a rough patch of copy, my eyes wandered to his and I was gripped by poetic fervor.

"Tell me, Edward, if I may be so bold to ask ..."

He merely raised his archetypical eyebrows.

"What is your substance ... that millions of strange shadows on you tend ...?"

"Sonnet LIII."

I could almost visualize the roman numerals in his eyes. He followed up my immortal quote-query with a question of his own: "Would you crack a window, Ari? It's stuffy in here."

"Edward! I just recited the most exalted line of English poesy, and all you can think about is the heat—?"

A smile between impish and sheepish crossed his lips. "I'm afraid you're much more the romantic than I am, my good friend." He gazed absently around the room. "Life has drained the romantic pulse out of me."

"Is that why you keep yourself shut away up here from the rest of the world?"

"It's why I write."

I thought he was going to retreat into the chambered nautilus of his ruminations, but he held his index finger aloft, an Edwardian leitmotiv signaling a statement about to be issued. "I like the change you made this morning in this final paragraph here, Ari ..." He held up a page from the manuscript, signaling me to take my seat on the rattan chair. I scooted to his side. (I should refuse a place by the throne?)

"That was a nice touch," I said, "adding the rue de Rivoli to your Parisian setting ..."

"*You* added it."

I'll say one thing for my Edward Vann: he gave credit where credit was due. And I lapped it up.

"I think it provides the perspective you need for your exquisitely romantic characterization of the Louvre."

" 'The infinity of marvel and mystery beyond the great museum'—that was *your* characterization, Ari."

I couldn't keep from quipping, "Who's writing this novel, anyway?"

He leaned across the space between us and ran his hand through my curls. It was his most physical expression of affection for me—or perhaps perplexity. He was getting used to the *idea* of me, if not to the *actuality* of a nice Jewish boy-editor within the hallowed precincts of Ocean House.

It was about then that the subject of the shower scrubbing came up.

"I think you've squeezed about all you can out of me today," Edward confessed, removing his hand from my locks and sinking back in his chair. "Besides, we've got to clear out shortly. Farleigh's sending someone to scrub down the shower in that bathroom over there ..."

I didn't want to take my leave of Edward, not right then. I was still feeling that gravitational pull, and hoping he'd invite me for drinks or a walk on the beach or to spend the rest of my life with him. Desperation is the mother of artful hints.

"What say we scrub down that shower ourselves, Edward?"

"Us—?"

Arching an eyebrow, I declared, "OK, I'll scrub it for you—let it be one of my tasks—and you can amuse me with droll tales while I'm toiling away."

"Tales of what—?" He raised an eyebrow in salute to mine.

"The most intimate moments of your life—for a start."

He picked up the house phone. "It's me here, Farleigh ... No need to send anyone to work on that shower ... but two gin and tonics, please ... that's right ... and nibbles ... thank you ..."

"Where's the Bab-O?" I asked.

His puzzled look clued me that I had some educating to do. "Cleaning powder."

"You'll find everything you need right inside that cabinet there."

I stepped into his Augean stable and opened the cabinet to uncover a variety of scrub brushes, a box of soap powder, and a container of sandpaper. I removed my sneakers, then rolled up the sleeves of my oxford buttondown, which I wore untucked over khaki Bermudas. And there I stood, a star of Columbia University, surrounded by brushes, cleansing powders, and filthy tiles—like Ruth amid the alien corn, *pour ainsi dire.*

"It started in France," came the disembodied voice from the study.

"*What* started?" I'd already dampened a brush and sprinkled it with that abrasive powder, which was about to abrade my hands.

"My sex life."

I scrubbed more vigorously.

"Whores and barmaids …"

I dispatched all the grunge and algae with my brush of Damocles. Edward had found a way to open up, and his bathtiles were beginning to gleam like a Parisian pavement in the rain.

"It was my first run-in with sex—*real* sex, mind you," he self-corrected.

"*Real*…?"

"I was caught—hook, line, and sinker—"

"Pecker …?"

"Couldn't get enough of those French babes, starving while their Jacques and Renés were at the front, in the sick ward, or still inside German prison camps. I was a stand-in, you might say, for the trampled flower of Gallic manhood …"

"You did it standing up?"

"Even went AWOL a couple of times—don't know how Dad got me out of that fix, the biggest laugh of all: my puritanical father paying for his randy son to fuck his head off with every streetwalker I was not too drunk to lay … and they loved the hell out of me, those little French tarts…. Why *me*, I can hear you wondering …?"

"I'm scrubbing …"

"… because I could speak their lingo, thanks to years of what I once considered useless French courses in prep school, where we read the classics—"

"Classics my assics!" I piped.

"Those French girls could tell me 'put it here,' 'touch me there,' and I'd comply to their *heart's* content …"

"Their *twat's* …?"

"You get the picture."

My world-weary writer, fucking his *tête* off in gay Paree—some picture!

"Sounds like you had a rollicking time over there, buddy …" I was giving those tiles the drubbing of their life, while tripping over every line in the sand that Edward had ever drawn between us. *Buddy*—? What happened to the Sun King …?

"Yes, it was good all right…. Trouble was, I brought it back with me."

"You brought a French whore to the States—?"

"Not literally; I was careful to keep my private life and private parts away from the unsullied terrain of Ocean House. What I'm trying to say is … think you're up for this …?"

"I've heard *much* worse." I midwifed his recollections. This Poor Protestant Goyboy needed to get it off, and who was a Nice Jewish Boy qua editor to stanch the flow?

"After the fleshpots of Paris … pardon my purple …"

Pardon it? I was thoroughly drenched in his purple by now. I'd just cleaned up a passage in his manuscript that originally read: "The thick, viscous blood oozed down his bruised and battered thigh, sloshing like maple syrup on a frosty morning into his flayed and filleted combat boots." Let me make a confession: you don't have to be a Protestant to know that maple syrup doesn't "slosh" on *frosty* morns.[2] To be fair, it was the guy's first novel.

---

[2] For the record, I'd not yet acquired the rarefied taste for "real" maple syrup. But I could speak for its plebian sisters—Karo, Brer Rabbit, Aunt Jemima—all three longtime inhabitants of Mama's kitchen cupboard.

"... I compartmentalized my sexual escapades, saving the nice girls for the teas and cotillions, the naughty girls for the rough stuff."

"Sounds like a sensible division of labor."

"They say Flaubert did the same thing."

"And he gave us *Madame Ovary*."

"*Un Fiacre nommé désire*. That's why, ever since, it's been hard for me to get it together with a nice girl. Oh, I have sex with them, but my spirit isn't always in it ..."

"Or," prompted I, "your dick ...?"

"In a word."

"So you're saying you need a mean mama to knock you about for it to work ...?"

"*You're* saying it.... But maybe ... that's it ..."

Before I forget, I remembered something that Olivia once mentioned in passing, and I'd meant to bring it up with Edward but hadn't found the right time. "Didn't you win a medal or something in the war ...?"

"Distinguished Service Cross, two Silver Stars ..."

His voice trailed off, and his pause made me wonder whether there might have been more awards than modesty kept him from revealing. That modesty is probably what made him change the subject. He stuck his head in the door, and after giving the tiles a once-over declared, "Fine job. I suggest you test your handiwork by taking a plunge. By rights, you should be the first to try out this sparkling domain. So step under that shower—refreshments are on the way."

"I have thrilling news—!" Fiona bounded into the study without a knock, a cleared throat, or a shuffling of feet at the door. If he'd been screwing Ned on the desktop, that wouldn't have stopped her. She might not have even noticed.

Edward screwed his gold Parker pen together, pushed the manuscript aside, and tried not to look long-suffering.

"I'm getting married–! We've just signed our prenup."

"Is there an escape clause?"

"Can't you be serious for one moment, Edward?"

"Who's the lucky guy?"

"The most wonderful groom in the world! Whom did you expect …?"

She sank onto the rattan chair, a hen settling her feathers, her mood too exultant to dampen. Ned had sat there just a short time before, when they pored over the latest chapter of his novel. It was their first session after the shared shower, and Edward noticed a new familiarity on Ned's part. Ned no longer deferred, didn't hesitate to interrupt, and instead of his polite "May I suggest …?"'s, he came out with clipped statements like "That doesn't work." They'd moved to a more equal footing. The transformative power of love?

Jewels of perspiration adorned Fiona's brow, and wisps of hair strayed about her head as if she'd been gardening in the heat. A refreshing sight, Fiona in mild disarray, instead of the well-coiffed hair tied back by a silken scarf, Miss East Side Manhattan. This felicitous deviation from her norm transformed her in her brother's eyes. The straight nose, high cheekbones, and penetrating hazel eyes might be enough to launch a thousand ships, if only she could hold her tongue now and then.

He reached for her hand and she let him take it.

"Why, Edward—I didn't know you had a sentimental bone in that body of yours."

"My favorite sister's getting married and I'm not supposed to be moved? I suppose you'll want me to give you away—or does that honor belong to Maximiliano the Mad?"

She removed her hand from his. "You'll do."

"When do you expect the blessed event to occur, Sis?"

"Not till after we're married, I should hope."

He caught her wry smile and matched it with one of his own. He couldn't remember the last time they'd enjoyed a bon mot together.

"Oh, Edward, I almost forgot—the guest wing, the rooms on the first floor you never use …?"

"What about them?"

"I'll need them for the guests."

"What guests?"

"All the family and friends we'll have to put up for the wedding, the ones coming in from out of town."

"Do we know anyone from out of town?"

"Mother's relatives, for a start."

"Did she have any?"

"Edward! This is the first and probably last time I'll ever get married. Won't you hush and listen to me, bitte schön—?" She unleashed her maddening trait of lapsing into German when she was cross, the vestige of a school year spent in Heidelberg. "Now, back to those guest rooms ..."

And that might have ended that, until she announced, "That boy who's been staying downstairs—he'll have to move out. Farleigh doesn't need him any longer."

"*Need* him? It's the other way around. He needs the room, he's recuperating from polio."

"But I'm getting married—"

"And Istanbul was Constantinople" (he whistled a couple of bars from the Four Lads' hit song) "... but what does your marriage have to do with it ...?"

"Do be serious, Edward. I can send someone to pack his stuff and deliver it wherever it needs to go."

The idyll of an eternity spent with Ned telescoped to a measly twenty-four hours, and that was pushing it. But he had to make one more protest, if only pro forma: "The poor guy's hardly back on his feet ..."

"Nonsense," she retorted, as if assuring him it couldn't possibly rain that day. "I've seen him around the place, and I'd be highly impressed if you walked as well as he does."

It was futile and he knew it: he could argue till the cows came home blue in the face. So he told her, "Spare yourself the trouble, you've got enough on your mind. I'll take care of it."

"You're a prince!"

She rose to go.

"I guess that's an improvement. The last time, you called me a butterfly."

"And a butterfly you were until recently."

Instead of leaving, she sat down again. "It's the most peculiar thing, Edward, but since that odd young man has occupied a room in the house, you seem to have come out of your cocoon."

"I have?"

"Even Farleigh mentioned it."

"What does Farleigh have to do with it?" he replied, his concern rising to an uncomfortable level.

"He's the one who hired him, silly."

"I'd forgotten …"

"Goodness, Edward—What do *you* care, anyway? Farleigh hovers over him like a mother hen. He used to bring him his breakfast when he first moved in. He just mentioned to me that he sees the boy out on the terrace or the beach every day."

"He does?"

"He caught him fooling around on the basketball court just yesterday."

"Fooling around …?"

"Farleigh said he makes a basket every time he throws the ball to the hoop."

Before Edward could think of a reply, she concluded,

"So much for rest and recuperation."

"But the good news, Sis, you've made a basket, too—you've got yourself a groom!"

"I already mentioned that." Fiona reverted to her signature deadpan.

The transformative power of love.

All was quiet next morning when the sun rose over a becalmed sea. Devout gulls had taken vows of silence. He lay awake for some moments, clutching his pillow close as a lover. Till a stabbing in his chest reminded him: he must ask Ned to leave. He threw on his clothes, hoping to catch his lodger before breakfast, figuring it might be easier to break the news while breaking bread.

He took the stairs slowly, and when he arrived in the foyer a familiar face met him.

Milly Tolliver wielded a multifeathered duster, her hair tied up beneath a wimple of white bandanna.

"Morning, Milly."

"I wish you a pleasant day, sir."

"If the gods are kind."

"Who, sir?

"Just a manner of speaking." He turned to go but she announced, "I have something for you, sir."

She fished a small envelope out of her pocket. Instead of handing it to him, she lay it on a marble commode beneath the foyer's gilded mirror, which reflected it back to him.

She then curtsied and vanished for all practical purposes.

Pocketing the note, he ducked into the pantry and, glancing over his shoulder, unsealed it.

I KNOW WHAI YOU RE UP TO

There was something comical about the cloak-and-dagger touch. The note, addressed to no one, bore no signature and was so general it might have meant anything. The *t* in "what" was not crossed, and there was no apostrophe in "you re". But why keep wondering? He could ask Milly later in the day. He'd meant to offer her a raise, and here was the perfect excuse to broach the subject.

Under other circumstances such an equivocal, if not sinister, message might have provoked alarm. But for the time being, he was so fixated on meeting with Ned that the threat of the note receded.

When he stepped back into the hallway, he caught sight of Ned on his way to the breakfast room. He seemed preoccupied.

"How's your appetite?" he asked, hoping to set a light tone.

"It's fine," said Ned. There was something childlike in the reply.

They sat down to a breakfast of scrambled eggs and salmon, fresh fruit, Parker House rolls, and a steaming pot of coffee. They'd hardly taken their seats when Farleigh appeared and asked whether he might bring them anything else.

"You've outdone yourself," came Edward's genial reply. His houseman was about to return to his duties when he noticed the envelope at Edward's place.

"I'm glad to see you've received your letter, sir."

So that was the path of the note, from Farleigh to Milly to him? Farleigh was the one to question about its provenance. He'd meet with him that afternoon, after offering Milly the raise.

"What are your plans for the day, Edward?" Ned asked as he poured them each a cup of coffee, as if they were so in synch that banalities sufficed for communication.

A radiant sun was streaming through the large window, which offered a splendid view of the beach. The idyllic setting would soon vanish with Ned no longer in it. He still hadn't figured out how to broach the subject, and the more he thought about it the more perplexed he became, until he blurted out, "There's something I've been meaning to discuss with you, my friend."

"That's funny—a concatenation of circumstances."

At least Ned was making light of the situation. Then Edward asked him, "Who wants to go first?"

"Well, sir, I believe that depends on who is presenting the weightier topic." Sunlight dappled the young man's head, forming a halo around it. Ned had never looked so beatific.

Making light of the situation, Edward said, "Mine is so horrific I hardly dare bring it up."

"In that case, I'll go first—I'm moving out." After a moment he asked, "Edward, are you breathing ...?"

Edward rose from the table and, without looking back, left the room and made for the beach. He forged through the yielding sand, his feet sinking in, the tide having only just pulled out. He turned toward the sea but a hand on his shoulder arrested him. He wrenched free and lurched forward, throwing himself at an aggressive wave thundering ashore. The wave drug him under as he ceased resistance.

He bobbed to the surface as the wave lost its force, and came face-to-face with Ned.

"No need for hysterics," Ned chided, sprigs of seaweed stuck in his thick merman hair.

"Why are you leaving—?"

"I'm just leaving your house—not *you*, you dummy! Time to be on my own again. Besides, my dad misses me, and I belong there."

As another breaker was about to hit, Ned lunged forward and pinned him to the sand. Then the wave struck while they grappled in the watery bed. Till Ned clamped him in a vise as the sea lapped around them with contented indifference, splashing its libation over their bodies, till Ned's head came to rest on his heaving chest.

"From Here to Eternity ..." sighed Edward.

It's not known whether the pair of tiger eyes that had followed them onto the beach shared that impression.

CHAPTER
13

I T WAS A HAZY, LATE-SUMMER MORNING when even trees and drooping shrubbery seemed weary from months of unrelenting heat. A garden hose led from the house to a sprinkler. He remembered children capering in its cooling jets in the days before air conditioning, when Ned was just a youngster. And to think he'd hardly noticed! All he could recall from that day long ago was a generic kid, a mere sketch of the boy who'd become—what else to call him?—his lover.

He made his way to the front door holding a wicker basket of fruit and two freshly baked loaves of bread. Ned occupied the doorway in undershirt and black corduroys held up by red suspenders. His young friend might have stepped out of a gangster film from the Capone era if it weren't for his wholesome looks.

Ned pushed the door aside and Edward offered the basket, wondering whether to shake hands or embrace him. But Ned directed, "Give it to Dad—it'll please him."

Ned led the way to the kitchen, where Silas Deane was preparing his famed pancake breakfast. A week before, the grateful father had mailed Edward a note thanking him for the care he'd lavished on his son and inviting him to a meal.

"Good morning, Edward." Silas was ladling batter into a cast-iron skillet. He wore a bib apron over a plaid shirt and woolen trousers. The room had a single window, over the sink. Pine cabinets lined the walls, and a table for two occupied the middle of the floor. It could seat three uncomfortably. A can of Bon Ami waited near the sink next to a bag of flour and a bottle of Wesson oil.

"Sorry I can't shake your hand," the chef apologized. "I'm at my battle station. We're honored to have you here, Edward."

"Honored to be here," returned their guest, setting the basket on the countertop. "Something for you and Ned here."

Silas glanced up and frowned. "*We* were supposed to supply the grub this morning."

"Farleigh forced it on me. I had no say, sir, in that matter."

"Speaking of having a say in matters," said Silas with a benevolent nod, "I'd have to say you're the perfect gentleman, Edward—your mama would have been right proud of her son."

"We weren't raised by our mama, Silas." Ned caught the glint in Edward's eye that Silas missed because of his focus on the pancakes browning in the skillet. "That woman you thought was our mother was a surrogate, hired to take us kids off her hands."

"Is that a fact, sir?" Silas glanced over his shoulder. "Pull up a seat for our guest, Ned, would you?"

Ned held a chair for the guest. "Here, Edward, we're dining in the breakfast room this morning."

"That's because we don't have a dining room," came the father's hopelessly matter-of-fact admission.

Edward took a seat and felt Ned's hands upon his shoulders. He reached back and gave Ned's leg a pat, the same leg that had borne the brace, straggled across the basketball court, wrapped around him.

Silas coughed and the son's hands flew off before his dad turned around.

"Pour the juice, Ned," Silas said. "I'll have these griddlecakes ready in a jiffy. 'Course, they're pancakes, but I like the other name better. Makes 'em sound more authentic, don't you agree? Ned, put that syrup on the table."

Silas piled the pancakes on their plates with generous sides of bacon, and all three were seated now. Without preamble he bowed his head and said a brief prayer. Images of censers and thuribles swirled before Edward's eyes, the pomp and circumstance of an Episcopal service that had once exalted him but eventually left him trailing behind the faithful. Surely his host's simple piety must be more pleasing to God, if there was one, than all the bishops in miters and deans in chasubles.

"That's melted butter in the pitcher," Silas informed them, "and there's more syrup if we run out. Now as they say in France, dig in!"

They ate in silence, knives and forks clicking arhythmically against the earthenware crockery. At some point, Edward declared, "Too delicious for words, Silas. You're a master chef."

"You, Neddy ...?" the father's gaze fell on his son.

"Qui ne dit mot consent."

Silas exchanged a glance with their guest. "Did you understand that? My son's learning Latin at Columbia."

"It means 'Best pancakes I ever ate'," returned Edward.

"That a fact? I didn't know they had pancakes when the Latins were alive."

"They had something similar, sir, and no pancake mixes in those days."

Silas reflected. "Did your mama, or that lady you said stood in for her, ever make pancakes for you kids?"

You kids. How strangely refreshing to hear himself and his siblings referred to by the neutral term. Weren't the Vann children once considered insufferable brats by the locals? "Yes, we had them every now and then ... Pass the syrup, would you, Ned ...? ... Thank you. And I can tell you, Silas," he asseverated, "These are even better than mother used to buy."

"Your mother *bought* your pancakes?"

"No, Silas, that lady who stood in for her."

"What's wrong, Neddy?" Silas had just noticed his son shaking with silent laughter.

Ned raised a hand to wave away further questions.

"I'd say Ned just has a rather mild case of the giggles," Edward diagnosed.

Silas took this in, resting his chin in his hand as he glanced at his two diners.

When they finished Ned said, "I'll clear the table, Dad."

"Thank you for this delicious treat," Edward began to the sound of water splashing over dishes in the sink. "I can't remember when I've had such a tasty meal, Silas."

"Well, sir, it's a very small way to thank you for … all you've done for my boy."

"Please don't mention it."

"Neddy's not used to the attention you've showered on him. He's a good boy, my son. He's not been spoiled."

"I hope *I* haven't spoiled him," returned Edward, reddening at his own remark.

"No, what you've done for him wouldn't spoil him. You've made him better. You've made him whole again before you gave him back to me."

The grateful father laid his hand upon Edward's as if sealing a pact.

"I must be going," said his guest, too overcome to face father or son.

"We'll see you to the door," said Silas.

The trinity made their way to the front of the cottage, where Deane shook Edward's hand, tears gathering in his eyes. Their visitor turned to go, he was on the threshold, when Ned wrapped his arms around him and hugged him so hard he nearly choked.

⋙✻⋘

What a tearjerker, the dad slobbering over his "griddle" (spittle?) cakes, the son and son's lover lapping it up right under his nose. To paraphrase an infamous wit, you'd have to have a heart of stone to read that passage and not laugh. But you must also admire their bravura. After all, neither gave a thing away. How seamlessly they carried it off—"Pass the syrup, would you, Ned …? … Thank you"—it's enough to make you think the poor dad was in on it with them! Of course, that would have been out of the question. Everyone was homophobic in those days in the climate of intimidation and blackmail fomented by J. Edgar You-Know-Whover. To be pro-homo was like being pro–child molesting. Even the priests, those faithful guardians *in loco diaboli*, kept it under wraps. Besides, Papa Deane had no reason to suspect his son of being anything less than a healthy hetero. He'd caught Ned necking on the front porch with more than one young thing—ad seriatim: Ned was no cocksman. As for Edward, his head filled with the mumbo-jumbo of thuribles and miters, he'd never fully left the church and was not about to count himself a pervert, not after being touched by the transformative power of love, if not incense.

Edward was never invited to our house for a meal, technically speaking, but he had one with us anyway, to my everlasting chagrin. I'll never forget that Sunday afternoon. I was in my room when I heard the doorbell importuning, then shortly afterward my dad's voice calling to me. "Someone to see you, Ari ..."

Someone? I hastened to the living room, where I was stunned to find Edward standing right next to Dad. How did he get that far? If I'd answered the door I'd have blocked his way! Edward Vann under the same roof as my parents—?

He held a sheaf of papers in his hands, imperturbable as I've ever seen him. I assumed he'd brought back some tax forms for dad to sign, but what did *I* know?

"Sorry to barge in," he began, the picture of serenity, "... but I was wondering, could we go over this chapter one more time—if it's not inconvenient?"

These were the first intimations that Edward was losing his sanity. Venturing into my house when my folks were home? What was he fucking thinking ...?

We'd hammered away throughout yesterday morning on an introductory section of his novel. It had given us both trouble. I thought it was overwritten; Edward thought it was too spare. The one thing we agreed on is that the novel hinged on it—we had to get it right.

Mama appeared in the doorway. She'd been listening to the goings-on from the kitchen.

"How are you today, Mrs. Edelman," asked our polite caller, tipping his imaginary hat.

"Hot as a fried latke," replied the inveterate truth-teller.

Before I could regain the power of speech, Edward pleaded, "I'll take just a moment of your son's time ..."

"Moment?" exclaimed my mama. "Listen to the man about a silly little *moment*! We expect you to stay to Sunday dinner, don't we, Irv?"

"Sure, why not?" Dad returned, his voice tinged with indecision. "We can probably stretch what we have."

"Of course, we can," encouraged Mama. "If we all eat a little less, there'll be enough to go around."

Edward tried to stop the madness. "I wouldn't *think* of imposing, Mrs. Edelman."

"Imposing? Who said anything about *imposing*? I don't have to eat a bite—there'll be plenty if I don't, honest. I'll find something to eat at the next meal."

"Seriously, Mrs. Edelman—"

"How long till the next meal, anyway?" Dad cajoled. "No one's going to starve if Edward eats with us—in all likelihood."

I'll always wonder why Edward agreed to sit through that meal. The only plausible explanation is that he was desperate to have my input for his novel. But the poor fellow would have to endure the excruciating table-talk of Sunday dinner at the home of Irving and Esther Edelman, aka Punch and Jewdy, not to put too affectionate a point to it.

It saved the day that Mama was a good cook.

Even Edward joined in the general merriment, quoting such apothegms as "After a good meal you can forgive everyone—even your relatives."

"Maybe *your* relatives, Mr. Vann," Mama rose to the bait. "Not mine, and certainly not Irving's over there."

Judging it judicious to change the subject, and no doubt frantic to powwow with me, Edward declared, "You know, you've got a regular prodigy here?" He glanced from my folks back to yours truly.

"Mr. Vann—!" My mama was so enthralled that she'd have granted Edward le droit de seigneur had he demanded it. But he was too full of latkes to frolic or fornicate.

"My Ari?" Mama resumed, "He takes after his father." She tossed Dad a freebie. When Dad failed to run for it, Mama added, "They say Ari resembles my cousin Saul, on my mother's side. At least, that's what they say. Of course, Cousin Saul was said to look like Harold Flynn."

"Errol, Mama," I winced.

"Harold Errol?—You've gotta be kidding—"

Kidding or not, we finished up and it's safe to say no one was still hungry; even mama had her fill. Edward took me aside and suggested we drive to the local DQ to go over his manuscript. I readily consented. As we were leaving, Mama called out,

"You'll have to join us again soon, Mr. Vann. Do you by any chance like kreplach …?"

It was imperative that I say something. "Boeuf bourguignon, Mama."

Edward inched the MG over the unpaved driveway while his heart raced ahead. A short distance down the road was an overlook with a compelling view of the sea. He parked there and leaned against the car as the bracing salt air filled his lungs. He was thinking about how the loving father, so concerned for his son, valued any kindness far more than it was worth. He felt shabby, accepting such heartfelt hospitality when the poor father had no idea of the much more extensive part that he, Edward, had been playing in his son's life. At least, no one could claim he dominated his young friend and protégé. Ned exhibited too much independence to be anyone's pawn.

That comforting insight settled none of his concerns, but he headed home refreshed and grateful that Ned had wandered into his life. Now, there was reason to thank the bishops and deans. The euphoria brought on by that train of thought blinded him to the motorcycle tailing him since he'd left the Deane cottage.

* * *

When he entered the house, he found Farleigh in the kitchen. His houseman was seated at the counter in shirtsleeves, with Milly near his side. An antique silver service for two dozen laid out on tea towels glistened before them.

"Good to see you, Mr. Ed." Farleigh pushed the jar of silver polish aside. A pungent whiff of the claylike substance transported Edward to the kitchen when he was a boy, cowering in the corner, expecting a blow from a vengeful Maxi. His brother would use any pretext to persecute him. Only Farleigh's quick intervention had spared him from Maxi's attack. The new houseman, who was busily polishing silver at that auspicious moment, had taken a liking to the younger Vann and became his shadowy protector in those difficult days of childhood, when Cecelia Vann was a remote presence in his life, his phantom mother.

"I left a message for you on the peer table."

"My thanks," he gulped down the words.

"Someone dropped it off around noon, while you were over at Mr. Deane's."

The image of an earlier letter flashed through his mind, and he started to ask who delivered it. But with Milly present, he opted for damage control and said nothing. Yet caution was for naught.

"I noticed there was no return address on it," Milly divulged. "I asked who was sending it but he said you'd know."

"You did the right thing, Milly."

He felt like a talking machine, his voice devoid of tone and timbre.

All but tiptoeing to the foyer, as if any sound he made would further incriminate him, he swept his hand across the peer table, gathering up the note without a downward glance. He retreated to his study and fileted the envelope. The handwriting was by now familiar.

TEN THOUSAND DOLLARS

He slid the note into its envelope and slipped it into the center drawer, where the earlier missives nestled. Not till he retrieved the note several moments later did he notice that there was more to the message: LEAVE ENVELOPE ON HALL TABLE TOMORROW P.M.

Whoever was making this demand was confident of its fulfillment, because the sender left no way for him to respond other than to comply with the request—or ignore it. Each time he tried to figure out who sent the note, his emotions clouded his reasoning, and after running potential suspects through the revolving door of his mind, he was as hard-pressed to zero in on the culprit as before he started. He had no enemies, he had no debts, he had no unfinished business that could have led to this. And then it dawned, and he recoiled in horror—this was about Ned and him.

Blackmail. It was not supposed to happen to you. Blackmail was like tattoos on sailors' arms, a practice of the down-and-out. Blackmail was a crime. The straight-shooter in him rebelled at the thought that the dastardly act was drawing him in.

Maybe he'd do better to contact his lawyer. Alden Brooks would know how to advise him. Alden was a first-rate attorney. But as he reviewed that plan, he feared it might only make matters worse. Did he want to reveal the reason for the blackmail? Even if he could face his lawyer after such an admission, wouldn't there be fallout for Ned? Did he have the right to compromise his young friend, or, what was worse, besmirch his reputation for the rest of Ned's life?

As the sun was setting and the waves whispered innuendos to anyone who'd listen, he tried to turn off his mind. Perhaps the sea would guide him. He sat and listened to the waves washing ashore and the drawstrings of the blinds clicking against the woodwork. Before he rose to take a shower, he made a decision: he would do nothing at all.

"We plan to drop in this weekend if you'll be home."

Vincenzo's proposed visit couldn't have come at a better time. He'd shut himself in his study for the past few days but hadn't typed a line. Instead of meeting with Ned to discuss "their" novel, he'd invented several tasks for Ned to do around the house after importuning Farleigh for suggestions. He'd meant to boost Ned's confidence when he explained, "You're in such fine shape now, it's time to put you to work again."

"Are you taking a break from the writing?" Ned had asked, an edge to his voice.

"Just a brief leave of absence."

"Everything okay …?"

"Take a seat."

As Ned sat down he declared, "I thought you might enjoy a change of scene for a couple of days, that's all."

Ned didn't reply immediately, so he asked again, "Are things okay with you …?"

"They're fine."

He expected Ned to leave him then, but he remained in the chair. After a moment he asked, "Edward, you didn't have a problem with my moving out, did you?"

"Not at all." Edward flashed a grin and tried to hold it.

"It's just that, I was thinking … if we're going to be, well, carrying on …"

"… you thought it makes sense for us to live apart …?"

"Yes," said Ned brightening now. "I'm glad you understand, Edward."

He squeezed Ned's hand. "I suspect we *will* be carrying on, as you so charmingly put it."

Ned got up to leave and brushed his hand through Edward's hair. At that moment, a homespun youth in nondescript plaid rose before the writer's eyes.

To Vincenzo he replied, "I'll plan a feast on the terrace."

"A picnic in the sand will do, but you've got to humor me in one thing, Edward. I've told Alex that you live in a bungalow near the beach—I want to surprise her. I'd like her to meet Olivia as well. And bring your young friend along—Ned, was it? Does he have a girlfriend?"

A picnic with friends would be just the thing to take his mind off the blackmail threat. He'd invited Olivia and mentioned it to Ned. "Maybe you'd like to bring Sally?" he'd suggested. "Sure," said Ned after a pause. "I'll ask her."

The picnic in the sand carried the day. Milly had asked for the day off and Farleigh was short-handed. So they'd make do without the servants. Edward packed the picnic basket himself and loaded up a cooler of drinks, while Ned and Vin spread a couple of blankets on the beach.

"Who needs the house?" Vincenzo declared expansively, his head in Alexandra's lap. "When we lie about in the sand like this, we're actually getting back to nature."

"I could hardly agree more," said Alexandra, a mischievous smile playing about her lips. "Chilled Pouilly-Fuissé, beluga caviar, fresh rolls stuffed with gruyere and cucumbers—this has got to be the most natural lunch I've ever tasted." She was still adjusting to Edward's "little bungalow" by the sea, which she'd fully expected to appear when Ocean House rose up to fill her view. Like many other first-time visitors, she thought the mansion was a country inn.

"All right, all right," grinned Vincenzo. Among his finest qualities, his best friends agreed, was not to mind whenever his overstatements were held up to gentle ridicule.

Ned had hardly taken his eyes off the statuesque blond since they'd come out of the ocean and settled on the blankets, though Sally leaned persistently against him. Alexandra sat across from him, with Vincenzo's head still in her lap. A pair of ivory "knitting needles" held in place the hair piled on her head.

Suddenly the head turned its eyes on Edward, who'd pulled his knees up to his chin. Olivia had taken her place at his side and adopted the same pose. Then the head asked, "What's so funny now?"

"I couldn't help thinking," began his host, unable to suppress a smile, "that from the angle where I'm sitting, your head looks— nothing personal—disembodied."

"Holofernes in person," exclaimed Olivia, whose one-piece swimsuit was not intended to turn heads, though it set off her trim figure to advantage.

"Don't you mean, *not* in person?" suggested Sally, who'd been quietly taking in the proceedings, "because the whole person's not there, or at least, not intact ..."

When all eyes, including the head's, turned toward her, she tacked on, "That is, if you consider the head a part of the person."

"I'm not so sure about that in this case," quipped Alexandra. She palpated Vincenzo's forehead as if to detect whether there was anything beneath it.

"Can I get you folks another drink?" asked Ned. He sprang up and opened the cooler. "Toss me that churchkey, Edward—"

Ned had been unfailingly helpful. He'd opened countless bottles and cans, and he retrieved their errant Frisbee from the sea whenever it went off course. His baggy T-shirt, with COLUMBIA emblazoned across it, nearly covered his bathing trunks. No sign remained of his limp from polio. He'd made a fine impression that day. If Edward had wondered about Sally's affections for her boyfriend, little doubt remained. She stayed close by Ned's side and held his hand in the water, as if to keep the waves from washing him away. Alexandra was taken with him as well, drawing him out whenever he offered an opinion. And Olivia—her playful banter seemed intended to put Ned at ease, as an older sister might do.

Edward envied the affability of the women with Ned, their flirtatious asides and affectionate pats and gestures. They seemed to be smoothing the way for him, as if he'd dropped in from another planet. Even Vincenzo was solicitous; when Ned volunteered to bring them more condiments from the house, Vin insisted on going with him.

"I think that boy's going to be just fine," ventured Olivia while Ned was out of earshot. "You've done a splendid job with him, Edward."

That evening they gathered behind the house to bid farewell to one another. Vincenzo was pleasantly high from the wine he'd consumed, and Alex insisted on driving them back to the city. Sally would drop Ned off on her way home.

"And you, Olivia …?"

She was walking toward her Impala, which the night had all but absorbed. "You know me, Edward," she replied evenly. "I've always got stuff to do in the morning."

"We all have stuff to do then."

"What do *you* have to do?"

"Me? I have to rise and shine."

He hoped his attempt at levity would lighten the serious mood that had overtaken them. When he held the car door for her, he offered, "You're welcome to stay over, Olivia."

"Don't worry about me."

Before he could reply Farleigh appeared at his side and handed him another envelope. "I didn't want to interrupt the picnic."

Edward slipped the note in his trouser pocket.

"I wish someone would send me notes at odd hours like this," observed Olivia.

"Be careful what you wish for," came the sardonic reply as Olivia drove off into the night.

Edward returned to the study and seized the letter opener on his desk. For an instant he considered shredding the envelope. The note read

IGNORING ME? YOU'VE FORCED ME TO UP THE ANTE

CHAPTER
14

AFTER TOILING TILL THE TILES sparkled like tinsel, I dressed and returned to the study, where I found Edward seated on the settee with the butler's table before him. A tray there contained two gin and tonics, a basket of crackers, and a platter of various cheeses, including no Philadelphia and no Velveeta. (Time to restock the fridge, Mama.)

Edward signaled me to sit beside him. A quarter lime was impaled on the rim of each glass and ice cubes bobbed against the sides. (Okay, glasses don't have "sides," just as Ping-Pong balls don't have "tops"—that's what comes from editing Edward.) Tell you something—each time I've tasted lime since that occasion, I'm transported back to Edward on the settee. That lime was my madeleine. Years later, I was having drinks with other Columbia alums when I slipped and actually ordered a Gin and Edward.

After several sips, as the gin percolated through my showered skin and soul, Edward surprised me with an invite.

"How would you like to meet some friends of mine?"

"Sure. When?"

"Just as soon as we finish our drinks. They're downstairs."

"Shouldn't we join them now …?" queried polite little me.

Edward looked amused. "They can wait."

"Is that really proper? (I was teaching etiquette to Edward Vann—?)

"They have nothing better to do. Besides," said Edward at his most beguiling, "I'm enjoying our visit too much to cut it short. It's not often I have the pleasure of your company, Ari, aside from our editing sessions—and that's work. You always make yourself scarce afterward."

Blow, Gabriel, Blow—! So I'd not come across as a pushy sycophantic worshipful six-pointed-starry-eyed yid from the wrong side of the shtetl …?!?!? And here was the Master of Ocean House planning to introduce, ahem, *present* me to his august friends!

"Ready for the plunge?" That merry look in his eye told me the gin had taken the edge off his edge.

At the bottom of the stairs, we confronted two individuals in the grand foyer that I would not otherwise have assumed to be a couple. The man was staring out a window that gave onto the infinite, while the woman, shackled in stilettos and a butt-sprung skirt, was sedulously examining her self-portrait in the mirror over the peer table.

"Vinny and Charlaine, I'd like you to meet my accomplice." Edward did the honors without revealing my name. It was a curious omission that made me wonder. But then, I wondered at almost everything Edward said and did. I'd been worrying about whether I was properly dressed to meet these aristocrats, when it became apparent my fears were groundless. Vin wore faded jeans and an untucked polo shirt; it was so short that the waistband of his budget-brand underpants showed (a no-no in those days). Charaine was decked out in a pink and white pinafore with clichés of ruffles, but it was so low-cut as to belie the innocence of the, well, cut. In comparison, I looked as if I'd stepped off the pages of a Brooks Brothers catalogue. (Does Brooks even have catalogues?)

"Pleased to meet you, I'm sure," Chareen exclaimed when Edward presented me. Her reply oozed insincerity when she grasped my hand while staring right past me at the lord of the manor. I'd let myself believe, foolishly, that my association with nobility (I was on a first-name basis with Fiona as well) would elevate me to their status in their friends' eyes, that I'd enjoy at least a reasonable shelf life in their exalted realm. What was especially incongruous to my discerning eye was this Charlotte's Gentile hair—bleached and dry as straw. My Semitic curls put her frizz to shame, but who was *she* to appreciate a nice Jewish boy like yours truly? I was probably the first circumsnipped guy she'd ever met.

Skinny Vinny (he was all of 130 lbs.) was one of those back-slappers who disappears when he turns sideways. He stunned me with his aside, "I hear Edward's promoted you to Odd Jobber in Chief ..."

"Something like that," I replied as politely as wounded pride would permit. But Edward quickly dispelled my misapprehension.

"This guy here—couldn't get by without him." This time he clamped his arm around my shoulders. My hair stood on end, its every follicle burning with fire and fury.

"Going back to college this fall?" asked Vinny Murnoz or Murmansk—I didn't quite catch his peculiar last name. It sounded threateningly Bolshevik.

"That's right," returned obliging me.

"Suffolk County Community?"

"Columbia City University."

That prompted bleached and blanched Carlotta to trespass into the conversation. "I have a cousin, goes to Suffolk Community. He's on the G.I. Bill. Says it's kinda hard there, science, them equations and such ..."

I allowed my head to loll in different directions—an all-purpose response in hopes Char would cease and desist from further discourse on the subject. She had absolutely no class. She drove a Studebaker.

Edward had been staring absentmindedly at his fixation du jour, but rallied. "You guys must be *ravenous*. Shall we go for a bite?"

Mr. M insisted on driving the Studebaker. I sat in the backseat with Edward, my pride fully restored. It was my first ride in this vehicular bathysphere, and I sat straight as a poplar so when we passed the big fish in town, they'd see me right beside the biggest catch of all.

We soon wound up at The Gullet, where a striking black performer made a big fuss over Edward. Her uninhibited approach was so appalling it fascinated me. She teetered over to our table in spiky heels and stopped to sing a verse of "Stormy Weather," nearly tripping into Edward's lap in her tight pants and sequined T-shirt.

Did she plan to spend the entire evening with us? Edward wasn't discouraging her. He smiled at her blandishments, a louche smile that I'd not seen before. Next, she launched into her sultry rendition of a song she announced as "You Go to My Head" (or was it "Bed"?), and I thought I'd lost Edward. But then I felt his spine stiffening as he cast his eyes from the singer to of all people—Olivia St.-John.

She was approaching our table with a gentleman in tow, Mr. Brooks, everyone's'-who's-anyone's lawyer. I considered Olivia a beauty, but today she seemed wan and sere, drained of vitality, a press-dried rose rather than the fragrant flower I'd often sniffed. Could Olivia have changed that much in such a short time, or were my perceptions changing?

Ever the gentleman, his leering smile now exiled, Edward stood to greet her, and I followed suit. That was when the singer took a powder, though I don't know whether it was because of Olivia or Mr. Brooks. Edward's illustrious guests from the Studebaker Sedan remained in their seats. Perhaps they were already acquainted with the new arrivals?

The rest of the afternoon was an anticlimax to my Great Expectations. Perhaps a lawyer in their midst put folks on guard, and the singer never rejoined us. We had an uninspired round of drinks for which Edward picked up the tab. But the biggest letdown came when feet began to shuffle under the table and Olivia asked Edward whether he needed a ride home—which he accepted! And how do you think Edward disposed of yours truly? "Vin, give my friend here a lift, would you?" My sole consolation as we shook hands good-bye (he'd taken me aside for this, his boozy parting remark): "In all external grace you have some part. But you like none, none you, for constant heart."

"Here comes the bride ..."

Fiona hummed *Lohengrin* while breezing down the stairway of Ocean House, a would-be star of the Metropolitan Opera. The polished balusters of the grand stairway formed a suitable backdrop for the scene. Our bride-to-be held a lacy white wedding dress to her chest as Edward and Melville, brother and betrothed, gawked from the ground floor. Melville's feet sported a pair of new tennis shoes that looked to be a good size sixteen. The wedding gown flopped and fluttered, assuming a life of its own.

Fiona tapped the banister every few steps to keep the audience aware of her grand entrance. As she approached the ground floor, her decisive soprano intoned the words of the wedding march. She might have been delivering an inspirational speech.

At the foot of the stairs, she rested her hand on the orb of the newel post. Edward reminded, "Don't forget to toss the bridal bouquet!"

She ignored her brother's outburst. "Melville, you may kiss the bride." She added in case he hadn't noticed, "She's here."

Her betrothed shuffled toward the stairs to his beloved. "You must lift your veil before I can kiss you, Pet ..."

"As for that," she tossed the gown to Edward, "... let's save your kiss for the actual unveiling—"

She disappeared down the hallway as Edward remarked, "You'll have your hands full, my friend, as I imagine you can see."

Melville Mellon-Glade drew in a self-confident breath. "I've been known to say—if you don't mind my quoting myself—'What woman worth her salt isn't a challenge?' "

Edward, with wedding gown in hand, was not inclined to disagree. The suitor's attraction to the formidable Fiona was incomprehensible to him. She'd never deferred to her intended or lavished praise or endearments. She'd done absolutely nothing to encourage the poor man. Yet he'd stuck to his suit with the persistence, if not the ardor, of a love-smitten swain. And now she'd absconded without a word as to when—or whether—she'd return. Edward was about to make an excuse for her when the unruffled suitor announced,

"Well, old boy, it's off to the court for me—"

"Are you being sued again?" asked Edward, still holding the languid bridal gown in his arms.

"Tennis—I've two sets of doubles at the club today. Cheerio and carry on," came his well-worn reply, as if his future brother-in-law were in charge of the bride.

Edward couldn't help but smile as he watched Mellon-Glade thump toward the exit. Those oversize feet would surely make their mark on the court. But their parting hadn't quite ended. Before he stepped out the door, the future brother-in-law called over his shoulder, "Give my regards to your lady fair—Lydia, isn't it ...?"

The notes remained in his desk drawer, and he was relieved a few days later that he had no more to add to the collection. He was tempted to reread the ones that he'd stashed there, to compare the handwriting, to search for clues to the sender's identity. But the thought of holding them again was repugnant. By midweek his fears were abating, and though he was still disinclined to "review" them, he felt less cautious about discussing them with someone he could trust. He came close to phoning Vin, but Manhattan was too distant for a visit. He at length resolved to call his lawyer.

He met Alden Brooks at The Gullet, after checking to make sure Liane wasn't performing that evening. Didn't life have enough complications? A few months ago it had seemed so simple: he'd only just met the singer, Fiona had no plans for marriage, and, most important, Ned was not even on the horizon.

Although the days were getting shorter, abundant sunlight still illuminated the backstreets of the seaside community, where looming shadows stalked pedestrians and tailed automobiles. He parked the MG and proceeded to their meeting place. A waitress was ushering him to a table when a waving hand caught his attention. His eyes adjusted to the dimness, and he made out the reassuring figure of his friend and lawyer. He'd not crossed paths with Brooks since he'd asked his help at the hospital for access to Ned's room. He was determined not to mention Ned today.

Brooks wore his trademark Brooks Brother's pinstripe and a colorful paisley, a useful conversation starter: "I nearly dropped it in my soup at lunch—do you eat vichyssoise, Ed?" He put the question as soon as they shook hands and took their seats. The writer turned it to advantage.

"Strange that you should ask, my friend. I'm in the soup myself—and not just my tie."

Alden waited for him to continue without appearing to wait.

"I'm being blackmailed, since you didn't ask."

"Two questions: Who and why?"

"I wish I could tell you."

"How much?"

"It started with five thousand or so ..."

"You sound as if you're expecting it to go up."

Vann nodded.

The attorney collected his thoughts while a combo began to assemble onstage. Drumsticks beat against a snare drum and a saxophonist filled the air with a shimmering melody, insinuating it was time to let go and live. Edward had the surreal sensation that the combo was gearing up just for his lawyer's reply.

"My advice for the moment," said Brooks, "don't pay up yet, not so much as a dime."

They'd ordered a second round of drinks, and it was reassuring that his attorney had probed no further than those initial queries. They'd bandied about the words "sex" and "romance"; Edward threw them in as part of the mix, a subtle way to introduce the subject, should it become necessary to disclose more later.

But Brooks segued to another topic: "I wonder if that singer who's been performing here will be on stage tonight ..."

"I haven't any idea," declared Edward, more precipitately than he'd intended, but the only rise he got out of his companion was his eyebrows.

"In any event," his attorney concluded, "I hardly imagine she's your type."

"*My* type? I might surprise you one day, sir," he returned. "Don't put anything past me."

"I shall take that under advisement."

They sipped for some moments in contented silence, till Brooks resumed, "My word—isn't that your singer now …?"

There must have been a last-minute change of program— Liane had come onstage as the combo muted their rendition of "Stormy Weather." She was wearing a bodice-tight vermilion gown that hung loosely from her hips to the floor.

"How the hell does she draw breath in that outfit?" Alden's voice oozed admiration.

"I can't help you there, my friend, I'm not a seamstress," he replied, "but time for me to make scarce." He left a large bill on the table to cover their drinks.

As they were parting, Brooks urged him to call immediately if the blackmailing front heated up.

He was as lighthearted driving home as before the notes began to arrive. Alden had just transformed his predicament into a simple business matter. The magic of lawyers. As he was about to pass the turnoff to the Deane cottage, he swerved on impulse onto the country lane. He hadn't spoken with Ned—his *accomplice*, as Alden had unwittingly dubbed him—for several days, though Ned had appeared each day for work. He hadn't realized how much he missed his friend, editor, lover till he pulled into the driveway of the bungalow. Dusk was falling, and stray gulls were sending their last messages before the advent of night. Perhaps one of those messages inspired him with a pretext: he'd invite father and son to dinner. Emboldened by this inspiration, he rang the bell of the enchanted cottage, wondering whether Ned would come to the door.

Silas Deane answered.

"I was in the neighborhood and thought I'd drop by."

Silas nodded. He looked confused.

"If it's not too late, could I take you and Ned to dinner …?"

"That's very kind of you, Edward, but …" He faltered as he tried to complete his sentence.

"Is something wrong, Silas …?"

Deane's head shook up and down, his sole response.

"Is Ned home?" Edward prompted.

"Yes, … he is."

"I'll stay just a moment, if he's busy …"

"He *is* here," said the befuddled father, "but I don't know if it's such a good idea for you to see him, I mean, at this particular moment …"

"To say hello …?"

When Silas began to wring his hands but with no further explanation, Edward ordered, "Take me to him."

The reluctant father opened the screen door, then led the way, his shuffling gait betraying his state of mind.

At the door to Ned's room, Silas paused.

"I'm very sad to tell you, Edward, he's not himself—"

"What's happened—?"

"Says someone or other tried to rob him." Silas knocked at the obdurate door, making little more than a tapping sound that was all but effaced by the rumble of a passing automobile.

"Neddy …," he called softly.

"No reply.

"It's me, … it's your father …"

"What's the matter, Silas …?"

"An accident," came the distracted reply.

"He's hurt—have you called a doctor—?"

"He doesn't want me to."

He edged around the father and pushed into the darkened room. It smelled of alcohol and distress. Ned lay on his side, his face to the window.

Edward dropped to his knees by the bedside. "Can you hear me, Ned …?"

Ned's head barely moved on the pillow. As his eyes adjusted to the dimness, Edward perceived the bandage covering his cheek and a smaller one on his forehead, near the hairline.

"Ned, … what's happened to you …?"

Ned reached for his hand. "Tell me, Ned," he insisted, "I want to help …"

Ned shifted position but still held Edward's hand. "You can't help me, Edward."

"You know I'll do anything for you—"

Ned shook his head.

"The cost doesn't matter, whatever you need—"

"You can't buy everything you want, Edward, and you can't fix this, no matter how much money you're willing to throw away."

He gripped Ned's hand more firmly, as if increased pressure would prompt him to say more, but no response. He gazed down at the face, its color only recently restored after his ordeal with polio. It resembled a mask, scarred and discolored, yet for all its abrasions, not without beauty.

He parked on the driveway, half-paved and potholed, then stepped into the humidity of late summer so viscous you could pull it like taffy. He'd not called ahead. He rang the bell and his stomach began to churn. Shortly the coffee-colored man appeared, wearing the habitual T-shirt.

"Wait here," replied the mouthpiece that nothing seemed to faze.

But the master of Ocean House was too hot and gone to take orders. He reeled toward the hall to her bedroom. A fluttering curtain partly covered the doorway to a patio. She was sitting at a table and he heard the voice of a man moments before he appeared to her. At a word from Liane, the man vamoosed into the surrounding woods.

He stepped onto the patio and she looked up as if she'd been expecting him, yet she declared,

"Why have you come?"

"For you."

"No, you've come for yourself."

He gestured toward the chair opposite her. "May I—?"

She nodded and he sat.

"Do you object to my visits …?"

"I'm entirely neutral."

"That's encouraging."

"I'm not trying to be."

"Do you want me to leave?"

"I invited you to stay."

"Don't you care for me, Liane …?"

"It's not about caring, as you so quaintly put it."

"What is it about, then …?"

"I've told you—your needs."

"What about my needs, as you call them …?"

"You bring them here. I deal with them."

"I give you money."

"It's a transaction."

"You don't think it's fair …?"

"It's not about *fair*. 'Fair' is used only by children, and only in the negative—*That's not fair!* You never noticed …?"

He pushed back and the wrought-iron chair tipped over. As he swayed and lurched to keep his balance, she smiled for the first time.

Sensing the futility of his visit, he looked her hard in the eye then got up and returned to the house.

As he made his way to the front, he slammed his fist against the wall but didn't bring down the temple. Her man had followed him. When he took his arm, Edward was inclined to strike him, but the fellow's grip was so slight, almost entreating, that he let himself be led into the room, submitting to desire. The man guided him to the sofa, where he slipped off Edward's loafers. Next, his nimble fingers unbuttoned his shirt, unfastened his belt, and removed his shirt and trousers. Again taking Edward's arm, he lowered him to the sofa, holding on till he'd maneuvered his willing prey to a reclining position. With the same quiet concentration, he pulled his shorts to his ankles, then glanced toward the doorway, where Liane had reappeared.

CHAPTER 15

T HE ROOM WAS ALIGHT with order and good taste; everything had its place and everything was in it—the cushions arranged across the bed, the teak rack for holding the bedspread, the oval table between two Louis XVI's, with black-and-white family photos, arranged by size rather than subject. The room exuded a stability that could dissipate if not carefully tended. It was more a room to observe than to live in.

The woman seated across from her was about to speak. She looked as if some fleeting thought had risen to consciousness, and she wished to express it no matter who might hear, or not hear, her. But she said nothing, perhaps fearful she might sound ridiculous. Who was that woman, anyway? She'd often pondered the question.

Olivia streaked a trace of rose pink across her lips and blotted them against a tissue. Everything was as it should be: eyebrows plucked, eyes lined, lips colored, makeup base smeared into her fair skin. Nothing was ever out of place—and she found herself wondering why. Why did she have to be perfect? Did that come with being a woman? Edward's mother always looked perfect, Fiona always looked perfect, even … she paused, then said the word aloud though there was no one else in the house: "Alexandra."

Yet Alex Cabot was entirely different from the other women she knew. Alexandra didn't take pains with her appearance. Most of the time she just looked effortlessly stunning. At their recent picnic at Ocean House, Alex hadn't bothered to paint her face. And when they met for lunch in the city a week later—at Alex's invitation—she appeared again without makeup, while stray wisps extruded from the hair she'd piled on her head. "Just got out of an exasperating meeting!" she'd explained when she joined Olivia at the restaurant near her office. Olivia was charmed by her new friend. Alex was one of the few women she knew who didn't fuss about her appearance; she'd not once caught her with a can of hairspray! Even with new romantic interest Vincenzo, Alex seemed unconcerned about the impression she was making.

There, her mask was in place, her hair tied back with a velvet ribbon. (Edward preferred it that way.) (Why didn't she express preferences for Edward's appearance?) She was all set for the drive to the station, where she'd meet Alexandra's train from the city. On sudden inspiration, or rebellion—she wasn't sure which—she yanked the ribbon from her hair, letting it fall where it would. Much of that lustrous hair fell to one side, her new look, asymmetry, a flapper from the twenties?

It was a warm, clear morning of late August, when summer's promise of blinding light, burning sand, and endless heat was now fulfilled. Dry shrubs and desiccated leaves dotted the seascape, and dog-day afternoons sapped survivors' energy. But hints of autumn were in the still, heavy air—sudden gusts of cool wind, the early sinking of the sun.

Olivia parked a block away and strolled to the little train station. Her silver Bulova with diamond chips, a gift from her parents for graduation from Smith, reassured her that she'd allowed sufficient time to meet Alexandra's train. She found a bench in the shade, where she was alone but for a teenage boy with piercing eyes and skin blotched with pimples. He was collecting a stack of newspapers that had been left for him to deliver. She watched his deft movements with the careless attention one devotes to insignificant events when forced to kill time till a friend arrives or a ship enters the harbor. He was banding the papers together before loading them into his bicycle basket; the bike was so battered it might have been manufactured secondhand. When he finished his task, he took the pack of Chesterfields that he'd folded into the sleeve of his skimpy white T-shirt and lit one, striking the match with a flourish. He took a couple of drags and expelled the smoke, then approached Olivia.

"Cigarette, ma'am?"

Her tight smile was a polite refusal, but he continued to hold the pack out to her, as if she might change her mind. She was prepared to accept the gift-giver as a well-meaning if intrusive adolescent, but the tattoo etched on his upper arm injected a trace of menace. Before she could think of a way to dismiss him, she heard the train nearing, its wheels grinding a dirge in the morning air. The teenager appeared to lose interest as she stood and walked toward the tracks.

The train hissed into the station, and soon Alexandra was walking toward her in a brightly printed sundress—a Kandinsky in motion. Her skirt stopped inches above the knee while the dress tied at the neck, leaving the shoulders bare. Her hair was piled on her head, but this time there were no stray wisps. "Sorry I'm late," she called out, with a glance at the station clock.

"We can blame the Long Island Rail Road for that." Olivia's sympathetic demeanor brought a smile to her guest's face.

"Could we make a wager?" Alexandra's critical eye bore down on her while they headed for the car. "I'll bet you make excuses for all your friends, so we don't have to accept responsibility for our actions." She tacked on, "There now, could anyone possibly be more blunt?"

"You're giving my good nature too much credit." Her reply suggested that Olivia was giving the matter some more thought as they approached the Impala. "If you'll stow your things on the backseat, we'll be off."

As they drove into town, Alexandra stole a couple of glances at her friend without picking up the conversation. They could do that later, if it was meant to be.

Shortly Olivia suggested, "Let's make a stop at the local bodega. I thought I'd get your input before filling the kitchen with food you don't like."

"How thoughtful. Have you and Edward been together lately?"

Olivia swerved off the road for several feet. "Yes and no. Depends on how you define 'together'."

"How do *you* define it?"

"Me? I'd say you shouldn't leave such definitions to me. I'm not very good at them."

"Definitions?"

"Relationships. Here we are."

She parked at the store's entrance and slipped out of the car before her friend could continue her questioning.

Inside the little emporium Alexandra observed, "Nice, salty tang in here, or do I have the sea on my brain?"

"They keep those large windows open to catch the breezes off the ocean."

Olivia was about to introduce a couple of denizens to her weekend guest when Alexandra exclaimed, "Say, don't we know that fellow by the ...?"

He was leaning over the frozen vegetables counter, his back turned to them. "My designer eye tells me that's Edward's young man, the one at our picnic ..."

Ned looked up and a smile of recognition overlay the blush that had poured into his cheeks. His pulse quickened as the two favorites approached. He still wore a bandage on his forehead, and the bruise on his cheek was now a bluish smear.

Olivia held back as Alex brushed past her to bestow a kiss on Ned's intact cheek. He put an arm around her waist while still holding the packages of frozen green beans and corn. Olivia awaited her turn, but her face fell perceptibly when she noticed Ned's abrasions.

Alexandra exclaimed, "Don't tell us—an unhinged door ran into you ...?"

A rueful smile and Ned pursed his lips, hoping he'd have to say nothing more about his condition. "I had an accident—nothing serious, too embarrassing to talk about …"

After an awkward pause Olivia said, "Alexandra is visiting for the weekend—"

"… and Olivia is letting me pick out the food I'm going to cook for us." Both grinned at her remark. "But who the hell wants to cook in this weather? I'm taking the two of you to lunch."

"The groceries …?" Olivia gestured to their empty cart.

"Leave them in the cart—we'll come back for them later, after we pick them out. What do you say, Ned?"

When he hesitated she insisted, "My treat—no argument."

The hostess seated them beneath a protective overhang against the sun. A block away, the sea impinged with impunity beyond the beach homes that lined the shore.

"I never paid much attention to this place before," said Ned as the waitress distributed their menus.

"It was once a private home," explained Olivia. "They say it was built by a sea captain who had five wives."

"That sounds like fun," quipped Alexandra, "for him."

"Not at the same time," Olivia clarified. She could barely squelch an amused expression.

Their banter cheered Ned. He'd been depressed since his "accident" a week ago. His refusal to talk about the ordeal had forced his dad to stop questioning him. Edward, too, had ceased to pursue the subject. When he reported for work the following morning in a haze of pain and embarrassment—his face stinging beneath the bandages, his arms and shoulders aching—Edward questioned, "Are you able to work?" "Of course" was all he replied. Edward asked him to clear a storage room filled with books and bric-a-brac to be shipped off to various charities. He'd cleared out most of the room when Edward dropped in for a visit yesterday. They'd exchanged nothing but pleasantries since the injury. He wondered whether he'd offended Edward by refusing to discuss his condition.

Did Edward not realize how much he needed his respect and approval?

"How's your appetite, Ned?"

"This is the first time I've thought of it, Olivia," he returned, "but I think it's popping back to life, now that two beautiful ladies are egging it on."

"Get a load of that flattery!" Olivia winked.

Alexandra had been watching Ned closely. "Are you excited about returning to Columbia this fall, Ned?"

"Yes, I am."

His neutral reply caused her to probe further. "You seem hesitant …"

He looked down at the menu. "It's been a special kind of summer for me. I'm not sure I can explain …"

"Special indeed!" interjected Olivia. "You've had polio and recovered from it. That makes you a hero!"

"Edward's the hero here. Edward pulled me through."

"You're both heroes as far as I'm concerned," exclaimed Alexandra. "Do we have a medal or two to pin on the gentlemen, Olivia?"

A distant look came over Olivia. "Can you imagine Edward wearing a medal, or any other kind of decoration …?"

"He's certainly earned one," said Alex, having heard about Edward's devotion to Ned.

"Edward's the soul of modesty. I'm afraid he'd be horrified if anyone pinned a medal on him. You'd never know," she added, lowering her voice, "that he was decorated more than once in the last war." She glanced down at the menu before asking Ned, "Edward's managed to keep you pretty busy, from everything I've heard?"

"He's been a good boss," said Ned, who noticed that Olivia's eyes remained on the menu.

"I never understood what sort of work Edward gives you," said Alexandra, signaling a nearby waitress.

"All sorts of odd jobs around the house, mainly."

"Aren't you forgetting your most important task?" asked Olivia, her eyes now meeting Ned's as Alexandra's settled on him as well. When Ned failed to speak she added, "His writing."

"Oh, so we have two writers in our midst?" asked Alexandra. "I didn't realize I've been traveling in elite company."

"Well, we're very elite out here," joked Ned, his shoulders going slack with the break in tension.

After a ripple of laughter Alexandra asked, "Are you writing a novel, too?"

"Not exactly," said Ned. "Not at this very moment."

"You mean, not here at the table?" Alexandra's mischievous response wreathed his face in smiles. She thought him uncommonly sweet and wondered why more men weren't like Ned.

The waitress arrived to take their order. Her cardboard tiara kept a mass of red curls off her forehead. She cast a flirtatious glace at Ned. "Say, kiddo—don't I know you …?"

Coloring slightly—his transparent skin betrayed him unfailingly—Ned replied, "That all depends."

"Listen to that one!" She shook her curls, an exercise in which she was much practiced. "Was it Kathy Carnaby, or Ginny Struthers …?"

"Hamburger steak, with ketchup, please."

She hesitated before her peals of laughter caused them all to smile. "I get it. You're dodging the question—you're ordering instead—!"

"Let's all order," interposed Alexandra.

The waitress soon served their orders of filet of fried codfish, shepherd pie, and hamburger steak, accompanied by sides of French fries and a frozen vegetable of their choice. They ate heartily, and when she returned to take their orders for dessert, a familiar voice inquired, "I hope I'm not too late to join you?"

"Edward—! What are *you* doing here?" Alex beamed.

"Crashing your party, if that's permitted."

"If it's not permitted, Mr. Vann," declared their outspoken waitress, his unsolicited ally, "I'll find you a table of your own …"

"Should we let him join us?" teased Olivia.

Edward gave her and Alex a peck on the cheek before patting Ned on the back and slipping into the seat across from him.

"How did you know where to find us?" asked Olivia.

"Your Impala happened to be grazing right in front of the restaurant when I was passing by. Welcome to our sunny town, Alexandra. What a pleasure to see you here again. I hope you left our friend Vincenzo in good spirits?"

"Vincenzo sends his regards, Edward."

"How did he know you were going to run into me?"

"He didn't know. I brought them along—just in case."

Edward's eyes rested on Ned. He wanted to say something reassuring to draw his young friend into the conversation, but he was interrupted before he could form the words.

"Strawberry shortcake with whipped cream, anyone?" the waitress proclaimed. "Our dessert du jour—that means 'today's special'." All four nodded and soon she was serving them each a portion, with coffee on the house.

It was midafternoon when the sun flattened their shadows against the dry, dusty terrain and their party broke up. Over Alexandra's protest, Edward paid the bill. As they prepared to depart, he asked, "May I give anyone a ride?"

"We girls are fine," said Olivia. "Ned, I'll bet you could use a lift …?"

"I was actually at the grocery store when these ladies picked me up."

"How did you get there?" asked Edward.

"Walked."

"I'll drive you back to finish your shopping."

Edward pulled up to the curb at the market and waited for Ned to make his purchases. He returned soon with a full bag.

"Home now?"

"Thanks, if you have the time."

"It's all I have."

They drove some distance in silence, when Edward asked, "How is that mess of a room coming?"

"Shaping up—I should finish within a day."
"Doesn't seem possible. You just started."
"Want me to show you?"

CHAPTER

16

A SQUALL OF RAUCOUS GULLS swooped over Ocean House, determined to get in the last word before they sailed out to sea across the mewling and purring waves. A playful sun exaggerated the size of the MG to four times normal as it rolled into the driveway. When it reached the patch of shade extending from the house, Edward drove it from chiaro- to -oscuro and parked against the bank of garages.

For the first time since they'd left Olivia and Alex, he faced his passenger. "Do you want to stow your groceries in the house, for safekeeping?"

"Nothing's going to melt here."

In a spurt of deviltry, his companion ventured, "Not even your heart …?"

Ned crossed his arms and the grocery bag lurched against the dashboard. "Sometimes I don't know what to make of you, Edward." He looked away as if seeking something on the horizon. "My heart's already melted—didn't you know?"

Edward started to speak but only smiled, a kindly, almost shy smile.

They mounted the stairs to one of the rooms above the garage that had sheltered servants in the days of old man Vann. When they entered, Ned asked,

"What do you think?"

Edward cast his eyes about the airless chamber. "It's starting to look empty—mission accomplished."

"Not entirely, but give me another day."

"No rush—I don't want you to strain yourself."

"I'm not straining."

"Ned—"

"Yes, Edward?"

"How are you?"

"Me? Fine."

"How are you—really?"

It was stifling in the room, a month of August immured there. Ned opened a window, and when Edward continued to stare at him, he murmured, "I'm getting by."

"Ned, what happened?"

The young man fixed his gaze on the bric-a-brac still on the shelves. "I'm okay—all right?"

"Tell me—what happened?"

Ned shook his head.

"Ned, I must ask you something I've never asked a soul before."

His young friend met his gaze as the surf's rumbling filled the room.

"Do you love me, Ned?"

Ned started to reply but the words caught in his throat. He rested his hands on Edward's shoulders and spoke so softly the sea nearly overrode him. "My turn to pose a question I've never asked: Does the surf wet the sand …?"

"Ned …" Edward wrapped his arms around him.

"… It was just before dark. I was walking home from the grocery, a bag in each hand. I didn't see him … he came from behind a tree, or the bushes—I've tried to put it out of my mind …"

"Go on," urged Edward, still holding him fast.

"He wore a bandana over his face, like those bandits in Westerns. He knocked me down and started punching me. I tried to fight him off, but my arms were pinned behind me. I had to kick my way free …"

The words spilled forth as if ink from an overturned bottle. " 'Queer!' 'Fucking homo!'—he kept snarling as he was punching me. Before I could get up, a car appeared around the bend. Its headlights must have startled him. He fled to the woods …"

His breath came in short wheezes. Edward continued to hold him, as a salty wind filled the room and the sea blended its muted consolations with Edward's soothing words. "Ned…. we'll find the bastard. We'll see that he's punished …"

"No!" Ned wrenched free. "You mustn't attract attention. I understand why he was angry, it's my own fault …"

"But, you've done nothing wrong—!"

"Try telling that to society."

"To hell with society!"

"You're a fine one to say that, Edward." Ned returned to the window and his gaze drifted out to sea.

Edward longed to reassure him that things would turn out right, he'd force them to. But he feared Ned's reaction. Was Ned alleging that his, Edward's, high station protected him from the kind of attack he'd suffered? He felt a gulf opening between them, as if they'd lost the ability to hear each other.

A dutiful sun had done its work for the day, but its rays still lit the clouds with vermilion while streaking a scarlet canvas across the heavens. Edward propped in bed beside a gin and tonic on the nightstand. He'd written sporadically after dropping Ned at home with his groceries, but inspiration was in short supply. As he directed his narrative toward a conclusion—the war winding down, President Roosevelt dead, the nation in mourning—he'd reached an impasse and knew he'd write no more that evening. Ned would help him through it tomorrow, wouldn't he? Ned filled his thoughts, and he began to realize how far he'd strayed from the Edward Vann of a time when nothing interfered with his concentration.

When they'd arrived at the Deane bungalow, he hoped he and Ned would resume the conversation they'd begun over the garage, when Ned disclosed his awful tale. Instead, Ned climbed out of the MG and said only "Thanks for the ride."

As the gin circulated through his body, he relaxed for the first time since leaving Ned. He was tempted to phone him, to hear Ned's voice again, to say that all would turn out well. But would it? Would Ned return to work next day? What if Ned kept him at a distance as they were finishing their collaboration, their intimacy at an end? Or worse, what if his friend didn't want to see him again, and the novel still unfinished ...?

Amid this swirl of concerns, another cropped up: Should he report the attack on Ned to his lawyer? What would Alden Brooks, in his burnished respectability, think if he told him the truth? Was there a way to alter the details to avoid implicating himself and Ned in what would surely come across as a sordid liaison? He turned out the light, his drink half-consumed, and tried to go to sleep. He was about to doze off, but a storm kept him awake, rattling shutters and scattering papers from his bureau. At last, a fitful sleep carried him away. Next morning he rose early and took a walk on the beach.

The storm had drained all color from the setting. Sky, sea, and sand appeared a pale brownish-gray, the color of anterooms and back corridors. Several times he strayed from his path across the moist sand into the wavelets lapping at his feet. The sea air helped him set his mind straight, and he resolved to contact Brooks as soon as he returned to the house.

"I wouldn't say that what I have to tell you makes an airtight case, but it's a significant detail, and I'm bringing it to your attention."

Edward's own formal lingo both surprised and amused him. He tried to relax in the lawyerly leather chair as his eyes swept over the plaques decorating the wall, showcasing Alden Brooks's awards and citations. How was he to tell this embodiment of respectability that the young man he'd taken under his wing had been brutalized for shacking up with him?

The response from his lawyer seemed at first to be a change of subject, but he perceived that it was meant to put him at ease. "Thank you, my friend." Brooks leaned back in his chair, as if he were about to doze off. "That was some confab at The Gullet the other day. You were in fine form."

"Was I ...?"

"As I recall, you were regaling the ladies with all manner of amusing tidbits and trivia, in all due respects."

"I was paying absolutely no attention."

"I was all but certain that singer was prepared to abandon the stage to you, especially after you honored us with a round of 'I've Never Been in Love Before'."

"Me, in love ...?"

"You were crooning at the top of your lungs, let's see ... 'wine that's all too strange and strong ...' "

"I'll have to ask my agent whether entertaining is allowed by my contract."

Brooks barely nodded. "As for that significant detail you mentioned ..."

Edward drew his chair closer to the desk. "It involves a vicious attack ..."

"On you?"

"On someone I know."

"Related?"

"To me, or to the case?"

"Either, or both."

"The case."

"And the perpetrator?"

"Identity unknown."

"How do you know the blackmailer and the attacker are one and the same?"

"Woman's intuition."

If he hadn't known Alden Brooks for some time, he'd have missed the slightest change in his demeanor, an inward turning of the lips as if he were going to purse them.

"That might not hold up in court."

"I don't want to go to court."

"Where do you want to go ...?"

"As our friend Hamlet once said, '*That* is the question'."

* * *

Bright sunshine awakened him. Momentarily disoriented, he recalled a hotel years ago after the war, when he'd got away with Caroline for a weekend before they married. They'd concocted a fib for family and friends to account for their absence. At the last moment, he'd revealed his plans to Dad, in case something went amiss. Dad's only remark: "If she does it with you, son, it'll always stick in the back of your mind that she might have done it with someone else."

Caroline's beauty dazzled him, her blond hair billowing about her oval face. Each time she resurfaced from a plunge in the waves, she brought to mind a mermaid floating in the surf. He had little understanding of beauty in those days. Beauty stood for an image of the woman of his dreams. It tethered him to her, though she maintained long afterward that she'd never meant to hold him, or even attract him. Yet there were periods when he believed he couldn't make it without her. That transfixing image of her beauty kept him from perceiving the actual woman beneath it. Years later, as she broached the subject of divorce, she avowed that he'd not once seen her for who she was.

Perhaps that was why he never accused her of leading him on—he was clearheaded on that point. Still, he'd never come to terms with the thrall of her beauty. His passion flourished, even in the face of her increasing indifference. She'd left him completely by the time he realized his "great love" had attached him to no one but a fantasy. Only when he met Olivia did Caroline's hold on him ebb.

He'd hoped Olivia would free him from the spell of his first wife. She encouraged his pursuit and seemed to relish it. But as he came to believe that she was accepting him as Caroline never had, his ardor waned. Vincenzo suggested one evening after they'd polished off two bottles of Cabernet Sauvignon that Olivia's "big mistake" was to give him "too much rein." Vin opined, "With Caroline, you had to fight for whatever you thought you got. Now that it comes easily, you're at sea."

While transported to another time and place, he'd hardly noticed that the sun's rays were filling the room. By then his evanescent reflections had vanished as suddenly as they'd arrived, and he was left to face the day. Would he sit at the typewriter and write, or just sit? He'd pondered the question all the previous evening, when he fretted that if Ned didn't join him, he'd no longer be able to create.

He dressed quickly and went for a stroll on the beach. Several gulls waddled by, giving no ground to the wingless intruder in their midst. When he came upon an outcropping of primeval rock jutting above the sand, he sat down to watch the waves cast themselves onto the beach.

The sea was majestic, imperious, querulous, capricious, haughty, and arrogant, heaving wave after wave upon the shore with utter disregard for the consequences. Despite the watery violence, he felt at peace after a morning of worry and fretting. He was tempted to sit tight, to wait for something to happen—a bottle to bob to the surface with instructions for him inside?—rather than return to his writing. But no bottle washed up.

He strolled back to Ocean House. After several false starts he was about to lose himself in his work, when the familiar footsteps caught his attention. Ned hesitated, as if waiting for a cue.

"I'm glad you came," he said, a smile breaking on his lips.

"Did you think I wouldn't?"

"I didn't know what to think."

"Well, here I am. Shall we get to work?"

The dialogue of two feuding gulls filled the room. A gust of wind swept in off the sea and whirled the fans overhead. Still the writer kept silent.

Ned pulled up the rattan chair and sat beside him. "Edward, are you all right?"

The gulls had flown off and the fans ceased revolving before he responded. "Of all the houses in all the towns in all the world, you walk into mine ..."

By way of reply, Ned hummed then sang the first bars, "You must remember this ..." Then he took the top page from the manuscript and ran his eye over it.

"I think you should add one more paragraph here on the French Resistance ..."

He returned the sheet to the pile. After watching Edward watch him for some time, he declared, as much in amusement as exasperation, "Hey, Edward, it's me—Ned.... Don't you see me, Edward ...?"

"I don't *need* to see you. I can feel you radiating toward me."

If Ned had meant to reply, Edward preempted him. "I'm risking everything by telling you this, Ned, but I don't care.

"I once thought I knew what beauty was. I didn't understand then that I was blind. Beauty—in quotes—was a caprice, something I imposed on someone who caught my fancy. It was purely the work of my imagination, and it overwhelmed any response from its object, who ceased to matter as an individual in her own right. I knew absolutely nothing about beauty that emanates from the soul and lasts through time.

"But it's no longer like that for me. I see you for who you are, Ned. I haven't imposed anything on you. My will and my imagination have been at bay since you first walked through that door. They've been directed at this manuscript, our close friendship notwithstanding ..."

The words were spoken so quickly that Ned leaned forward to catch them: "You came into my life and I let you be yourself, I did nothing at all—until, inexplicably, I fell in love with you. I've never loved like this until you. I'm coming to realize I've never loved before—without wanting to possess, to control ..."

"It's important you understand this—I have no intention of holding on to you, of making you a prisoner—"

"The Narrator and Albertine ..." Ned murmured so softly he wasn't sure he was heard.

"There's nothing I want from you now, except to love you, whatever that means, however things have to change—or stay the same—between us."

His words trailed off, as if he were losing the power to project them. When Ned kept silent he sighed, "I suppose you consider me a blithering idiot."

"No, Edward," Ned took his hand. "You're just like any other man, only more so."

CHAPTER 17

T HEY WORKED WELL INTO THE AFTERNOON, punctuating the dense August air with brief verbal exchanges and the shuffling of manuscript pages, till problems were solved or tabled. The sea had lost its voice, and the day had settled to a stillness that could make you forget who you were or what you were doing. It was past four, and the winds were whispering promises they didn't mean to keep.

Edward cupped his head in his hands and let go for the first time that day. "We've made progress," he observed as Ned was still scrutinizing a paragraph. "You've brought us closer to our goal than I could have ever imagined when we first met."

Since the brutal attack, Ned's spirits had not resurged, and he strained to put on a good face. He returned a wan smile and was about to speak, but a gull settling on the window ledge distracted him. When the bird flew off, he said, "You give me too much credit, Edward."

"Don't sell yourself short, my friend. Look how far we've come since you came aboard. My words, *our* words leap off the page now. The prose is fleet, wry, gripping. It glistens with polish and reveals a deeper melancholy. I couldn't have done it without you."

"Do you ever think about what's going to happen next, Edward?"

"Next novel—?"

"After we finish revising this one, after I return to school?"

Edward had been leaning back in his chair. Suddenly its front legs gaveled the floorboards. "That's too far ahead for me to think."

"I'll be gone in a couple of weeks."

"No need to remind me of a date I've been dreading."

Ned left his seat and went to the window. Farleigh had raised the blinds that morning to a peerless view of the ocean. Edward came up behind him and put his arms around Ned's waist as the surf hummed a soothing lullaby. "I don't understand what's happened to me, Edward—"

"Nothing's happened, you're fine—"

"Please let me speak. I have to get this out." When he was sure Edward would keep still, Ned resumed,

"When I came here as a stranger, you gave me work. You shared your writing with me and respected my opinion. You cared for me when I was sick and nursed me back to health. Yet all that time, you expected nothing in return."

"There was nothing more to expect—you'd heaped riches enough on me."

"This is all so strange, Edward."

"Strange? What don't you understand?"

"My feelings—I can't explain them …"

"What must you explain?"

"For one thing, we're men, both of us. So this shouldn't be happening."

"It shouldn't …?"

"You talk as if it's normal."

"Is it abnormal?"

"That's just the thing—I don't know."

"[F]eeling guilty is foolish. I am a deeper and warmer and kinder man for my deviation. More conscious of need in others, and what

power I have to express the human heart must be in large part due to this circumstance." — Tennessee Williams[3]

At length Edward ventured, "It's easy for me to sit here and preach to you. I'm isolated in this big house, and you're the one who's had to pay a terrible price for our friendship—"

"Don't worry about that—"

"I *do* worry about it, all the time. And I should probably tell you that I've spoken to my lawyer—"

"My god, Edward—!" Ned wrenched away. "I thought we'd agreed not to say anything about this—to anyone!"

"I don't recall that we agreed to anything—"

"You're making it worse—"

"I think you're wrong there. No one should get away with beating you up."

"What good is a lawyer when there's not a thing we can tell him—?"

"Blackmail is a federal offense."

"Who said anything about *blackmail*—?"

"Someone's been trying to blackmail me—"

If he'd meant to pacify his young friend, his revelation had the opposite effect.

"You didn't tell me—"

"I didn't want to worry you."

"Who's blackmailing you—?"

"I get these cryptic notes, every now and then."

"Do you know who sends them—?"

"They just appear in the house. Farleigh gave me one, I found another on a table ..."

"When—?"

"Now and then, the other day ..."

"You should have said something to me."

---

[3] *New York Review* 10 23 14, p. 30 (Review by Geoffrey O'Brien of *Tennessee Williams: Mad Pilgrimage of the Flesh*, by John Larh, Norton).

Ned had never reproached him before. In hopes of defusing the tension, he declared, "Could we get something straight here? You and I haven't done anything wrong. Can we at least agree on that?"

Ned inclined his head just perceptibly.

"I have the sense that, what we've done ..." he hesitated as Ned continued to stare, "... it's the first time for both of us ...?"

Ned nodded.

"It's not as if we'd set out to make this happen ...?"

Ned's grin was the affirmation he'd hoped for.

"In other words, it just happened?"

"The first time you touched me ... or the first time I touched you ... I hardly knew what was happening. As you said, it just happened ... It had been a horrible day. I was afraid you were put out with me, and every time I tried to approach you, you seemed to move farther away ..."

Edward's own recollection of that day flashed back, the frustration, the despair. It was cruel comfort to realize they'd experienced it the same way.

"Then I found myself in your arms and I felt ... somehow ... as if I was ... home."

For a brief eternity Ned's words blotted out the menace of blackmail. He returned to his seat and gestured for Ned to join him.

"Mind if I ask, what is your experience in this department?"

"What department—?"

"The sex department."

"I've gone all the way a few times, starting once in high school—it just happened."

"I understand—it just happened to me once, too ..."

The mutual confessions cleared the air, and they became a couple of guys sharing war stories. The confidences they exchanged, which dispelled the tensions over lawyers and blackmail, might have lasted indefinitely——but for an untoward interruption.

"This will take just a minute."

Fiona had entered the study and neither of them had noticed.

"On guard, everyone!" warned Edward. "Fiona's minutes have been known to last indefinitely."

"Would you *hush*, Edward—!" She advanced on the desk, her dismissive tone reminding him of their childhood spats.

"What's troubling you, my dear?"

"*Troubling* me—?" She was about to correct his choice of term, but remembering that she'd come to ask a favor, she softened her tone, which still verged on imperious.

"I need to borrow your young man." Her eyes pinned Ned to his seat.

"You're an editor, I hear?"

Without awaiting his reply she explained, "I'd like to have a sharp eye go over the wedding materials before I send them off to the printer."

"Is it counseling you seek?" asked her brother.

"We can dispense with your input, Edward. Would you please come with me, Ted ..."

The diktat brought Ned to his feet. He exchanged a quick glance with Edward as he followed her out of the room.

Fiona led him to her office on the first floor. It contained a bouquet of crimson peonies whose cloying fragrance crowded out most of the oxygen. On the walls were framed diplomas and group photos from Fiona's days at various prep schools, culminating in Wellesley College, filled with ambitious young women eager to launch their careers.

"This is what I'd like you to do," she began, gathering a sheaf of papers from her desk and transferring them to a side table. "Please sit down, won't you? I think this shouldn't take too long, if you're diligent..." She fixed her eyes on her watch. Did she mean to time him?

While she was glancing at her Longines, Ned took a mental snapshot. The resemblance to Edward was startling, though he couldn't have said whether she was a feminine version of her brother or he a masculine version of her. The features in common seemed stronger in a female physiognomy but no less handsome: the mismatched lips, sea-green eyes, and light-brown hair, hers streaked with tasteful platinum. He felt a stirring in his sex, and he wondered whether the appeal of this woman who resembled her brother stoked his desire for him, or could it be for her …?

"I have always been curious about the effects of the transposition of a friend's or loved one's face from the masculine sex into the feminine and vice versa." — Marcel Proust[4]

He was surprised she was lingering. He expected such a perpetually "busy" person to have been on her way. He wondered whether she'd forgotten him, then she spoke again.

"May I ask you something—?"

"Sure."

"Is Edward's writing any good?"

Before he could reply, she appended, "I know it's a terribly indiscreet question, but he *is* my brother, after all, and I have the distinct impression that you've spent quite a bit of time together this summer …"

"Your brother is a wonderful writer, and a wonderful man."

"I'm glad you think that."

Next she made those rustling sounds your hear when someone's preparing to depart, but she caught him off-guard again.

"What does he write about?"

"Edward …? Life."

"What does Edward know about *life*?"

"Read his novel."

She took a step back for a more critical view of him. "You're a self-assured young man, aren't you?"

"I'm sure of my editing, if that's what you mean."

"I don't know *what* I mean." It was the first time he'd found her to be anything but supremely self-confident.

---

[4] William C. Carter, *Marcel Proust* (New Haven: Yale Univ. Pr., 2000), p. 643.

"I'm worried about Edward."

He rose to the bait. "What has Edward done?"

"It's what he *hasn't* done, you see ..."

"I'm not sure that I do."

"Of course you're not sure. You hardly know him. What I'm trying to say ..." She relaxed slightly, like a thick stalk barely bending in a strong gust. "... you don't know him the way I do."

"Surely not."

"To you, my brother is just a quirky older man, shut away like a monk in his cell, where he spends days and nights fussing over his writing."

"I certainly know that side of him," he responded, matching frankness with candor. He dared to add, "but I'm sure he does other things as well."

"You're quite an ingenuous young man, if I may say so."

"You may—since you have."

"You've not been tried by life, have you?"

Before he could even imagine how to reply, she exclaimed, "Forgive me—I'm being much too personal, bad form. I'm speaking frankly because I think you like my brother—genuinely so. I can't imagine Edward allowing anyone to see his writing if that person hadn't won his confidence—and his respect."

He decided to let her unwind.

"He's never trusted me to read a word of it, except once, when I grabbed a page from him and ran away with it. But you could hardly call that trust, could you?"

"It's not for me to judge. But I'm sure he understood you were genuinely interested in his work."

"How could I not be? But I fear while he's cooped up with his writing, life is passing him by."

"What would you have him do, instead?"

"Get a job—nothing taxing—create a business, travel, for a start. I've been onto him about signing up for a cruise; I was thinking the honeymoon cruise that Melville and I are planning to take ..."

"You think Edward would enjoy being on someone else's honeymoon?"

"You have a point there. But he needs to get away from here—move to England, spend some time in the south of France, or perhaps half a year in Tuscany. We have villas in all those places, he just has to pick one."

The mention of those far-flung locales where she was trying to exile her brother unsettled him. Though he himself would soon go off to school, it hadn't occurred to him that Edward might leave Ocean House. What did this overbearing sister know about her brother's needs, and desires—!

"Perhaps you should show me what you wish me to do ..."

"Of course," she mused, as if she, too, had been caught up in her thoughts. "Could you look over these announcements and menus, proofread them, dot the *t*'s and cross the *i*'s, so to speak—you'll know how to proceed ..."

She placed the papers in front of him. "If you have any questions ..."

"I'll holler if I do."

Edward's eyes scanned the line where sky meets sea while waves broke at his feet. The unreachable locus gave him perspective on the miasma of existence, and he hardly noticed as three young boys approached with their spaniel in tow. It was hard not to smile at their rowdy exuberance, screaming childish insults at one another while stopping now and then to pet their dog or order him to do some impossible trick, commands that Fido blithely ignored.

As the boys passed by, their shouts and cries blending in harmonious discord with those of the gulls, his mind turned to Ned's upcoming departure. He kept reminding himself that the city was not far away—seventy miles as crows fly, a couple of hours by car. Once Ned was at school, they could visit each other whenever Ned had the time. He'd send a car to bring him to the Island and combine the trip with a visit to his dad. He'd be doing all three of them a favor.

With that consoling thought, he resolved to return to his writing. But a kick from behind sent him sprawling. Someone's foot was on his back, pressing him into the sand. He glanced up and caught a glimpse of the figure standing over him.

"Son of a bitch—" If anyone else had knocked him down, he'd have repaid in kind, but from force of habit he could cuss his brother out without expending much energy.

"Gotcha where I wantcha—!"

Maxi stepped back as Edward rose to brush the sand off his slacks and shirt.

"What's with you?" He scowled.

"We have an account to settle. We can resolve it here or a place of your choosing, where we won't be overheard."

"Unless it's a duel you fancy, I suggest we stay right here. The waves don't gossip."

Maxi gazed seaward. Even dressed in beachwear he looked disheveled. His Madras shirt was missing two buttons, and his cotton shorts might have come off the rack permanently rumpled.

"Invitation accepted." Maxi sank into the sand. He removed a flask from his back pocket and took a swig, then handed it to his brother, who leaned as far from him as he could while still able to reach the flask. He downed a generous draught.

The sweet, slightly sickening odor of the bourbon filled Edward's nostrils as the liquor burned down his throat. It had been years since he'd tasted the stuff—he was a scotch & soda man. It transported him to the banks of the Rhine as the Allies were making their push across that fateful waterway. They were closing in on the Germans, and everyone knew it was but a matter of time. His company had been ordered to hold back to maintain the Allied presence on the river, as the forward troops of the Allied armies fought their way into the Reich. He and his buddies had downed so much bourbon in their advance that any number of memories might have returned now: bombed French villages, dazed inhabitants, a fox terrier he'd adopted. He'd always longed to write a fictional account of his war experiences, and now Ned had helped him realize that dream. He almost forgot that his brother was sitting next to him as he took another swig of memories before returning the flask.

"Let's get down to business," Maxi continued. "I have something for you here." He reached into another pocket and pulled out what appeared to be a letter. "Shall I read it to you, or do you prefer to do the honors yourself?"

Maxi handed him the missive, whose appearance was identical to the anonymous notes he'd received from the blackmailer. His eyes swiveled from note to brother before he slit it open to read

THE GAME IS UP

CHAPTER 18

"WHERE DID YOU GET THIS—?"

Maxi's lips curled into a sneer, a relic known to Edward since childhood. "I didn't get it from anywhere—I *wrote* it."

"You—?"

"You fancy yourself the author here, while my writing has been circulating all summer. Funny, isn't it?"

Maxi reclined on his elbows and his feet made a show of kicking up the sand. When he stopped, one loafer hung by his toes.

"Why …?"

"Of all this family's many needs, a cocksucker isn't one of them."

"What do you want?"

"For a start, I want you to stop hanging out with that little fairy you've been keeping around the place."

"He's a fine young man—he's on a scholarship to Columbia University."

"Spare me the sentiment, Eddie. If I thought he was a fly-by-night, would I bother to bug you …?" He pulled a pack of Luckies from his pocket and lit one. "Have a smoke?"

"You may not remember that I've never smoked, but here's something we both know—you're jealous."

"Why would I be jealous of a queer?"

"Because he's the kind of man you'll never be."

"A fucking fairy—?"

"He's hard-working, dedicated—he's going to make something of himself."

"The only thing he's making is a monkey out of you."

"What I don't understand is why you care what company I keep. Tell me what you're really after. But before you do, why did you have to brutalize a poor kid who's barely recovered from polio—?"

"I never touched him."

"Your goon, then."

"I don't know what you're talking about."

"I don't believe you."

"Then we've reached a standoff."

A wave came within lapping distance, and Maxi scooted closer to avoid it. "I had nothing to do with what happened to your pretty boy."

Then why these notes …?"

"To soften you up. I figured the suspense would break you down."

"How much do you want—?"

"You're starting to make sense—five hundred thousand."

"Impossible!"

"Of course it is."

"Why should I fork over five hundred grand even if I could?"

"To buy peace of mind—and get me off your back."

"You're not a threat to me."

"I'm not? Wait and see."

"I'm pleased with your work. Do you think I could borrow you again sometime?"

"Sure. When?"

"Right now."

Fiona had intercepted him at the foot of the stairs. If past practice was a guide, she knew he and Edward were wrapping up a session.

"I'm free."

Her approval flattered him. It didn't matter that she was treating him like a subaltern. He was glad to take on more "assignments"—anything for the college fund. And he could foresee the end of his editing venture. He'd managed to curb Edward's penchant to re-revise and re-re-revise—a sure recipe for never completing the book. The writing was much tighter than when Edward first asked him to collaborate. His mind returned to that fateful day when his new boss put him on the job.

He'd not seen the inside of Ocean House since he was a boy, when Dad took him and his sister to Christmas parties for Vann family employees. As he mounted the stairs, he imagined himself on a movie set, about a reclusive writer in the Hamptons, an East Coast *Sunset Boulevard* with the leading lady a male.

When he walked into Edward's study, he'd knocked so softly his future employer didn't hear him. And the startled look on the writer's face when he glanced up—he'd obviously forgotten their appointment! Mr. Vann seemed as unsure of himself as his visitor. It was a case of mutual embarrassment, till the subject of literature filtered into the until then awkward conversation, and he was invited—it was still hard to believe—to step into a new world— the writer's novel …

"Please come with me." Fiona tossed her head in the direction he was to follow. Her crisp linen dress might have just sprung from the ironing board.

She led him to a cubbyhole near the kitchen that he'd taken for a large closet. Then he saw the narrow stairway at the back. Fiona forged up the stairs, her white patent flats click-clacking on the floorboards. At the top they came to a sitting room, where she opened the curtains and sunlight flooded the space. It was filled with white wicker furniture and overstuffed cushions. A feminine touch pervaded—ruffles on upholstery, needlepoint "paintings" on the walls.

"Be seated, won't you? Here, next to me. I don't bite."

As he sank onto the sofa she amended, "That is, not usually."

"I'm reassured," he returned deadpan.

"Know something—" she began, as if to get a weight off her chest, "it's hard to imagine you could be intimidated—if, in fact, you are (… are you?)—by the likes of me when you've been dealing all these months with my overwhelming brother."

"Edward's not such a monster."

"Edward's a pussycat—I'm referring to Maximiliano."

He tried not to react.

"Besides, poor Edward is utterly besotted—with Olivia. I doubt he has time to think of much else, but his writing, of course. But that's a sideline."

"Olivia …?"

"His girlfriend. Surely you know about Olivia …? He runs off to see her at odd hours of the day and night. It's amazing she hasn't lost her reputation by now. Edward could save it, her reputation, if he'd only propose, but Edward seldom gets around to starting—or finishing—anything, as you've been learning. That's why I'm glad you've been helping with his novel."

"How do you know he's running off, as you say, to Olivia?"

"Maxi tells me. Maxi knows everything. In fact, I'm glad you introduced the subject. He's the reason I've sequestered you here."

He couldn't begin to imagine what that *reason* might be.

"I'd been planning for Edward to give me away … at my wedding."

"He mentioned it."

"Did he? That's curious."

"Why so?"

"Edward rarely remembers anything he says he'll do. He means well, poor dear, but his mind is usually where it shouldn't be. Father thought it was the war. He was completely changed when he came home—we all noticed. Father was at his wit's end for a while, till Edward found a job in publishing, then started writing books."

"Maybe that's why he writes—the war?"

"I couldn't say. But back to more important matters. You've done a splendid job. I should have asked you to write my invitations yourself. Then they wouldn't need editing."

A benevolent smile, which was out of her usual character, crossed her lips and she continued. "With regard to this ticklish situation we're in, you've been helping Edward with his writing; how do you suggest we get him off the hook. I don't want to hurt his feelings."

"Edward doesn't strike me as the kind of man whose feelings get hurt easily."

"You know him so well—that's good. So I can count on you—?"

"To what …?"

"To tell him."

He stared hard at her.

"… that he won't be giving me away after all."

"You really prefer Maximiliano to Edward?"

"You sound skeptical—incredulous, even."

"Both—but I'll do as you ask."

Summer has a way of catching up with me—it usually ends abruptly, when I awake one morning and realize that fall's in the air. But my pleasant routine had lulled me into thinking that this fateful summer would last forever. I'd immersed myself in Edward's novel to the point that time came to a standstill. Edward and I were living that fictional work while we edited, wrote, and rewrote. Though I noticed little else as the season progressed, something peculiar *did* grab my attention: the more our conversation strayed from his writing, the more his mind seemed to unhinge. Perhaps "unhinge" is too strong a word, but my Edward was showing symptoms of a mysterious malaise. He could be arguing a plot point with great lucidity, then when the subject turned to everyday matters, his mind would fog up and he'd speak in non sequiturs or repeat himself. When we dwelt in his fictive world, he seemed more and more at home, but stepping outside it into reality was becoming a challenge.

When this happened the first time, it came on the tail of a conversation he had with the illustrious Fiona, who, by the way, had started to pay me some attention at last. I had the distinct impression I was no longer an adjunct to her brother but an individual in my own right.

She stopped me in the grand foyer one morning as I was heading to Edward's lair and not only addressed me by name but got it right this time.

"I've been hoping our paths would cross, Ari," she began, her tone both businesslike and cordial. It was pure velvet when she came to "A-r-i," which she'd articulated formerly as Harry, Gary, or Jerry (as if I were one of Donald Duck's nephews?). How she prolonged those two little syllables—*A - ri*! It was all I could do to keep from exclaiming *Whatever you desire, my Goddess!*

"Whenever you have a spare moment," she resumed, her questioning tone intimating she was casting herself on the mercy of my totally open schedule, "we could discuss an inconsequential matter. I'd like your opinion."

Her regal countenance underscored that nothing she said could be inconsequential. To keep from groveling, I looked at my watch as if even *my* time had an infinitesimal value.

"Apologies if I'm detaining you ..."

My awkwardness may have come to my aid, by making it seem as if I were carefully weighing whether I could spare her those precious moments from my inexhaustible supply.

"Perhaps when you return tomorrow?"

My masterful reply salvaged my amour-pourpre: "Let's not put it off."

"How kind of you," she instantly returned, as if she'd assumed I'd instantly comply. "I'm probably making a mountain out of a molehill, but I wondered whether I could count on you for a small favor ..."

I followed her to the side parlor, at the front of the house. She made sure the door was partly ajar so she could see whether anyone approached. We sank onto matching loveseats across from each other.

"There'll soon be a slight change at Ocean House, and if there's anything that gets to Edward, it's change. You must be aware of this peculiar trait by now—?"

I looked as attentive as possible, as if *I* were the one who'd requested the interview.

"It's become apparent to me that Edward and you are rather close, so I thought it wouldn't be too presumptuous to impose on your friendship." She sat straighter here as if something had startled her—was it the smoke arising from my ears burning with pride and glory?

"I shall have to be away for a couple of weeks, and someone has to be in charge at Ocean House during my absence."

I was on the verge of committing a colossal gaffe—I almost pointed my thumb at my chest, as if Fiona were anointing *me* as the new Overseer of Ocean House.

"Maximiliano has agreed to move in while I'm away."

That *was* news, and not the best kind. Edward regarded his older brother with disfavor and had as little to do with him as possible. Did Fiona notice that my eyebrows were approaching my hairline? Before she could say more, I asked,

"If I might be so bold as to inquire, isn't Edward the one in charge here?"

"Yes and no" came the pert retort. "You see, Edward does as he pleases—no gainsaying that. It's what he *doesn't* please that concerns me."

My eyes flashed her a question to which she responded, "Staying on top of the bills, paying the staff, mundane matters like those—not the sort of things a writer likes to worry about. You're wondering why I'm calling on *your* help? Because I believe you really care about my brother."

"Yes, I do." I gulped modestly.

"It's settled then."

"But how can I help?"

"Think of ways to get him out of the house now and then, that would do him a world of good."

"Like walks on the beach?"

"Yes, but better still, get him away from the property. Drive him to dinner, to the movies—anywhere."

She rose and, taking a small key concealed inside a lacquer box, opened a drawer of the Louis XV escritoire nearby. "I've left a hundred dollars for you here."

"How do I get Edward to go out with me?"

"I'm sure you can persuade him. Edward has told me about your editing. Quite an accomplishment, considering I could never get him to let me look at a word he wrote."

She took my stunned silence for consent. "We have a deal, then? I was sure I could count on you, Ari. I wish you luck."

Dusk had fallen though a dying light reflected off the sea. It cast shadows against the wall of the stairway as Ned climbed to the second floor. His own shadow moved a few steps ahead of him, daring him to follow. The silence inside Ocean House had a quality of its own, like an echo you await any moment but never quite hear. It was dark upstairs but for the amber glow escaping from one room, but when he reached the study, he found it empty. He'd arrived on time, eight thirty. Where was Edward?

He advanced along the hall until he heard the voice of Perry Como crooning "No Other Love," a Hit Parade favorite. It issued from Edward's bedroom. It reminded him that he had more to tell his friend than Fiona's message about her wedding. But he couldn't decide how to broach the subject of a change in his life. Despite their closeness, he had no idea how Edward would react.

"I imagined you'd search and find me," Edward grinned, propped in bed behind a copy of *Look* while the radio played in the background. He seemed in good spirits.

"I'm glad you asked me to come back."

"We've done enough work for the day. Our book is nearly finished—you said so yourself." Edward gestured for Ned to take a seat beside him.

He lay back on the pillow and Edward reached for his hand. How could he have secrets from him, Ned wondered?

"Are you okay?" he asked when Ned didn't speak.

"I'm fine."

"You sure ...?"

"No."

"What is it?"

"It feels like the walls are closing in."

Edward's eyes rested on him for several moments. "Where would you like to go?"

"Anywhere. Out."

Edward turned off the radio and slipped on a pair of loafers. "Let's go."

He steered the venerable Cadillac, one of several denizens in the garages of Ocean House, along back roads till they came onto the highway. He drove only a short distance till a brightly lit marquee appeared around a bend in the road.

"We're going to a drive-in movie ...?" Ned took a bill from his wallet.

"What's that for?"

"My treat."

"Save your money."

"Going out was my idea."

"Doesn't matter."

"Don't drive another inch till we settle this, Edward. I have to tell you a thing or two, and it wouldn't be fair for you to pay for the privilege of listening to news that might not please you."

Edward took the bill and drove to the window to buy their tickets. Attendance was sparse. Several cars were bunched in twos or threes, but most of the love-vehicles had parked several spaces away from their nearest neighbor. Edward drove the lumbering vehicle to an empty row at the back of the lot and stationed the Cadillac next to a speaker.

"I didn't notice what's playing," Ned remarked as Edward hooked the speaker to the car window.

"A new release—*The Caddy*."

"We're watching Jerry Lewis tonight—?"

"Who's watching? We've come here to talk."

The previews started and Edward turned down the speaker till it was barely audible. "Now, what's on your mind?"

"How would you feel if Maxi was the one to give Fiona away at her wedding …?"

"Give her away? He'd be more likely to *sell* her."

His eyes were adjusting to the darkness as he tried to read Edward's expression. "Then you don't mind …?"

"How did you find out? Maxi told you?"

"Fiona." He shifted position, anticipating the next question. "I suppose she thought I'd be better at it than she was—at telling you."

The feature filled the screen, briefly illuminating the interior of the car.

"I suspect my sister's become rather impressed with you."

"I don't know why."

"She sees you as a wholesome influence."

"If she only knew."

"Maxi knows."

"About us—?"

A short, quick nod.

"I'm sorry—truly sorry, Edward."

"Don't be," he returned, moved by Ned's pained expression. "But what was that other thing you had to tell me?"

"Oh, that ?" He leaned toward him as if to offer a reassuring pat on the shoulder. "Sally and I had sex."

Edward turned up the speaker, as if suddenly interested in the soundtrack. "She's a nice girl. I hope you treat her well."

They sat in silence as the flat, nasal twang of Jerry Lewis filled the car with unspeakable inanities, which were spoken nonetheless. At length Ned declared, "Then you don't mind …?"

"Am I supposed to?"

"No, I just thought that—"

"What did you think—?"

"I don't suppose I thought anything. It just happened."

"You had nothing to do with it?"

"That's not what I mean."

"What *do* you mean—?"

"We were fooling around one night, in the swing, in my backyard. It happened."

"Why are you telling me this?" Edward turned the volume higher.

"I don't know." Ned was startled by the sound of his own voice. "Because I thought it might matter. Because I thought you might care."

"What's there to care about?"

"I don't know."

"Don't you know *anything*?"

They remained for the duration of the film as its madcap antics mocked what each of them was unable to express. When Bugs Bunny hopped across the screen courtesy of Warner Bros., Edward returned the speaker to its holder and put the key in the ignition. "I'll take you home now."

The Cadillac lumbered over the driveway to the Deane cottage and stopped in front while crickets chirped and katydids spread their tidings. Ned opened the car door and Edward said, "I'll see you in the morning?"

"I just remembered—I left my bike at your place. I can't get to Ocean House without it."

A car zoomed by on the highway, its headlights slicing through the night. "I'll pick you up in the morning."

They said farewell and Edward drove off as Ned watched the proud Cadillac of tailfins and copious chrome vanish into the ink-black night. He returned to the house and crept to his room, where he undressed and slid under the covers. But sleep refused to come; his mind was awhirl with images of Sally and Edward. He tried to reach out and touch them, but they flitted away each time. He finally opened the blinds and gazed into the backyard. The moon's gentle light detailed the outline of the swing where he and Sally had taken their pleasure. She'd dropped by and said she was just checking on him to be sure he was all right …

"Why would I *not* be all right?" he'd asked.

"You've had a rough summer, sweetheart, and I was concerned. I saw your dad in town and he said he'd be at a Rotary meeting this evening, so I thought it was as good a time as any to see you."

"I'm fine," he'd replied, both touched and somewhat thrown by her visit.

It was a starry night and she suggested they go for a walk. They set off across the lawn, and before long she'd taken his arm. He'd always been the one to initiate physical contact. But why resist? He cared for Sally as much as for any other girl he'd known, and she'd stood by him during his struggle with polio. Between Sally and Edward, he was attended around the clock.

They circled toward the backyard when the swing came in view.

"I've never noticed it before," she exclaimed. "May we go for a little ride? I'd so like to try it—!"

A copse of trees concealed the swing from the road. After he was seated, Sally found her place on his lap and began to caress him. The only complaint of the durable structure was a low creaking as they rocked back and forth. But soon the swing fell silent as the two lovers gave in to desire. When they finished, Sally kissed him once again and asked him to remain in the swing while she went to her car.

He'd hardly anticipated this turn of events but was glad it happened. It restored a sense of self that had faded during his bout with polio and his unfathomable liaison with Edward. He wasn't sure what to make of it, this sexual involvement with two people at the same time, of opposite sexes at that. But would it matter in a few weeks, when he'd return to school? He wasn't sure. But for the first time all summer, he felt intact.

CHAPTER 19

A N ANXIOUS SUN SPILLED ITS RAYS across the broad, flat sea as if on deadline to release them. The tattered cloud cover reflected the rays in every direction, and it was hard to tell whether day was coming to life or dying. Gulls dove and swooped over the waves in urgent missions as a sultry breeze off the sea empowered the indolent ceiling fans in Edward's study. Their blades revolved with renewed vigor, if not will.

Edward was leaning over the manuscript, his left hand curled beside it, while the right held an eager pencil above those highly edited sheets. As the hand moved closer to the page, a warning broke the writer's concentration.

"I hope you won't make any more changes. We've fixed everything—I'm sure of it."

Ned clamped his arms over his chest, daring the writer to defy him.

"I keep thinking there just *has* to be a way to improve this ending …"

"What's wrong with it *now?*"

"Does it have sufficient impact? We've cut so many words from it—"

"Those extra words were bogging it down."

"I'd chosen them so carefully—"

"I deleted them with just as much care."

Edward continued to run his eye over the page. "Think it's all right now, do you?"

"I'm sure," came the confident reply. "Too much tinkering can unravel a well-knit passage."

"Thanks for the apt image." He glanced up for the first time since he'd sat down to review Ned's "final" pass. "So I'm a tinkerer, am I—?"

"Among other things." Ned slid onto the rattan chair by the desk. "You're also kind, generous to a fault."

"Go on, I like this."

"... a good lover ..."

Edward looked up but said nothing. The room was darkening as insistent gulls clamored for attention along the shore.

"Are things all right, Edward ...?"

"What things?"

"You, ... me ...?"

"Us ...?"

"No, the man in the moon—of course, *us*!"

"Ned," Edward hesitated, "you're the only perfect person I've ever known."

A breeze blew through the room on its way to nowhere. Ned's eyes brimmed. Edward dabbed them with his hankie. "Don't be sad."

"I'm not sad. ... I'm actually grateful—and relieved." Ned gently pushed the hand away that held the handkerchief. "When I told you about Sally and me, I was afraid I'd hurt you—"

"She's your girlfriend, you care about each other ..."

"Yes, and I care about *you*."

"That doesn't mean you shouldn't lead a regular sort of life."

"I said you were generous, Edward. At the risk of repeating myself, I'll say it again. You're the most generous man I've ever known."

"I can afford it."

"I'm not talking about money."

In the distance, the swelling sea all but drowned out the sparring gulls.

* * *

They met again later that day to tie up loose ends. One paragraph occupied most of the session. Edward had declared, "It has to work—period." Ned was certain of one thing: it had to be pared down from Edward's dense style, which, if compared to a painting, would be a canvas covered in layers of impasto, some highlighting, others obscuring the subject.

It was so still he could hear the clock ticking over the fireplace. While Edward's hand circled above the page, searching for a place to strike, he asked,

"Have you given any thought to your next book?"

"I was considering a novel on the subject of the terrible power of love ..."

"Autobiographical?"

"You're thinking I should write something about you and me?"

Ned frowned. "What could you write about us that wouldn't land us in jail? It's against the law in some states, you know—I've checked."

"Never thought about it, though not surprised to hear it."

Something lingered in the air, though neither was quite prepared to own it. A knock at the door interrupted their discussion.

"It came for you a minute ago, sir." Farleigh handed him an unstamped envelope. As Edward took it, Farleigh withdrew his hand as if from a hot burner.

Edward read the note. After the briefest hesitation, he ripped it to shreds that flittered onto the manuscript. "I have to go—"

"I'm coming with you."

"Sure you want to see the ugly side of this family—?"

Ned followed close behind him. When they came to the stairs his pace slackened, while Edward descended with the tread of a cat. Ned detected an argument in progress. He waited at the head of the stairs, hoping to gauge the tone of the exchange. Pitch and volume increased, till he could catch isolated phrases.

"...not have to pay a price, big shot—?" Maxi's voice rang out.

"There's nothing to pay for!" came the sharp retort.

"I've got the evidence to put myself on your payroll for the rest of my life, pal—"

"You don't have a thing on me—or Ned!"

When he heard his name, Ned started down the stairs. He moved with dispatch but had the sensation of staying in place, as if taking strides in a nightmare though not advancing. He could catch all Maxi's words now as he neared the ground floor. The thought flashed through his mind that he'd collapsed here when polio struck.

"This has nothing to do with your little queer boy—!" Maxi gloated. "Here's proof—"

He waved a photo before Edward's eyes as Ned approached the foot of the stairs. He held it still just long enough for the viewer to glimpse a couple in flagrante, with another naked male at their side. The woman, holding a whip in one hand, perched over the first man.

At that moment, the figure herself emerged from the sidelines, the sensuous performer of middle years. She mounted the stairs till she came abreast of Ned. Enclosed in a saffron sheath that a seamstress might have sewn to her body, she directed her resonant alto to the young man, her onyx eyes casting a knowing look at him.

"So this is the face that burnt the topless towers of Ilium— or maybe it was Ocean House …?"

"What's your precious Olivia going to think about this?" taunted Maxi, brandishing the photo again. "And all those swells at your country club—do you think they'll want to be caught in your company, once they've seen you fucked over by a brown-skinned mama—?"

Edward threw a punch and Maxi staggered back, his hand to his jaw, while the woman watched as if amused by the melee. Then Maxi lunged forward and grappled Edward to the floor. They rolled over the carpet, their limbs tangled, though Maxi's outstretched arm still held the picture beyond Edward's reach. The woman slithered down the stairs and nabbed the photo, but Ned crept behind her and snatched it away. He sprang up several steps to take a look, and his face radiated shock. He slipped the incriminating photo between his chest and his undershirt.

"You little bastard—!" Maxi dragged Ned to the floor and his legs locked him in a vise. He pummeled Ned's face till Edward wrenched him off, then knocked him out with a left hook. He lay inert at Edward's feet.

The woman abandoned her watch post on the stairs and, despite her tight sheath, rushed to Maxi's side. She knelt beside him and wiped his face with a handkerchief she took from his pocket. When he came to, several moments later, he snarled, "So this is how you want it—? The photo will be all over town before the day's out—! ... I've made copies, of course."

"No it won't." Edward glared at him, his voice oddly assured in the face of the threat.

"Think you can stop me?" Maxi glared, a stream of blood trickling from his nose.

"I don't plan to lift a finger against you—you're not worth the effort."

"Nice bluff—!"

"It's not a bluff," Edward replied in the same calm tone, "and my threat will top yours, you ass."

"What threat?"

"The tiara, to begin with."

"Tiara?"

"Fiona's emerald tiara—"

"The one she lost or misplaced—whatever the story she cooked up ...?"

"The one you *stole*."

Maxi was sitting up now, wiping more blood from his nose with the back of his hand. "You have nothing on me—!"

"I was there."

"What's that supposed to mean?"

"I watched from the doorway. I saw you take it. I saw you stuff it in your pants pocket. You were wearing a pair of striped trousers, the ones Fiona bought you for the church charity bazaar.

You hightailed it through the foyer—I nearly lost you—and drove off in your Ferrari. You disappeared for a few days after that."

"You have no proof but your imagination."

"Imagination my ass—I've got proof all right! And in case you're too dense to get that, it's not just about a purloined heirloom. You wrecked Fiona's relationship with Mama—they barely spoke afterward—and that's when this family really went downhill, not that you give a damn. Imagine how she'll react when she hears about this."

Maxi turned pale, not only from loss of blood.

"And that's not all I have on you, you son of a bitch—"

A sullen Maxi dabbed at his nose as if it required all his attention.

"You and Dimitris," Edward continued, "those times he came to visit, and the two of you'd drag me off to your room ..."

Maxi stopped dabbing but didn't glance up.

"The things you did to me—"

"You can take that up with Dimitris—if you're still bearing a grudge."

"This has nothing to do with grudges or Dimitris. It didn't stop when Dimitris left, when you had me to yourself, tied to the bed or handcuffed to a doorknob—" Edward choked back a sob, the pain of memory showing in his face. "You know how much it hurt, not just my ass but my heart, to be raped by my brother, someone I trusted—!"

Liane pinned her eyes on Maxi. The sea had receded and no sound could be heard besides their voices, which seemed to increase in volume through the resounding stillness.

"Your imagination's run amok, Eddie," Maxi glowered, "if you think anyone's going to buy your crap."

"I wouldn't be so sure," Edward shot back, and for once Maxi directed his full attention to him. "I have an unassailable witness."

Maxi's expression neutralized.

"Farleigh knew. He didn't do anything about it—he told me later he feared no one would believe him. But he comforted me. And he took me to the hospital once—I was bleeding. I imagine they still have the records."

Behind them, a throat cleared. "Yes, I imagine they still have them."

The houseman stepped out of the shadows as the sound of the surging sea presaged Liane's command, "Drop it, Maxi—you can't milk this anymore."

She helped him rise. After he steadied himself, he shambled away, the sheath edging close to him.

Farleigh and a housemaid advanced upon Ned and Edward, alarm covering their faces at the sight of blood dripping from Ned's nose and swollen lips.

"Let's give a hand here ..." Farleigh hovered over Ned, his sorrowful expression betraying intense feeling for the young lodger he'd watched over since his release from the hospital. He offered a supportive arm, but Ned was still too dazed to rise. His houseman's gesture reminded Edward that Farleigh had told him some time earlier, "Young Deane—he makes me think of you, sir, when you were that age."

Edward rose to his feet as the maid stood by, reaching out as if to help but not touching him. He regained his balance, staggered over to Ned, and sank down beside him.

"You okay, man?" His eyes searched Ned's as the servants looked on. The maid had taken a cloth from her apron and held it to Ned's nose to stanch the bleeding.

"I guess I'm no worse off than you, Edward..." A bluish cast shadowed Edward's right eye. "Quite a shiner you got there."

"Pardon the intrusion, sir," Farleigh began, "but we should get you to the hospital."

"I don't think that'll be necessary," Edward faltered. But the maid exclaimed, "Mr. Granger's right sir. I ain't a nurse, of course, but you're both bruised and battered, if you don't mind me tellin' you."

Ned took a closer look at Edward. One eye was swollen shut and blood seeped from a corner of his mouth. "Maybe we should go, Edward ..."

"I'll get the car," urged Farleigh. "Edna, tend to them 'til I come round again."

I've tried to imagine how lives might have taken a different twist if I hadn't answered Super-Guy's summons to go for a spin that fraught and fateful afternoon. I could practically hear my trusty steed calling—*o-c-e-a-n-h-o-u-s-e* ...

The year had advanced to September, and I was enjoying a golden afternoon while packing my trunk for the return to Columbia: typewriter, Frisbee, forty-fives, carbon paper, rubbers (both varieties), and a pin-up calendar for my dorm room. Also a fourteen-carat gold letter opener from Edward. When he presented it one morning after we'd slaved over a thorny passage, he said it symbolized my work in "liberating" his prose from the "manacles" of his mind.

The sight of this pseudo-sword reminded me of our most recent session. I'd made the finishing touches on that much-fought-over manuscript, and we agreed that it was time to ship it to the publisher. Edward said he'd mail it later that day—he had to make one final pass—instead of accepting my offer to drop it off at the post office. I should have known better about final passes. Were things ever *final* with Edward's writing? Maybe that's why I stopped packing and mounted S-Guy to return to Ocean House. I had to be sure that manuscript was on its way to New York.

I hopped on my steed and took a back road near the shore, which dead-ends at Ocean House. As the Guy and I rounded that crook in the road past which the mansion rises majestically, as if from the ocean's depths (I'm starting to sound like Edward—oy!), a memory flashed through my mind of the basketball game I'd wandered into several weeks ago, when Edward and The WASPs were cavorting on the court. I'd come a long way since rubbing shoulders with the elite. With no invitation, I was paying a call on Edward Vann.

The afternoon sun spotlighted the back of the house like a giant movie screen. I didn't bother to knock or ring. Even the stalwart Farleigh accepted me now as one of the elect. He was puttering in the grand foyer as I entered. We exchanged knowing nods while I made my way to the stairs. He'd opened all the doors and windows facing seaward, and the sound of crashing waves accompanied my ascent to the second story. Despite those rambunctious waves, I was conscious of my every footstep as I approached the study.

I found Edward at his desk, but he must have dozed off because he was leaning over it. Several manuscript pages were strewn about the floor. That seemed odd; those seven windows were shut tight, the fan blades were frozen, and there was no breeze. I felt a twinge of impatience when I saw that our writer hadn't taken his book to the post office yet. My impulse was to replace the fallen pages in the manuscript and make off with it. But as I stooped to pick them up, I spotted an open vial in their midst from which a couple of yellow pills had spilled onto the floor.

"Edward—?"

I ran my hand across his back. No response.

"Edward!" I shook his shoulders until his chest thumped against the desktop. Then everything happened at once. I ran to the stairs and shouted to Farleigh at the top of my lungs, raced back to the study, shook Edward again, pounded him on the back, reached for the phone, dialed 9-1-1. They responded after two rings to hear me gulp, "Ambulance—Ocean House—*quick!*"

Farleigh rushed into the room as the phone hit the receiver and I ordered him to bring cold water from the bath. I continued shaking and prodding my moribund friend, all the while calling his name. Farleigh returned moments later with the water. We raised Edward's head and doused his face with a cold jet. It was then he gave the first sign of life, a low moan.

"Shouldn't we call someone—?" Farleigh asked as we continued shaking our limp charge.

"Go down and wait for the ambulance—I'll do what I can up here—"

The faithful houseman vanished as I held Edward's head and patted his cheeks, till one eye, then the other, slit open.

"Edward—!" I implored, "Oh, Edward—!" In response his head lolled from side to side as if coming loose. Visions of Fiona sprang up before me—the woman above all others I'd tried to please all summer, desperate to be noticed, eager for her approval. She'd entrusted me with the care of her brother, and he tries to take his life—on *my* watch!

They were in the hallway leading to the emergency room of the same hospital where Ned survived his bout with polio. An all-too-familiar scent caused him to lag behind Edward and Farleigh. The mix of floor wax and antiseptic summoned a vision of Edward keeping watch by his bedside as he burned with fever.

"They'll fix you both up nice and fine, never you fear," encouraged Farleigh, masking his concern with a jovial overlay. An orderly approached as they entered the emergency room and asked them to be seated prior to admission.

"There's no need for you to hang around here, Farleigh." With a benign smile, Edward added, "I'll call when we need a ride."

His houseman started to back away, as if uncertain he should take his boss at his word. Edward's eyes swept the room before he added, "Keep mum about this—no need to alarm the natives."

When Farleigh was beyond hearing, Ned cuffed Edward on the shoulder. "Where'd you learn to throw such a punch?"

"The army, France."

"France? I thought you—"

"My adventures there weren't all in the boudoir."

"What are we going to tell them?"

"We'll think of something."

Ned sat quietly, deep in thought. At length he ventured, "Edward, that photograph …?"

His companion's head bobbed slightly as he considered a reply. "I asked if you wanted to see the ugly side of my family …."

When Ned remained silent, he added, "Another side of *me*, to be perfectly frank, if you must know ..."

"I think I *should* know, Edward. I'm ...," he groped for words, coming up with, "... I'm not a prude—live and let live, and all that—but I thought ..."

"What did you thought?"

"Well, that we were ... you might say ... kind of special to each other ..."

"Special ...?"

"Why did you pick me, if you were fucking someone else?"

"The sixty-four dollar question," Edward mused. Then with a troubled expression, he added, "I can't answer you right now. But you deserve an explanation, and there *is* one. ...Can you give me a little time?"

"I probably shouldn't make such a fuss—after what I told you about Sally and me."

"Thanks for helping me off the hook," he lay his hand on Ned's shoulder. "But that's an entirely different situation, in all due respects."

"Not ultimately."

"You're much kinder than I deserve." He removed his hand.

The trace of a smile appeared on Ned's lips as a matron of full figure approached. With a complacent smile, she intoned, "I hope you gentlemen haven't been brawling."

"If that had been the case, my good woman," quipped Edward, "my friend here would be looking much worse and I'd be unscathed."

"I don't suppose, then, that you tripped over a banana peel, the both of you?" She could hardly have sounded more neutral.

"Yes, as a matter of fact."

She held up her clipboard as if to make a notation. "Was it the same peel...?"

"Two separate ones," Ned replied.

"No, there was just one," Edward contradicted.

The nurse took a seat beside Edward and adjusted the frameless spectacles on her inquisitorial nose. "Can you tell me where this mishap occurred? I want the god's truth from you."

"On the highway. I skidded off the shoulder and we rolled over a couple of times." The unflappable reply elicited no reaction.

"It was a nasty curve in the road."

"Someone hit you coming 'round the bend? That should be reported to the police," the matron admonished.

"I can tell you in all honesty, ma'am, no other vehicle was involved."

"Who was driving?"

"I was."

"No," Ned interrupted. "I was."

"You couldn't have been," corrected Edward. "You were asleep."

"That's why we had the accident."

"Well, sir," exclaimed their interrogator, you must have bruises and cuts elsewhere on your bodies if they look anything like those faces. Come along with me—I'll get someone to examine you. You're Mr. Vann, I believe …"

As they were being discharged from the emergency room, their wounds dressed, Edward received a message that Miss. St.-John would be at the hospital soon to drive them home. An orderly led them to the visiting area near the front desk, which was catching the dying rays of the sun.

They took a seat on the timeworn sofa, then Ned asked under his breath, "What's this about a tiara?"

Edward's eyes swept the tight little room. "When Fiona was planning her wedding, the first one, our mother gave her a priceless emerald tiara. It had belonged to an English lord related to her family. It was the first time we'd ever heard about it, because she kept it in a safe somewhere. Fiona was in a flutter over it, as you can imagine, and pranced around the house and god knows where else with it on her head, despite the strenuous objections of Maman. One day, she couldn't find it. They had the whole staff search the house high and low, called in the police, detectives; they even raked the sand around Ocean House, but no sign of it anywhere. Our mother was not of a forgiving nature, and the loss—let's call it a *loss* for the moment—created a rift between her and Fiona that they never bridged."

"Do you know what became of the tiara?"

"I eventually tracked it down. I started with a local jeweler. I was sure Maxi would be shrewd enough not to park it with him. But that jeweler gave me the names of other establishments in the vicinity. My hunch was that Maxi wouldn't go far to dispose of it— he was always desperate for ready funds. That hunch proved to be correct, and I soon found a jeweler who'd made a record of the transaction."

"You never brought this up before?"

Edward glanced around the room. "I had to go abroad for several months and had little contact with home. I might have stayed away indefinitely, but mother died and I returned for the funeral. I thought about revealing the truth then, but everyone was already upset enough, so I kept mum."

"And Maxi never guessed that you'd found out?"

"No, fortunately."

"Why *fortunately*?"

"Because I can use it against him now. Can you imagine how Fiona will react when I tell her?"

Ned nodded, then sank back on the sofa, relaxing for the first time since Farleigh brought them to the hospital.

"The strange thing is," Edward resumed, "this blackmail business was never about you and me—Maxi wasn't gunning for us after all."

Before Ned could reply, a familiar voice greeted them from the doorway.

"Farleigh told me where I'd find you." Olivia's eyes scanned their faces. "I just happened to call and was suspicious, of course, when he seemed at first not to know where you were, then his prevarications ..."

Edward took her in his arms and kissed her.

"Careful, dear, I don't want to hurt you—"

"A kiss never hurts."

She stepped back. "Judging from your faces, I'd say you took a bad turn on the highway."

"The highway—?" questioned Edward, forgetting the fib he'd concocted.

"They told me when I called the hospital."

Ned's rueful glance prompted him to add, "We got off pretty easy, all things considered."

"How about the car ...?"

"Just a scratch or two, miraculously."

"Thanks for coming to the rescue, Olivia," said Ned, chagrined they were performing the same charade for her as for the matron. "What did Farleigh say had happened?"

"Something about an accident. He assured me you'd be all right. He said he'd leave the details to you. So of course I didn't quite believe him."

"The gruesome details," Edward grimaced. "Let's leave the details for later. This young man needs to get home and rest. He's going back to Columbia soon."

No one spoke again till they stepped onto the front porch of the hospital. It was then Olivia declared, "How nice to see you walking away from this place, Ned. The last time we were here, you were barely able to move under your own steam."

Ned led the way to the car.

CHAPTER
20

T HE WEATHER SEEMED TO KNOW it was a big day as Edward drove them to the station. A cloudless sky heralded a new beginning, as if the year were starting four months ahead of its dreary January debut. As they approached each intersection along their route, the lights managed to be green, the wind barely blew, and traffic kept to a brisk pace, while schoolchildren tagged along the streets and byways on their march to knowledge. It was fall at last.

He parked near the station, then he and Ned hopped out of the Cadillac and opened the back doors for Sally and Olivia. Edward sensed something momentous in that simple act. They'd spent the summer together in various combinations, and now this close society was about to leave him. The heightened significance of moments spent in bus and train stations, a time of irrevocable change arriving as implacably as the next incoming train, filled him with nostalgia. Yet he'd done nothing to prevent this outcome. When Olivia told him she'd taken a job as assistant editor at Alex Cabot's magazine—"a beginner's slot, but what else am I doing with my life?" she'd asked when she announced the news—he was quick to congratulate her, as if she'd been striving toward that goal all along. He might have said *I'll miss you* or *How will I get by without you?* But he didn't. It was certainly not that he *wouldn't* miss her; she was the most important person in his life, his summer fling with Ned notwithstanding.

Fling? He stole a glance at Ned, who was gripping Sally's bags as well as his own as they prepared to cross the street to the station. Was that the way to view his relationship with the young man, his lover and, yes, son, for most of the summer—a fling?

Ned's expression suggested he couldn't be happier, his Leonardo smile radiant and mysterious. Would Ned forget him after his return to the hurly-burly of college and the thrall of New York? That was a chance he'd have to take. If there was any consolation for him in their parting, it was knowing he'd let go of Ned so he could return to Columbia. He hadn't tried to hold on to him as his editor—and lover. Several times that summer, Ned had mentioned in passing that he was worried about having the funds to continue his studies. He'd replied each time, "Don't worry." He'd not added *I'll make it happen.* In any event, there was no future for them as lovers. That was something he could *not* make happen.

Sally led their little group to the station, head and shoulders forward. She was off to Barnard College, a future geneticist. For once, her presence didn't irritate him. As the sun tinted and streaked her dark curls, he now saw an admirable young woman forging her path through life by her own efforts. He quickened his pace and came up beside her, they were shoulder to shoulder. He felt quite small that he'd let jealousy cloud his vision of her. Her devotion to Ned when he was down with polio matched his own. He felt ashamed he'd withdrawn from Ned, if only briefly, when Ned confessed that he'd become intimate with her. Later, he came to understand his withdrawal: he feared he was losing Ned to a rival. But wasn't *he* the rival? What would Sally think if she knew about Ned and him ...?

They reached the station, and when they came to the ticket line he pushed ahead, announcing he'd pay their fares to the city— his going-away gift.

Olivia protested but Ned wisecracked, "Let him, Olivia— he's paying to get rid of us!"

He wheeled around faster than intended. He hoped his hurt look wasn't obvious.

When he disbursed their tickets, Olivia made a startling discovery: "Mine's a roundtrip—"

"Mine, too," echoed Ned and Sally.

"Proof positive," Edward smiled in triumph, "that I'm *not* trying to get rid of you."

Olivia slid her arm around his waist and kissed his cheek. It wasn't the swooning farewell she'd envisaged from the Fairy Princess to the Prince of Ocean House. It was a workaday embrace with the durability of calico rather than the sheen of silk. All summer her beau (it was safe to call Edward that, wasn't it?) had had ample opportunity to monopolize her time, throw himself at her feet, carry her off to a tropic isle. But Prince Charming had been far too diffident for such passionate engagement. Yet, he'd been especially tender since she told him about her job offer, attentive to a fault, encouraging, sensitive, loving. And last night, when he'd taken her to bed, he was urgent and insistent. That was something new! His face gazing down at her—despite its cuts and bruises—had never looked more handsome as he drove them to climax. And that ridiculous story he'd concocted about the car wreck with Ned—what did he expect her to make of it? They'd obviously gotten into a scrape they weren't ready to own up to.

But Edward's past excuses, prolonged absences, even his unengaged lovemaking were no longer her immediate concern, the operative term here being *immediate*. She was not stepping out of Edward's life by moving to New York; she wasn't worried that accepting the job would mean losing him. Rather, she'd answered opportunity's knock and was embarking on a big adventure, or as they say in the present age, moving out of her comfort zone. Junior League parties, showing opulent homes to rich buyers, community beautification campaigns had their attraction; but did she want to spend her days as a pampered matron at church functions and county fairs when she still had time—Alexandra put it perfectly—to reinvent herself?

How serendipitous, her new friendship with Alex Cabot. They'd hit it off from the first, without a thing in common. Till one day over a hurried lunch in Midtown Manhattan, Alex asked, "What do you plan to do with the rest of your life, Olivia?"

At the time, she took the question as a conversation gambit, nothing more than an opener. The French bistro was crowded and noisy; perhaps it was a city girl's means of cutting through the niceties? But before she could reply, Alexandra affirmed, "I mean it—what's going on with you?"

"Frankly, nothing."

"You don't beat around the bush—I won't either."

Her new friend and apparently mentor then proceeded to expound her theory of the "modern woman"—"who should never be dependent on a man for her upkeep—"

"… or probably for anything else," Olivia concurred.

Alex hesitated for just a moment. "Am I making mean—?"

"You're making sense."

Alexandra reached into her purse and withdrew a sheaf of paper. "This is a copyediting test. Take it home and do your best. You can use a dictionary and any reference books you choose. Then mail it back to me, okay?"

A week later she found herself in the office of Alexandra's boss, entertaining a job offer. She accepted on the spot, found an apartment on upper Park Avenue, and returned to Long Island early that evening. When Edward met her train, the first thing she said: "I've moved to New York."

The train had slowed on its approach to the station and appeared to be barely moving. Edward took Olivia's suitcase and tried to gauge where the train would stop and the doors open. His eyes on the approaching behemoth, he didn't notice that Sally was standing beside him. She threw her arms around his neck and, holding him fast, murmured, "Thank you, dear Edward, for everything you've done for Ned and me."

"Well, I should be thanking *you*, my dear," he returned, quite moved by her forthrightness, "for helping him get back on his feet."

"It wouldn't have happened without you. Without you, he might not have made it."

"Take good care of him, you hear?" He held her close and breathed in her curls brushing against his face as the train pulled up and belched to a stop.

"Break it up, you two!" Ned offered his arm to help Sally onto the train, while taking Edward's outstretched hand and pumping it. "Watch out for yourself, old man—and don't get into any more scrapes without me."

Edward forced a smile. There was much he wished to express, as though he were a prisoner just offered the chance to bid a final farewell before they'd lead him away. But Ned was already stepping into the train and Olivia was about to board. It was all he could do to wave and mutter something he couldn't remember even moments later. Then Olivia was hugging him good-bye and the conductor said something stiff and irrelevant and the door clanged shut, its top half hanging open as the engine wheezed and the wheels began the grind of their journey. Yet the train was barely moving for all its sound and fury.

Despite all the racket, he heard his name, sharp and distinct in the crisp morning air.

Ned had returned to the door and was waving frantically. Edward jogged forward as the train was gaining speed. Leaning precariously over the door, Ned cried out, "You have a permanent place in my heart, Edward, no matter …" the runner almost missed the rest, "… how far from me you might be."

Gasping for breath while sprinting beside the train, he managed to shout, "I'll always be there …"

He returned to his desk amid a divertimento of surf sounds and gabbling gulls. The house felt empty without Olivia and Ned, and he knew the emptiness in his heart would be with him for some time. But it was good to be back at work. His imagination was a kitchen of pots simmering, kettles ready to boil. Time to begin his next book, and he hardly knew what it would be. But he was up for a breakthrough; it would not be long before his thoughts would take shape and his fingers would be pushing into the keys of his Smith Corona. Maybe he'd purchase one of those new electric models. An idea was crystallizing, and he was about to type the first sentence. But a light rap at the door drew him out of his imaginary world, and his fingers slipped off the keys.

"Pardon the interruption, Mr. Ed ..."

His houseman hesitated into his presence, and when he reached the desk, he threw a quick glance over his shoulder toward the doorway behind him.

"A young woman to see you, sir."

The writer's eyebrows rose.

"Says she's a friend of young Deane and Miss Sunshine. Says she hopes you might find work for her here at Ocean House. Says she can type ..."

⋙❋⋘

"Please don't fret, he's going to be perfectly fine, you *must* believe me."

"How can you be certain ...?"

"I'm sure—trust me—scout's honor."

My hand made an ersatz Boy Scouts pledge to Fiona the Fair and Fabulous. As soon as I learned that they'd taken a pump to poor Edward's tum and he was no longer in danger, I'd tracked her down with Farleigh's help and she joined us an hour later. We were facing off on either side of his hospital bed. Her beautiful visage alternated between expressions of concern for her brother and admiration for yours truly. I lapped it up. I could hardly believe that I'd assumed the mantle of authority in what was a very personal Vann family matter.

Before Fiona appeared, I'd spent a bleak two hours with our near-suicide. The staff assumed I was next of kin and asked my permission each time they took Edward's temperature or checked his blood pressure. An administrator in suit, tie, and slicked-back hair visited our patient and advised me in dulcet tones that they'd entered a diagnosis on Edward's chart: gastric disturbance. He was followed by a trio of well-wishers consisting of Dr. Kirkpatrick, Alden Brooks, and the priest who officiated at the Episcopal church that the Vann family patronized. News traveled fast. Edward's body, mind, and soul were in capable hands.

Fiona and I kept vigil over Edward like relatives awaiting a decedent's last will and testament, making small talk about the weather and neighborhood gossip. It was nearly an hour before Edward gave a sign that he was emerging from his ordeal. His color had resurfaced; the pallid cheeks with which he'd been admitted were now suffused with rose. His breathing, spasmodic when I rode with him in the ambulance, was regular and reassuring. Just as I was starting to feel comfortable with the most imposing female I'd ever known, Edward's eyes blinked.

"Looks like we got him back." I fanned the flames of Fiona's hope as she listened for her brother to speak.

Edward sat up in the iron bedstead and fixed his eyes on us, but he remained silent.

"Really, darling—you gave us such a scare," Fiona chided, as if his attempted suicide were a prank. "Whatever got into you, mein Schatz?"

It must have chastened her to register how far the illustrious Vanns had tumbled to earth from their pedestals. Edward lay in that narrow hospital bed—heaven knows how many derelict souls had occupied it before him—while his proud sister must have been imagining the succession of newspaper columns that might have reported Edward's failed attempt, foiled, as it were, by an astute young Columbia scholar. Was Fiona losing her godhead?

Edward struggled to regain his bearings. I wondered whether he believed he'd died and gone to an Afterworld in which his sister and I were now a number. His head had dropped to his chest, and he murmured so softly that we leaned in to catch his words.

"I'm sorry to put you to so much trouble—I truly am ..."

"You can thank this young man for saving the day, Edward," Fiona exclaimed with another admiring glance at me. "What got into you, anyway?"

"I couldn't let it go, not as it was …"

"Couldn't let *what* go—?"

"His novel," I chimed.

"It wasn't ready," he stubbornly maintained, all my editing notwithstanding.

"What do you mean 'wasn't *ready*'? You've been at it all summer," Fiona scolded, as if the passage of time could bring off a work of fiction.

He turned his pleading eyes on me. "He understands …"

"I think I know what was bothering you," I improvised, "and help is on the way. I've got a finalized version of that pivotal paragraph that's been hanging us up."

"Your finishing touch?" His wan smile teased a tear from me that I blinked away as fast as I could.

"Call it that, my friend. Let's just get you out of here—and the manuscript out of your house."

A nurse stopped by to announce that Edward could be discharged after he'd rested sufficiently. Fiona had a hurried conversation with her in the hall, and they decided it was better for the patient to spend a night in the hospital. She offered to drive me home, and I promised Edward I'd bring him the final "piece" of his manuscript the following day.

Fiona's swan chariot—a sky-blue Cadillac—awaited us in front of the hospital. An orderly was holding the door for her as we stepped into the cool air of early evening, when the sun's rays still lingered over our town. In a white silk scarf that I could take for a wimple, she reminded me of Ingrid Bergman in *The Bells of St. Mary's*. Yet as we drove toward my house, I had trouble maintaining the vision of Fiona Vann as a nun. While dusk was falling, she'd turned into a starlet.

As the swan Cadillac approached my street, she asked me to light her cigarette. I said I didn't carry matches.

"You don't?" The tang of incredulity permeated those two tiny words.

"No—should I?"

"A gentleman should carry a book of matches at all times."

"If he doesn't smoke ...?"

"To light a lady's cigarette."

She instructed me to use the car lighter. I pushed it in to fire it up, then held the burning brand to the tip of her Pall Mall, until a puff of smoke rose into the air. As she pulled away from me, the streetlight hit her face. It was then I noticed crow's feet at the corners of her eyes and streaks of gray in her hair, strands that had once passed for platinum in my adoring fancy. I believe it was then that the transfiguring light turned her into a mortal. She'd ceased to be the woman of my dreams. It was no small transformation—from goddess to nun to human in one afternoon.

This change of heart, or gonads, might have been reinforced by the change of scene as we swerved off the main road and passed in front of Sadie's house. I'd considered Sadie my girl for some time now. We'd spent many evenings together that summer on the beach or at the drive-in, whenever I could wheedle our woebegone Nash Rambler out of Dad. I'll confess I hadn't gone as far with her as I'd hoped when summer began, that time when Edward surprised us on a stretch of beach. But a curious thing was happening. The more time we spent together, the more I was willing to accept the boundaries Sadie set regarding the ripe fruit of her body, corny as this might sound. Besides, she'd received that scholarship to Barnard, and I was looking forward to having her in the city after my return to Columbia. I put my lust on wait-and-see.

Next afternoon, Super-Guy and I cruised over to Edward's. The gorgeous fall day promised things to come, or maybe it was my sense that one era of my life was ending and a new one was about to launch. I hadn't bothered to announce my arrival in advance; that's how familiar I'd become with the Master of Ocean House.

I parked the Guy near the back door and popped into the kitchen, where I was sure to find Farleigh. He was instructing Milly in polishing flatware—a promotion for the girl—when I made my appearance.

"How's our writer?" I inquired, with the feigned cool of the recently initiated. (I'd lit Fiona's cigarette, after all.)

"Quite well, I'm sure you'll find him," replied the judicious houseman. I assumed his ever so slight nod toward Milly signified that the maid knew nothing about the previous day's calamity. The diagnosis "gastric disturbance" had made the rounds and was universally accepted. Edward even went to the kitchen every day for a week after the episode and swallowed an ostentatious glass of bicarbonate of soda in front of the staff, to lend credence to the hospital's, shall we call it, prevarication.

I climbed the stairs to the second story with the feeling that it was the last time I'd pass this way. The reassuring sound of Edward's typewriter greeted me when I reached the top of the stairway, but it was softer than usual. I stepped into the study to discover he'd bought one of those electric machines.

"Do you have to think faster now, too?" I jested, hoping to dispel any awkwardness over yesterday's mishegas, for want of a better expression. For the first time, I took a seat on the rattan chair by his desk without being invited.

He looked up and grinned. "Most of what a writer does at the keyboard is sit and think and wait. I guess I must learn to wait faster with this new contraption. By the way, you saved my life."

"All in a day's work."

"I knew you'd say something like that."

"That makes it no less genuine."

"Sit down, would you."

"I'm already sitting." Hadn't he noticed?

"I wanted to tell you—"

"Why you did it—?"

He glanced out to a sea mottled by a flotilla of fleeting clouds. "I thought it was the end."

"Why? You've finished your novel, it's soon to be published—"

"Maybe that's it."

"You'll begin another one."

"You'll be gone."

"I'll bet you've already started it—in your mind ..."

"My mind ... let's not talk about *that*."

"You'll be fine, Edward, believe me. I know that for a certainty."

"You're so sure of my future—I'm just as sure of yours." He reached into the desk drawer and handed me something.

I thanked him and pocketed the check without looking at it. It was time to bid a fond farewell, time to be grateful and give thanks, time to summon memories yet look ahead, time to open the heart and state the inexpressible.

Instead, we shook hands and said good-bye.

I didn't look at the check till Super-Guy brought me home. In the privacy of my room, I took it out and examined it. In the notational blank at bottom left, Edward had penned EDUCATION. The sum would more than cover the rest of my studies.

So farewell, Ned, you've come a long way. When you first showed up at Ocean House, I feared you'd spend your summer doing nothing but menial tasks. What foresight to have spoken your mind about his writing, that first day when Edward asked you to read a few pages of his magnum opus, and to have stuck to your guns. Keats or Shakespeare—who could possibly win that argument? You were brave not to give in. You were the original innocent, but you knew your own mind, and that's what Edward loved about you. It wasn't your body. Edward was as straight as they come—he loved your spirit. Until you, no one had ever stood up to Edward, except Fiona and Liane. He was stuck between the rigid propriety of the one and the forbidden freedom of the other. You were his way out.

I'm in your debt, Ned, for humoring my quest to lead a more glamorous existence than the one that played out at Ocean House that summer of 1953. Sure, it was a thrill to work with Edward and his manuscript, to rub shoulders with him and his Patricians the day Super-Guy and I wandered into their basketball game. But how much more uplifting when Edward brought you literally to your feet when he took you to the court to shoot baskets. How he hovered over you to guard you from harm, his body blending with yours as you tried out those awkward first steps back to life.

Despite your humble beginnings, for all your infirmity in your struggle with polio, you succeeded at one thing I've never been able to master: you made someone love you without even trying. Is there a greater triumph?

The manner in which the world of appearances imposes itself upon us, and the manner in which we try to impose on the outside world our own interpretation—that is the drama of our lives. The resistance of facts invites us to transport our ideal construction into the realm of dreams, of hope, of belief in a future life, which is fed by all the disappointments and disillusions of our present one.

—André Gide
The Counterfeiters, p. 205

Questions for Discussion

1. *The Counterfeiter* is a novel within a novel. What is the purpose of this device?

2. How are Ari Edelman and Ned Deane alike? How do they differ? Why does Ari have this fantasy of Ned?

3. Is Edward Vann the same person in the novel and in the novel within the novel? Why or why not?

4. Compare and contrast Edward's relationship with Ari and with Ned.

5. How would you describe Edward's attitude toward women?

6. Fiona, Olivia, Liane—describe their influence on Edward. Does one predominate over the others?

7. The sea, surf, sand, and gulls are said to be characters in the novel. Elaborate.

8. Part II is titled "Reconciliation." What might that mean?

9. If you were to make this book into a movie, how would you deal with the story within the story?

10. Alexandra Cabot is a minor character in the novel. What function does she serve?

11. The book is set in the 1950s. Does it seem true to the period? What makes you think so?

12. What does the narrative say about class structure in the 1950s, and how does that contrast and/or compare with today?

In Gratitude

All kinds of people have a hand in birthing a work of fiction, from the imagination to the printed page. In the case of *The Counterfeiter*, I am thrilled to thank my conceptual editor, Barbara Hoffert, who shaped the story and untangled its many illogicalities and inconsistencies; Margo LaPierre, who copyedited every line meticulously; Gilbert Fletcher, whose artistry proves that a picture is worth a thousand words; and Steven Hayes, who oversaw all aspects of production and held my hand through every nerve-wracking stage. My heartfelt thanks to all of you! If there is a single person whose encouragement and expertise made this book possible, who kept me going when I ran out of steam and no safe harbor was in sight, it is my very good friend Shira Nayman. I guess that makes you a muse.

About the Author

E d Cone came to New York from the South to study for a master's degree in international relations at Columbia University—and stayed. He pursued a career in publishing while writing novels and short stories on the side. He is a father, writer, editor, book reviewer, former tap dancer, and licensed New York City tour guide. He lives with his wife and children in Manhattan. *The Counterfeiter* is the first of his fourteen novels to be published.